I Love You, Charlie Tanner

Lynne Golodner

Scotia Road Books

For Mommy Sonny, who appreciates the importance of loving family no matter what

ADVANCED PRAISE

"Haunting, powerful, and intimate... *I Love You, Charlie Tanner* explores what happens when a woman dares to discover who she is beyond the man who once defined her."

Jean Meltzer, bestselling author of *The Matzah Ball*

"Passionate and full of mystery, Lynne Golodner's *I Love You, Charlie Tanner* is as breathtaking as Cape Breton's rocky coast. But the novel also tackles bigger themes, like the ache of regret, and the tangles of family and faith. Golodner's Charlie is fully realized, a heroine who discovers a second chance at love, at independence, and at becoming the person she always hoped she could be. Golodner understands that grief and desire are two sides of the same coin, and by the end of this powerful story, so do we."

Christopher Locke, author of *Without Saints*

In this evocative novel from Lynne Golodner, a rich tapestry of love, loss, and second chances unfolds against the backdrop of breathtaking landscapes. Fans of *Where the Crawdads Sing* will be captivated by the lush, vivid descriptions of nature, drawing readers deep into a world where the land itself is as alive as the characters. The story weaves together the delicate threads of the human heart with the raw, powerful rhythms of the natural world.

Sarah Ansbacher, author of *Wave After Wave* and *Ayuni*

BOOKS BY LYNNE GOLODNER

Fiction

I Love You, Charlie Tanner

Cave of Secrets

Woman of Valor

Nonfiction

Forest Walk on a Friday: Essays on love, home and finding my voice at midlife

The Flavors of Faith: Holy Breads

Stand Out from the Crowd: The Your People Guide to Beside-the-Box, Funky, From-the-Heart, DIY Marketing, PR & Social Media

Hide & Seek: Jewish Women and Hair Covering (Lynne Schreiber)

In the Shadow of the Tree: A Therapeutic Writing Guide for Children with Cancer (Lynne Schreiber)

Residential Architecture: Living Places (ghost-written for Dominick Tringali)

A Patient's Guide to Understanding Cutaneous Lym-

CHAPTER ONE

Backed against the living room wall, I could watch everyone. The room hummed—men and women in huddles, young children scurrying under the adult conversations. In the center, a table of food brought by my neighbors. If they couldn't take away my sadness, at least they could feed me. But I wasn't hungry, standing there against the cold wall. I was numb. I'm not sure they even saw me, or maybe it was practiced looking-away, unable to bear the anguish in my eyes.

Winter in Nova Scotia, the air biting, even inside the poorly heated house. The windows were laced with condensation, and outside, the late-winter winds off the lake seethed and howled. I could see it with my eyes closed after nineteen years living at the edge of the Bras d'Or Lake in a quiet corner of Cape Breton, its shifting waters black under a cloud-quilt sky. I'd come to know its moods: irritable in a winter storm, glassy in the thick humidity of summer, roiled in humid confusion as the seasons shifted and tried to find their footing.

Boden plucked an oat cake from a basket and popped it into his mouth, scanning the room. I nodded when his gaze found mine. When pity pooled in his green eyes, I had to look away.

The urn was hard and heavy in my left hand, cradled against my right arm, like the baby James and I never had. If only he'd wanted a family. Then at least I'd have a piece of him to keep forever. But all I had was his burnt remains in a cold canister, a catalog of memories and a few old photos. Not even any recent ones. When the community became digitally connected, he'd railed on about how it would be the end of us, too much time spent posing than really living. He was preachy like that, but I hadn't minded, or maybe I'd just gotten good at tuning out his rants. I was used to him after all our years together, my great love.

James had wanted to be cremated, even scribbled his final request on a torn sheet of paper. He'd never been the kind of man to plan ahead for what-ifs. Rather, he'd sailed on the wind, confident it would carry him, and if problems arose, someone else would take care of them. Me, probably. James hadn't been a worrier. I did that enough for both of us. I couldn't believe I'd spent twenty years, half my life, with him, and all I had to show for it were his ashes in a canister and an empty house with an echoing closet where his clothes used to hang beside mine. At least his parents hadn't taken his ashes, too.

Cool, wet air rushed in as the door snapped shut behind another trio of well-wishers. Damon, Evie and little Conor. I nodded toward them, trying for a smile and failing. Conor ran over.

"For you, auntie," he said, handing up a crayon drawing. I knelt to his level and took the paper. Mostly scribbles and a sun with big fat yellow rays. I mustered a smile, biting back the tears, and patted his cheek before he scampered off.

"I'm so sorry, Charlie, hon," Evie said, gripping my shoulders and leaning in for a cheek-kiss. I let her. I didn't have the energy to resist or to return the gesture. Damon nodded and glanced at his feet before the pair of them ambled over to the talkative others.

Everyone around me was talking, the low hum of chatter a buzz that held the room. Not me. As soon as I'd heard James had died, my throat had closed and all my words disappeared.

Would they ever return?

Boden came back into my sight line, his eyes searching mine. I don't know what I projected back to him, but he came over and pulled me to him. I grunted as he jostled the urn.

"Sorry, love," he whispered, stroking my hair. I couldn't remember the last time I'd washed it and wanted to apologize for the greasiness. At least Boden understood my silence and didn't push me to talk. He'd been my best friend for fourteen years and my refuge all the long nights when James forgot to come home, or chose not to, and I pretended he was out late working in one of the greenhouses Anam Cara was known for.

Anam Cara—Gaelic for *soul friend* and the name of the commune where I'd been a resident for half my life. I hardly remembered any life before this one. James had consumed my focus for two decades, and now I was all alone on the edge of the world.

The kitchen door swung open, and two elder aunties came out with trays of sandwiches—egg salad and chicken salad. Little ones swarmed over, grabbing what they could reach with grubby little fingers, before the ladies waved them off. The plates settled on the table, they surveyed the other dishes—little sugar tarts called pork pies, molasses spice cookies known as Fat Archies, an urn of home-brewed tea, a pitcher of rum punch and a steaming pot of vegetable soup, all handmade and brought as a temporary salve for my loss.

Were they here for me or just because it was what you did in our community in times of crisis? How many of them even knew me, the real me, deep inside?

I'm not sure I really knew myself anyway. Just the version James had dictated to me, over and over again, for nearly twenty years.

I gnawed on a fingernail. A flush crept up my neck from the heat of too many bodies in close proximity. The urn grew heavy in my arms. Did a baby grow too heavy when held for a long time?

At Anam Cara, we worked in the greenhouses and, in warmer weather, the fields, day and night according to a shift schedule, but mine had been cleared for a week after James's death. It was customary to give people time and space to grieve and even still, I begged for a shift. Warm, soft soil sifting through my fingers, and I'd forget, for a few moments at least, the heaviness that had settled on my chest. But they wouldn't honor my request, pursing their lips and looking at me with pitying eyes. *Rest,* they urged. *Let the sadness wash over you. You'll make mistakes in the work if you're distracted. Give it time.*

For a brief time, I'd gotten swept up in the aftermath of his death. Everyone was asking me for input on memorial planning, when to burn the body, pulling me into spontaneous hugs or dropping off homemade food, even though I couldn't stomach anything. Then his parents swooped in from Boston to collect his things and argue about his remains. I'd always wanted James to marry me, but when they arrived, I was glad we'd never tied the knot. I didn't have the energy to speak, let alone argue on his behalf. James had always done the talking for me, the planning, the thinking, and when his parents fought with the community leaders, I watched from afar, understanding finally how he'd come from this clan. In life, he'd insisted that he didn't share their big-money entitlement, but I saw the similarities. They were stunned that their wealth and their influence had no impact in the heart of Cape Breton. James had been like that, a bit too big for this place, a bit too self-important. I'd envied his self-confidence for so long; it kept him in a bubble of contentment, outside the harsh truth of reality. He lived easy while the rest of us toiled.

Earlier in the day, most of the Anam Cara community, plus James's family, had gathered in the Lodge for a meditation and drum circle, our version of a funeral service. I could read the discomfort on his parents' faces, the disdain on his siblings'. They'd kept their distance from the commune and from James. Or maybe he'd kept them away. I honestly didn't know why we never saw them or heard from them, where it started and where the family ties ended. At the service, Boden sat at my elbow, wrapping me in a blanket when I started to shake, dotting my streaked cheeks with a tissue as I silently wept. You'd think James's parents would have come over to me, embraced me, even if just to ask about their son—but they didn't even look in my direction, let alone offer a hello or a nod to the role I'd played in their son's life for two decades.

Was it possible they didn't know about me?

After, I returned to the house in the new-fallen snow to find them racing through the rooms I'd shared with James, throwing his sweaters and jackets and books and photos into garbage bags to take with them. They didn't ask if any of it was mine or if I wanted to keep any part of him, to let the scent of my life partner linger in the house we'd shared. I opened my mouth to say something, but no words would come.

"We have to get back, you understand," his mother said as they whisked out with the force of a winter gale. Her single strand of pearls gleamed under the lamp light. How had he come from a woman like that? So refined and elegant. And my James, in his frayed flannels and fisherman sweaters worn at the wrists where he'd pulled the sleeves over his hands for warmth.

I came out of my reverie when a throat cleared, and the chatter petered out. At the center of the room stood Armand, Anam Cara's bold leader. I turned my head and found Boden hovering at my elbow. I leaned against him, his body warm against mine.

"I think it's time to say a few words about our James," Armand said, sending a sympathetic smile in my direction.

I nodded.

He was tall, his bald head gleaming under the ceiling lights, his dark eyes blazing.

"I can hold it for a bit if you want," Boden whispered, but I shook my head and clutched the urn closer. I'd pulled one of James's sweaters over my plaid dress, a cushion for the urn, which was growing heavy in my arms. But I couldn't put it down. I wouldn't. Someone might take him from me, and then what would I have?

"James was the light of this community, a force and

an inspiration," Armand chanted. "Everyone loved him." From a far corner, someone whimpered. Though Boden's hand gripped my shoulder and his body kept me from falling, my face was finally bone-dry. I had no tears left.

"A true visionary, he left the expectations and structures of capitalist society to live in sync with the land," Armand continued. "He brought purpose and zeal and passion to everything he did."

He paused, swallowed awkwardly, sipped water from a paper cup one of the old aunties handed him. He nodded and offered a soft smile in thanks, handing the cup back.

"I remember when James came to Anam Cara, with Charlie on his arm." He glanced in my direction, and all the heads in the room turned to stare at me. Some offered weak smiles, others pitying gazes. My heart raced. *Look away*, I begged. When he continued speaking, their heads turned back to our charismatic leader and they forgot about me, and I exhaled a bit too loudly, a few heads glancing my way. I clutched the urn closer, rubbed the smooth, cold metal as if it were his warm, soft skin. Boden's breath was hot on my neck, and I swatted at him to move back.

"He dove into the planting that first year with such enthusiasm—I'd never seen someone so motivated to become part of the heart of this community."

A few uneasy titters rippled through the crowd, and Armand giggled.

"Don't be offended. All of you are glorious members of

Anam Cara, so valued. But today is about honoring James and his contributions."

A few heads nodded.

Armand was good at placating people. It was why they'd chosen him almost unanimously as our new leader five years earlier. No one questioned his authority or vied to replace him; they wouldn't dare.

He continued extolling James's wonderful traits, a few of which were inflated or outright fabricated. He told a funny story, then a sad one, and ended with a poignant example of how generous James had been in helping lead others to the right way.

Had he been generous? I'd loved him, shared his bed, given up everything to live at his side, and with him gone, I felt like a limb had been ripped from my body and exposed to the raw, dry air—but I didn't remember him as remotely generous.

Everyone applauded when Armand finished speaking. Leave it to him to turn this into his own performance instead of memorializing James. I shook my head. My mouth was so dry, my throat like sandpaper. Where was an auntie to hand me water?

I left the comfort of my spot on the wall to go in search of a cup and anything wet to pour into it.

"Aw, Charlie, so sorry," voices rang out. Hands patted my shoulders, my arms, my back as I passed.

I winced, shook my head to fend them off. I didn't want

their pity. I wouldn't share my sorrow. I couldn't—no one had known James like I had. And if I saw pain in their eyes, I might question whether the story I told to comfort myself was indeed true.

It would be so convenient if the words would just spring out of my mouth right about now. I opened my lips and wagged my tongue, but no sound came.

"Here." Boden thrust a paper cup of fresh-pressed apple juice into my hand.

I gulped it down and held it out for him to refill.

He ran off and returned in less than thirty seconds with a full cup.

Then, Armand was standing in front of me, all six-foot-two of him, with that angry jaw and big hands. I looked up. His chin was dotted with day-old bristle.

His arms came around me as he pulled me to his chest, pressing my nose against his ribs. His heart thumped mad-ly, but his voice was slow and deep.

"Poor, sweet Charlie," he said, petting my hair.

I cringed, tried to shrink in his grasp, the urn bulky between us.

"I know you can't see it now, but you will feel better in time. I promise. You may even find a new love someday."

He stood back and peered into my eyes almost as a challenge. Or an invitation? The gall! Talking about finding a new partner less than a week after the great love of my life died suddenly and left me all alone, hinting that he might make a good replacement. If that's what he meant? I couldn't see clearly. Bile rose in my throat, and I choked it down, not wanting him to see my surging emotions.

I bit down on my bottom lip and nodded, hoping my face looked soft, that he couldn't read my thoughts. It must've worked, because he nodded and patted me twice more before heading for the door. Two aunties ran over with his coat and a wax paper package of warm oatcakes. The door slapped shut, a wisp of new snow and cold air swirling over the mat.

The crowd was thinning as people packed up to leave. They'd been here for the better part of the afternoon. I was tired. I wanted them gone. Boden followed me around, my persistent shadow. He was the only one I could stand.

I hadn't seen her anywhere in the crowd, but suddenly Indira appeared, a beautiful young woman who had been raised in the community and was raising a daughter there all on her own. I didn't much like her, and for good reason, but I kept that to myself. She came right for me. Didn't even stop walking when she got within a foot and threw her arms around me in a firm, hot hug, pressing me close, as if we were best friends. Her tears spilled onto my cheeks and in my hair, and I tried to pull away, but she held me tight and shook with sobs.

"Oh, Charlie, what will we do without him?" she wailed, and some of the others came over to coo at her and pat her arms, and all I wanted was to be out of this room, alone in the bedroom I'd shared with James, with the door locked and my memories to comfort me.

Then, her weeping quietened, and she leaned closer, her mouth open next to my ear.

"I know the truth," she whispered, slipping a small piece of paper into my pocket. "I'll tell you when we're alone."

She kissed my cheek and left.

What *was* that?

And the truth about what?

Chapter Two

I found my voice at the border.

I had no choice, really. I rolled down the window and smiled at the guard.

"Passport, please." His face was serious, the dark blue of his uniform emphasizing his tone.

I handed it over. If James had known I'd been secretly renewing my American passport each time it expired, he would have yelled at me, maybe even confiscated it. He would've said something like, *What do you need that for when we have all we need here?* Which was why I'd kept it hidden in a box beneath the bed, alongside my mother's letters.

The guard scrutinized my passport then checked my face against the photo.

"Why were you in Canada?"

I licked my lips, begging the words to come.

"I was living there for the last twenty years with my partner, who just died, and I thought it was time for a change, so I'm coming home," I said all in one breath.

He sucked his lip and peered into my car. "Roll down the back window, please."

I did as he asked and watched as he angled his neck to see into the back of the old Volvo, the car I'd puttered in to college two decades earlier and kept in running condition all these years.

"Looks like you've got a lot of stuff back there," he said. "What is all that?"

I turned to glance into the back seat at the boxes and suitcases piled high. I hoped he wouldn't ask to look in the trunk, which was packed as tightly as it could be with all the rest of my possessions.

"Everything I own," I said.

"Everything?"

He craned his neck again for a closer look.

I nodded, glancing in the rearview mirror. There were no cars behind me. It was just past sunrise. The border from New Brunswick into Maine was usually sleepy, with few cars crossing and little flak from the border guards. It was actually a perfect place to run drugs or guns, if you were into that sort of thing.

"You on the lam or something?"

My heart raced. Was I?

I shook my head, gnawed on my bottom lip. Most border guards weren't this chatty. When would he let me through?

"What was he like?"

"Who?"

"Your partner."

Really? Was he bored on this shift? Lonely? I sighed and fell into the conversation, taking a big breath before letting it all out.

"I thought he was the love of my life, but now I'm starting to wonder," I said, going for full honesty in an effort to end this inquisition and get moving. I needed to be on the other side of the border, safe in the United States, the miles between Anam Cara and me growing farther by the minute. I resisted the urge to look behind me, to see if anyone had followed me. Why would they? No one knew I was leaving, and few people were up that early anyway.

I'd spent the whole night packing my car full of everything I wanted to take—clothes and books and dishes and photo albums and anything of James's that his parents hadn't seized, plus a few shared items like the revolutionary gardening books that had been published to great acclaim by the Anam Cara founders. As soon as the car was packed, I'd left the keys to the house, which had never been mine, on the dining room table and quietly closed the door. I hadn't looked behind me as I coasted out of the community, the first fingers of light shining on the other side of the lakes.

I was nobody in Anam Cara, other than James's partner and a quiet gardener. I'd spent most of my time in the greenhouses and garden plots, fisting soil, trimming plants, pulling weeds and checking the earth for moisture and temperature according to the growing parameters laid out by Eamon and Edith Andrews, the kooky hippies who'd evaded the Vietnam draft by escaping to Canada and creating this commune. I was boring, vanilla, not remarkably memorable.

James was my first and only love. I'd never slept with anyone else, and unlike many Anam Cara members, I didn't believe in free and open love. I far preferred books and the tea I made from lavender, mint and nettles than the rum many of my neighbors passed in a shared bottle during one of the popular swinging campfire nights.

The headlights of the car behind me were bright in the rearview mirror.

"Do you miss him?"

I raised my eyebrows at the border guard. *So we're really doing this.*

"I did at first, but now I don't know," I said.

He nodded, considering my words. With one more glance into the car, he waved me on.

"Welcome home," he said.

A thrill rippled through me at the words. I rolled up the window and drove off.

I hadn't realized how tightly I'd been holding it all in until the commune was far behind me, on the other side of the border. Five miles from the crossing, I pulled over to the side of the road, put the car in park and dissolved in heavy, gasping sobs. A thick forest of balsam fir and eastern hemlock stood about twenty feet from the two-lane throughway. When the sobs faded, I killed the ignition and got out of the car to trudge in the snow. I stretched my arms overhead and angled my face to the white sky. The scent of the forest was invigorating, and calming.

It was quiet and cold. Tufts of snow dusted the ends of branches and the peaks of the trees. A hawk circled overhead. My breath puffed in front of my face, and for the first time in a long time, I felt safe and free.

Chapter Three

A bell on the door rang out as I opened it.

"Hiya," a woman called out from the back of the store. "Need any help?"

I shook my head as if she could hear me and stared at the shelves. I'd come back when it was time to plant, but for now I needed a snow shovel more than anything. The aisles didn't seem to be organized in any particular order, but I wasn't in a rush, so I trailed up and down until I got to a corner display of heavy-handled shovels and ten-pound bags of salt.

"Whatcha need?" The woman rounded the corner and looked at me. She wore an unbuttoned flannel over a waffle-print long-sleeve, Carhartt khakis and heavy work boots. Her long gray hair was braided into two plaits.

"Found it," I said, picking up the shovel I wanted.

"You new to town?"

I nodded and followed her to the checkout counter. The store was cute, quaint and had everything I'd need to make the house and its small property my own. I'd be back here, often, so I thrust a hand to the woman.

"Charlie Tanner," I said by way of introduction.

She grabbed my hand and clasped it. "Mary Hobson, proprietor."

She rang up the shovel then looked at me. "Drive icy?"

I stared at her, not understanding.

"Your driveway. Is it icy?"

"Oh. Sorry. Um, probably."

"You're that new, ah," she said. "Well, we sell salt, but I don't abide by it. Not good for the land. Anything is better, and we've got it all—wood chips, straw, sand. Some people put cat litter down. We got that, too."

She looked at me expectantly, waiting for my response.

"I'm good for now," I said. "I only just arrived. I don't know yet how bad it is. I'm sure I'll be back."

She nodded, and the register dinged. It was an old-fashioned thing with round keys. "Twenty-two bucks," she said.

I pulled cash from my pocket, and she handed me a paper receipt and the shovel.

"Thanks. I'm sure I'll see you again soon," I said, turning to leave.

Mary waved me off.

It was funny that the one thing I didn't think to pack was the snow shovel. Not that I could've fit it in the car, but I'd lived in cold climates all my life, had hefted new snow to clear walking paths and streets for driving since I was old enough to follow my father, stepping in his deep footprints. I'd always loved the sound after a new snow, when the whole world falls quiet and I can hear my breath. It's one of my favorite times, when I can think clearly, when anything seems possible. James never understood why I piled on layers and slid into my cushioned, insulated boots to walk outside the minute a storm ended. *You're crazy,* he used to say. *You'll die in the cold.*

It's not like I wandered into the wilderness or went out without a flashlight, though I never turned it on. The moon or stars were always bright enough to see by, and there was no real danger around Anam Cara. I liked the suspense of waiting for my eyes to adjust to the natural dark and could never understand what he'd been afraid of.

Before James died, I'd never considered that he might want me out of the picture. I'd believed we were happy, in love, connected. Even on the nights when he didn't come home, I chose to believe that we were fine, that work or a friendly conversation kept him even though I knew I was lying to myself. From the start, he'd told me he was wary of monogamy, didn't think it was natural. I disagreed. I couldn't bear the idea of him with another woman, but I couldn't really do anything about it, especially not after I followed him to Canada. I mean, I guess I could've left, gone home to Traverse City, but I loved him. And he loved me. I still believe that.

I'd walked into town to get the shovel. It wasn't far, a

mile up the road from the little cottage I'd rented, so the walk back in minty winter air was just as quick. I unlatched the gate and walked through as delicate flakes fluttered down from the sky. I tilted my head and opened my mouth to catch a few on my tongue.

The sky was pearly white, a blank and vast canvas above the fir forest. God, I loved Vermont! I leaned the shovel against the house and went inside. It was perfect for me, cozy and just enough space to not get cabin fever—a bedroom at the back, a small cozy kitchen with a small table, and a living room with a soft plaid couch against the wall, a matching chair and an end table with a lamp made from deer antlers. The sole bathroom had a clawfoot tub with a shower head and a circular linen curtain. A wood stove warmed the sitting room.

Small, simple, with everything I'd need to start over. And the best part was the garden. In the back, there was plenty of room for rows of produce when the cold broke, and the owner had said I could build a greenhouse on the side of the cottage to start my seedlings.

A small mud room at the back of the house offered a fairly new washer and dryer plus a closet where I stored my suitcases. The bedroom closet was big enough for my clothes (I didn't have much), the bathroom had a cart for toiletry items, and in the living room, a trunk served as a coffee table and held extra blankets. I piled the blankets onto the couch and the bed and filled the trunk with photo albums and boxes of letters. And at a thrift store two towns over, I'd found an old bookshelf that I placed in a far corner, which was big enough to hold all my books.

I scanned the interior of the abode and sighed. Mine, all mine.

I'd perched the urn with James's ashes on a shelf in the kitchen closet. I still hadn't decided if I'd fulfill his dying wish or not. It was all so curious. He'd scribbled on the back of a flier for a sound-and-movement class that when he died, he wanted his body cremated and for me to scatter the ashes off the northern coast of Cape Breton at Dingwall. And while I did this last task for him, he wanted me to sing "The Piper's Refrain" by Gordon Bok.

I couldn't make sense of it, and the image of me warbling out a tune I hadn't known while James was alive made me feel like I'd been duped.

I still didn't understand why he'd written this request in the first place. Had he known he was going to die? But how could he? I mean, it was a heart attack. At least, that's what Armand said. That can happen at midlife, and James was fifty when he passed. Armand had assured me that there was nothing fishy, only sadness, surrounding his death. I hadn't asked to see the coroner's report. It hadn't even occurred to me that I might want to see it. Why would I? It was bad enough to be thrust into this sudden nightmare of loneliness and pseudo-widowhood. I didn't need more information that I didn't understand to spark questions and muddy everything up.

But then, his written instructions and this song that I didn't know…

Why had James chosen it? I'd researched it at the library. It was beautiful and sad. I'd listened to it about twenty times since Indira had given me the note that day at my house. (And why did she have it, instead of me?)

The song lyrics told a story about a fighting troop of Scottish Highlanders during the French and Indian War, but it also mentioned the battle of Ticonderoga in the American Revolutionary War. I was well steeped in Cape Breton's Scottish lore. Bretoners were proud of their lineage and the hard-won freedom their ancestors had claimed by coming to this continent. Gaelic was still a second official language there, the place deeply influenced by the wave of Scots who fled the 18th Century Highland Clearances for friendlier shores and ended up in the rocky landscape of Nova Scotia's north.

But what did Duncan Campbell, the piper in the song, have to do with James Grace, my long-time partner?

I knew James's family had descended from Scots many generations earlier. But the legend in the song had to have a deeper meaning for James to invoke it in his memory. Was it a message to me from beyond the grave?

I replayed the song over and over, listening to the lyrics from some clue. Duncan wakes one night when a friend knocks at the door, begging to be hidden. Someone's chasing him; Duncan pledges to keep his secret. When the search party comes, accusing the friend of killing his cousin, Duncan keeps his word. But then the cousin's ghost appears and foretells that Duncan will die at Ticonderoga. Years later, he does indeed die in battle there.

Okay, great story, but what did it have to do with my man?

Until I knew, I wasn't about to fulfill his strange request. And I might not anyway because it was so damn strange. Besides, I was not ready to return to Cape Breton, to go anywhere near Anam Cara. And, James was no longer here to watch my every step, render judgment and berate me for making the wrong choice.

I flicked the kettle on to warm the water and scooped loose tea into a mug. I fingered one of the soft yellow towels I'd bought for the kitchen. James would've hated these. He'd had opinions about everything. I reveled in the freedom to arrange my home the way I wanted to, finally. Certain colors and fabrics had offended him, the towels had to be hung just so, no canisters on the counter, ever, because that made clutter, and physical clutter clouded the mind. In Vermont, I'd bought white ceramic canisters for flour, sugar and oats and smiled as I looked at them on the counter in full sight. *I'll show you, James.*

The kettle whistled, and I doused the tea leaves, leaving the mug to steep. I'd baked cherry-chocolate biscotti and bit into one, raining crumbs down on the floor. My heart raced as James's voice barked at me: *You're a mess! Eat over a napkin, or don't eat at all.* If he were here, he'd grab the cookie and toss it in the sink. I shuddered at the memory and took a bigger bite.

Why had I loved him? Why couldn't I see clearly how controlling he'd been when he was alive?

The newspaper thudded on the doorstep, and I went to the door to collect it before it could get saturated with snow. As soon as I'd arrived in the town of Present, I'd subscribed to the local paper so I could learn about the place I now called home. It was thin but well-reported and held an events calendar, a robust classified section and interesting little articles about the town council, the garden club, a community book exchange, the schools and houses of worship, which included a little Jewish congregation in the basement of a church.

I hadn't been around Jews in decades, though I came from them. Growing up, we'd never done much with religion. Besides, Traverse City, Michigan wasn't a hotbed of Jewish observance, though there were two liberal synagogues there. All I could remember was a pair of brass candlesticks my mother stashed in a kitchen cupboard that had come from Ukraine when her great-grandmother emigrated in the nineteenth century. I had a faint memory of my father whispering Hebrew on the anniversary of his father's death every year and lighting a candle that burned for a full day and a full night. But that was all.

Religion wasn't welcome at Anam Cara. We believed in the Spirits and the Gods and the Land, or so went the teachings of Edith and Eamon Andrews. James was heatedly opposed to organized religion. When his parents came to collect his things, they'd expressed dismay that he wouldn't get a proper church service and an Episcopalian burial.

"Please," his father had begged Armand, who made all the decisions for us. "It's only right. He was our son."

Armand's eyes had blazed in response.

"This is what James would've wanted," he'd said. "It's how we live here."

James Senior had wanted to fly his son's body back to Boston for a memorial at the Episcopalian cathedral and a burial in the family tomb. He'd looked so much like James that it was chilling. The same reddish-brown hair, though streaked with silver and cut close to the scalp. James had always worn his hair long and knotted in a bun atop his head, and his bushy red beard seemed to set his whole being afire. In contrast, James the elder, a banker, wore a blazer and button-down with polished loafers and pressed pants.

Anyway, it had been too late. By the time they'd arrived at Anam Cara, James had been burned to ashes and funneled into the metal urn that now sat in the dark recesses of my kitchen closet.

That night, I lay in bed, a shaft of moonlight bright

through my window. I hadn't bothered to close the curtains. It was toasty warm and quiet, and though I wanted sleep, it wouldn't come. I reached a hand below the blanket, into the warmth of my flannel pants to the place between my legs that had been neglected for far too long. I closed my eyes and tried to conjure an image of James, his sleek, strong body, lean and ropey with muscles, his skin so pale it would match the moonlight. I pictured him lying beside me, his thick fingers finding their way to the center of my being, pressing until I couldn't help but moan with delight.

For as tough as he'd been, we'd always had passion. Maybe that's why I'd never left. I arched into my own hand at the memory, wishing I could feel his hot breath on my neck, his lips raining kisses along my collarbone. Before his death, we hadn't made love in months, but I didn't interrogate that now. I didn't want to replace my warm memories of James with the cold truth I was becoming too aware of. I wanted to remember his passion, his burning eyes, the way his fingers knew my skin, the fact that he'd chosen me, that he always came home to me. My heartbeat slowed, and I withdrew my hand, bringing it to rest on the soft flannel sheet. Now, I'd sleep, and hopefully without the intrusion of disconcerting dreams.

Chapter Four

When we met on the campus of the College of the Atlantic, James was the most mesmerizing man I'd ever encountered.

In the low-ceilinged dining hall during lunch one of my first weeks on campus, he'd stood on a chair and raised his arms to grab everyone's attention.

"What fires you up?" he called to the crowd.

Hands pumped in the air, and a few students hooted. He was tall to begin with and taller still on that chair, the top of his head nearly grazing the ceiling. I'd looked up at him and thought I was staring at an angel.

His golden-red hair, haloed by the ceiling lights and the sunlight streaming in the windows, was silky and long, twisted up into a messy top knot. His brown eyes shone, and his red beard glistened as if it were electric. He wore a fisherman's sweater over dark jeans rolled into cuffs at the ankles and worn-in Timberland boots, the leather tarnished by dirt, the laces loose and undone. His teeth gleamed bright as he spoke.

"You're here to make a difference—not just on this campus, but here on earth, in this life," he chanted.

"Yeah!" a student cheered.

A couple of the girls at my table blushed and looked away. He was so handsome, so dynamic.

"Who is that?" I whispered to Sivan, my roommate who'd come from Israel to study the cohabitation of marine life off the coast of Maine. We were the only two Jews in the place, and I was uncomfortable with the connection, though I liked her brash confidence. While I didn't identify as any religion, my roommate was loud, unapologetic and proud of hers. Ours, I guess. I both admired and abhorred her.

"James Grace," Sivan said loud enough for the whole table to hear.

I cringed as heads turned in our direction. The other girls murmured unintelligible words between them.

"Yeah, but who is he?"

"Everyone's favorite professor," Sivan huffed.

I turned to look at her. "You don't like him?"

"I don't trust him," Sivan said. "Just look at him."

I followed her gaze to the man on the chair, who was gaining momentum as the crowd cheered him on. He was beautiful and sexy and pulsing with an energy that drew people to him. I had the feeling that anything he'd say would ring like a bell in my ears. I could almost feel my body drifting to his side. I couldn't look away from James

Grace.

"Oh boy…" I sucked air through my teeth.

"Don't fall for it." Sivan elbowed me. "He's a wily one."

"But so hot," I muttered.

When I walked into his classroom the next Tuesday, for the popular Language of the Land class, I nearly did a one-eighty and walked out.

"Not so fast," he called to me as I hesitated. And then he was standing before me, looking down on me, a terrifying smile on his face.

"And you must be Charlie Tanner," he said, one hand on his hip, the fingers of his other hand loosening a seed from between his teeth. "Sorry about this," he said, freeing the offender and flicking it to the ground. "That's what you get with homemade grainy bread."

"You make your own bread?"

I couldn't stop staring at him. His eyes were like sparkling jewels this close up, and he had a way about him that pulled me into his orbit.

"Of course," he said. "I love to pound the dough. Gets out all my angst."

I laughed nervously and slid into a seat, dropping my bag on the floor. Other students were trickling in, choosing desks, getting comfortable.

"How did you know my name?" I asked. The room wasn't big; anyone could hear the conversation from any desk.

"I know all my students," he said, winking.

It had started that day, the chemistry between us, the pulse of electricity and wanting. After class ended, James—he'd told us all to call him James, not big on titles or formalities—had called out, "Charlie! Can you stay a minute?"

I hung back as the other students looked shiftily at me and filed out. The classroom empty, the silence pulsed. My underarms were wet.

"Yes?" I said, hugging my books to my chest. I'd been too distracted by his request to slip them in my bag. My heart beat in my temples, and I found it hard to swallow. I didn't have much experience then being around men. Boys, maybe, but not a full-grown, confident man like him.

"You had some interesting insights in class," he said. "I like when students participate so eagerly."

I nodded. He hadn't needed me to stay just to say this. He was fishing for an excuse to corner me. He'd felt what I'd felt, the buzzing energy like heat coming off him. My face went warm.

"Have dinner with me?"

It was the first month of my freshman year, but I knew better than to get involved with a professor. Except that logic and common sense sailed out of my head the moment he asked. I was a walking cliché. Far from home, lonely on a campus of strangers, dreaming of someone picking me out of a crowd—this was exactly what I'd wanted, the stuff of cringeworthy romance movies.

I'd left Traverse City to build a life of my own far away from the boring, small life of northern Michigan. Not that Maine was any bigger, but here, no one knew me as Mellie and August Tanner's daughter. My parents were revered educators in the liberal artsy northern Michigan enclave, my father the high school principal who knew everyone's name and family and my mother the doting kindergarten teacher. They were adored by everyone and spent their days lavishing attention on children, leaving me to fend for myself.

I'd chosen College of the Atlantic as much for its distance from my family as to learn sustainable practices on a self-created study path mixing ecology and environmental studies. I wanted to one day lead a visionary farm that would feed poor communities and impart skills to empower people to sustain themselves on any plot of land they could plant. I wanted to find a place where I'd be known just as me, where I'd make friends who saw me, who chose to spend their time with me. A place where I could make a name for myself.

But it was such a small school, and while I had friends and loved my coursework, I was often lonely. And who was I kidding? I've never had the personality to be loud and noticed. I always preferred the shadows, to quietly watch and absorb.

I chewed on my lip as I considered James's invitation. It was the stuff of romance novels, only now I was the main character. A slip of hair dangled loose from his bun, trailing along the side of his face. It was endearing.

"Are we allowed to do that?" I said coyly.

He came closer, hooked a finger under my chin and tilted my head up.

"We can do whatever we want," he said in a low rumble.

Shivers rippled through me, and my heartbeat quickened. His finger was gone from my chin as quickly as it had landed there, and I knew it was crazy, but I missed his touch.

"Sure," I said.

"Cool." He smacked his gum as he said it. "My place? Seven o'clock?"

"Tonight?"

He smiled and snorted. "Why not?"

From then on, James inhabited my thoughts, my calendar, my bed. Somewhere, in the back of my mind, a little voice cautioned me not to fall for his bad-boy cool demeanor, but I couldn't get enough of his exploring fingers, his lingering mouth, the taste of him on my tongue. I tried things I'd never even heard of before. Before I met James, I hadn't been too sexually aware, though I was hungry to gain knowledge and learn new tricks. I'd never known my body this closely, nor the body of another, my only sexual experiences before him relegated to fumbled pawing in the back of cramped vehicles or on musty basement couches with high school boys who knew little about how to please a woman.

James knew exactly how to please me in ways I'd never known possible.

By day, I sat in the front of his classroom, my eyes blazing as I watched him come alive with the course material. He could be talking about coastal erosion or disappearing habitats or the challenges of sustainable planting in the cold north, and I'd be mesmerized by his moving hands, his electric voice, the little pieces of spittle that flew off his tongue and into the air, a crass anointment in the church of James Grace. Half the time, I didn't even pick up on his words, my pen trailing across my notebook in uneven scribbles. I just watched his body move, the contour of his jeans over his firm behind, the rippled chest that hid behind button-downs and sweaters. I held a secret knowledge of this beautiful man that made me feel special.

So when James took his inspiring voice out onto the campus square or a cafeteria chair and chanted to end modern-day slavery, to stop taxing the masses to prop up the rich, I followed. As did hordes of other students.

By the first snowfall of that academic year, I was hooked. Fat flakes came down in silence on the bristled ground, coated the soft arms of the evergreens. I flung a wool scarf around my neck, burrowed into James's fisherman sweater that I'd nicked after our last dalliance. *Should've dug out my winter coat from the closet*, I lamented as I sauntered across campus. But I'd wanted everyone to see my claim on James, bright as the new snow.

Sivan caught up to me and matched my pace.

"Where were you last night? You came home so late."

I tucked one lip into the other and grinned.

"Not going to tell me?"

I shook my head. We'd agreed to keep our relationship quiet for now, until it was safe to reveal. James hadn't specified when that would be, and I was desperate to shout our connection to the world, but I'd promised to keep quiet, and I never broke a promise. It was daring of me to wear his sweater in public, maybe even stupid. But that little voice inside me was growing louder, stomping its feet, hands on hips, demanding to know what I thought I'd get from this hapless coupling. But I was getting equally good at silencing my logical conscience, banishing it to the dark recesses of my mind.

"Nice sweater," Sivan said.

I looked down then felt a flush spread across my face. I was so excited to show a clue to the public when I'd pulled the sweater over my head, but now, in the bright light of campus, I felt exposed and foolish. James might be mad. How immature of me to think this was a good idea! I stopped walking, thought about turning back to my room to change into my own clothes, but I had just five minutes until class would begin, and I'd miss half of it if I went back now.

I gripped Sivan's arm and pulled her close. "Promise you won't tell anyone?"

She nodded slowly.

"I was with James," I whispered.

Students scampered past on their way to class.

Sivan was still nodding, her brown eyes boring into me. "I didn't want to believe it," she said quietly.

I stared at my roommate and stepped back. "Why?"

Sivan sighed heavily and ran her right hand through her golden hair. "Because he's a player, and he's going to hurt you," she said. "I didn't think you'd be stupid enough to fall for his shtick."

I took another step back and shot daggers at her. Aghast, and hurt, I couldn't find the words to respond.

I chewed on the nail of my ring finger, little chipmunk gnawing to give me time to think.

"You really think you're the only one he's with?"

The little voice squeaked louder. *Told ya so,* it said in a taunting sing-song. *Shut up,* I bit back, and the voice went silent.

"It's new. We haven't said we're exclusive."

Sivan nodded, a satisfied smile on her face. "But you want it to be."

My nod was slow, as I pretended I was trying to decide, but deep down I knew the answer already.

"Ask him," Sivan challenged. "Ask if he wants to be

exclusive." She moved closer, her fingers closing around my forearm. "I just don't want to see you hurt," she said in a softer voice, close to my ear.

She patted my arm and said, "Let's get to class. We're late already."

Chapter Five

"I need some proof that it's okay to take a chance on you," the Realtor had said when I applied to rent the little cottage in Vermont.

I understood that twenty years of no career, no tax returns, no proof of my existence wouldn't convince the bank to loan me money to lease a residence. Which was why I'd brought the shoe box with me. It was like I was invoking my grandfather, who'd never trusted banks and had kept all his money in pillowcases under the bed.

I'd found it when I was packing up the house at Anam Cara. It was late, the black of night, all the stars hidden behind thick clouds, which made the darkness inside the house press closer. The box was deep and wide, with money stacked in neat piles all the way across. I'd found it hidden behind a panel in our closet, which I hadn't known was loose until all the clothes were packed in duffels and garbage bags, and I saw the missing screw. The piece of plywood had hinged open like a gap-tooth. I'd swung it wide and peered inside.

It was dark in the space, but the silhouette of a box was clear. I grabbed a flashlight and pointed it inside, and there it was, a box full of money, left by James. At least I assumed it was his. It certainly wasn't mine. Where it came from or how he'd collected it, I had no idea, but a wave of relief washed over me as I realized that now I had the means to escape and find a place to live on my own. Before that moment, I'd been afraid my only chance at leaving Anam Cara was to crawl home to my parents, who I hoped would take me in, even after I'd cut them out of my life for two decades. I wasn't ready to confront that mistake or find out I had been wrong to distance myself from my past. With no savings, no bank account even, no work history to vouch for my abilities and no way of earning money, I had few choices. For a smart woman, I'd been very stupid for a very long time.

I pulled the box out from the hidey-hole, dusted it off and carried it to the bed. In the low light of a single lamp, I lifted off the lid and took out, one by one, bundles of cash held together by rubber bands. Twenty stacks of $5,000 each. A heavy sigh escaped my lips, and I sat down hard on the bed. I'd never held so much money in my hands at one time. Never even contemplated having this much to my name.

When had my dreams shrunk?

My heartbeat quickened as I realized how dangerous it was to have this at Anam Cara. A principle of the community was communal living; no member was permitted a bank account, but then, no member had to pay rent either. We were given a place to live that suited our family situation, and in return we worked the fields and tended the greenhouses. We also had other obligatory tasks—cooking, baking, cleaning the communal spaces, setting up for meals and washing dishes afterward. Plus the rotation for the farmers markets and sales outings. Each able adult served at least five shifts a month, giving over all the money generated from those outings to the community treasurer, who kept count and reported to Armand.

That's where James must've gotten the stash. Twenty years of pilfering an average of $5,000 a year. It could be done—especially since James had volunteered for additional shifts and spent some time as the community's treasurer. That brazen man! I'd always wondered why he was so eager to drive around in the Anam Cara van, negotiating with shop owners and grocers and sitting in the blowing wind at farmers markets.

I played it cool that day, and when night fell, I packed everything I owned into my old car and waited until the community was soundly sleeping before daring to leave.

I'd wanted to wait until morning to say goodbye to Boden, Lily and Charmaine, my three closest friends and allies in the world. But I couldn't wait. What if Armand caught me leaving? Did he suspect that I might? This was a lot of money stashed away from the community's coffers over a long period of time. I couldn't believe no one had become wise to it over the years.

Or maybe they had? And if so, how long would it take to follow the trail back to James?

As the first fingers of dawn peeked over the horizon, I coasted on quiet roads out of Cape Breton, thinking of Indira's hushed whispers to me at the memorial, her promise to reveal some mysterious truth when we were alone. I'd shrugged it off, turned my back on her because I hadn't want to confirm her intimate relationship with my life partner.

Banishing these unsettling thoughts, I pressed the accelerator heavier, increasing my speed away from all these questions. The box was shoved deep inside a last garbage bag I'd found in the back of my kitchen pantry, secured beneath a tight double knot. I thought of my last glance around the house that had been my home for two decades, the way it had been shrouded in total darkness once I extinguished the light, and the bravery I'd needed to summon to imagine a different life and to leave.

Why hadn't I found this courage sooner?

Chapter Six

How did I not see it all back then?

In the early days, I could've charted a different course, ended things before I got in too deep. And I don't believe that I didn't know, on some level. So how did I make the leap from innocence and hope to actually believing James Grace was the love of my life and giving up my dreamy future for him?

The bell on the door of Planter's Heaven dinged as I walked in.

"Back so soon?" Mary called down the aisle.

I nodded. I'd come every day if I could. What could be better than a shop filled with gardening supplies and people who loved working their hands into the warm soil?

I would start seedlings inside the house, and I needed a lot of supplies and tools to get going. A shelving unit and lights to mount above each shelf. Trays to hold tiny pots of baby plants. I'd stashed some heritage seeds from Anam Cara in a box when I left, marking each envelope with a piece of tape bearing the type of plant it would grow. This alone would've sent Armand into a rage, but he had no way of knowing I'd swiped a handful of seeds. Our inventory control had been primitive, at best, and by the time he was voted in as leader, Armand had been pretty far removed from the agricultural processes of the community. And anyway, I had no idea if they would grow here, in such different soil and sun and wind conditions compared with Cape Breton.

Still, it was comforting to carry a piece of my former life to Vermont. It would've been cleaner, and easier, to make a total break, turn my back on the last twenty years like I'd done when I went to Anam Cara. But I still shook inside from the loneliness and James's absence. All these snippets of discontent, all the questions that were now popping up into the daylight, couldn't erase what I'd believed for so long: that we had a unique and special kind of love. I missed the loving moments with him, even if I didn't want to.

In the gardens, James had lavished attention on the most challenging plants in the hard Cape Breton soil, determined to see them sprout and flourish. Sort of like what he did with women. He'd wanted to see if he could raise tomatoes outdoors, grow nightshade plants like eggplant in the short summer there. He almost always succeeded. I don't know if he talked to the plants when I wasn't looking or came out and danced naked in front of them under the light of the moon. Whatever magic he unleashed, the produce he nurtured grew strong and tall and robust. Those eggplants, cooked to golden with a taste so precious and smoky. The tomatoes, sweet when popped into my mouth right off the vine and tangy when simmered into sauce to can for winter.

From my pocket, I pulled the weathered piece of paper with my list of gardening needs and unfolded it, smoothed it out so I could read it. Mary wandered up behind me and peered over my shoulder. On the back side of the page was a diagram I'd scribbled in pencil of the garden I would build and plant behind the house when the air grew warm and the soil pliable enough to play with.

"Big project?"

I shrugged. "Just getting started. You know how it is at the start—you need everything."

She nodded. "Where're you keepin' the plants until summer hits?"

"In the house." My voice rose at the end, as if it were a question.

Mary shook her head. "Won't work, hon."

"Why not?"

"Don't have enough natural light in there. I know that cottage. It's close and dark."

I'd traded one small village for another, but Mary was right. There wasn't a lot of light in my little house, which might be why I escaped each morning for a long and winding walk in the forest and always ended up in the town. I'd often spend the whole morning at a lone table in the little café, reading a book and sipping too many free refills of coffee, or here, talking and planning with Mary. I didn't need to be here so many days. I just liked the sound of another human voice.

"Thought about building a greenhouse?"

I had. In fact, it was something I was eager to do, come spring. Maybe I should shift my focus and do that now.

"I'd be happy to help ya," Mary said, and I was surprised by how warmth coursed through me at her offer. Perhaps she'd become a friend. "Evenings, after the store closes," she said.

"I'd love that," I said a bit too quickly. I felt the blush creep up my cheeks until my whole face was hot.

We'd wandered up to the front of the store and stood on the customer side of the counter talking. Mary scribbled a phone number on the back of a business card and thrust it toward me. "Give me a call, and we'll sort it out."

I left without buying anything but felt happier and more optimistic than I had been in a long time.

Chapter Seven

Months after James and I started sleeping together, he'd professed his love for me late one night, and I'd basked in the glow of his pronouncement.

"I just want to be with you, Charlie-love," he whispered, his hand under my hair gripping the back of my neck. I leaned back into his strength and closed my eyes. With his other hand, he trailed a finger along my throat. Shivers danced along my skin.

He leaned down to press his lips against my throat, his hand on my neck gripping harder, as if he alone held me up. Eyes closed, my head buzzed, my chest throbbed.

"Come away with me," he whispered close to my ear.

My eyes flipped open, and I sat up. "What?"

"Come away with me," he whispered again, pushing me back on the couch and biting my ear.

"Like a weekend trip or something?" I said, trying to stay focused, but his insistent kisses wouldn't let me. I swayed and fell back against the couch, letting my eyes close.

"Let's leave this place," he said. "Let's start over. You and me. Somewhere we can live our values."

I sat up again and took a deep breath. "James, what are you talking about?"

He shook his head and sat upright opposite me. "Well, you know how to take all the fun out of this," he chortled.

But I wouldn't let it go.

"What are you asking me?"

He stood and feathered a hand through his hair, which he'd loosed from the bun. It shimmered around his face and down his shoulders, curtains of golden-red. He was pacing, his forehead wrinkled. We'd lost the moment, and now all I wanted was to lie back on the couch and feel his mouth on my body.

"Come here," I said, reaching for him, but he pulled away, agitated. "Don't be like that."

"Don't you be like that," he spat. "I was saying something adventurous and romantic, showing how much I love you, that I only want to be with you, and you rebuffed me."

I sighed. *Here we go.* James could be dramatic, and once he got going, there was no stopping him. I'd first seen it a month after we'd slept together, two months into our relationship. We hadn't been exclusive at the time, and with Sivan's voice in the back of my head, I'd broached the topic. He'd said things like, *I can't be pinned down*, and *I can't believe you want to pen me in*, and *don't rush me, Charlie.* He couldn't have known that I'd never had sex before him, never been truly in love. It was heady, and I couldn't think about anything else—not schoolwork, not friendships, not my own life. I was all turned around, and I both wanted to throw myself on him and pledge my undying love and also run fast in the other direction.

I'd called my mother in the midst of it all, hoping that she might offer a voice of reason, some loving advice.

We hadn't spoken in a few weeks. At first, it was all enthusiasm and joy. "Charlie, darling, I'm so glad you called! How is school?"

She could hear it in my voice right away, and she downshifted. "What is it, honey?"

I told her about James, how beautiful he was, how I was in love, how he had these emotional moments where he'd be loving and sweet and calm and then agitated and annoyed and I didn't know what I'd done to upset him.

I heard her breath catch between her teeth, and her voice changed.

"He sounds unstable," she said. "Maybe not a good choice for a relationship?"

I grew defensive, angry. How dare she question my choices! I was an adult, fully formed and living on my own. I hadn't been home in months, and I was doing fine. On my parents' dollar, of course, but I didn't say that nor did she. Her voice grew smaller, quieter. She didn't want the call to end, but I was on a tear and I couldn't stop. I said some things. I heard her whimper. An arrow pierced my gut, and I felt bad for hurting my mother, but then, she'd hurt me, too, didn't she know? Then my father was on the phone, and his voice was gruff, strong, deep, and he was defending my mother the way a lover should defend his partner, and I wondered if James would ever sound that strong on my behalf, defend me if I needed defending. I collapsed into the phone and sobbed. My parents went silent. It was a disaster of a call.

Later, when James came out of his funk and crawled back to me, all apologetic and loving and quiet and so incredibly tender, I told him about the call. He went dark for three days, not returning my calls, not looking at me in class, refusing to talk to me when I stayed after all the other students had left and made myself late for the next class. He completely ghosted me, and I didn't know why I waited so eagerly for him to see sense and come back. I somehow knew he would, and I'd wait for it because this was love, wasn't it?

And when he did come back, I took him in, believed his apologies, let him cry, his head in my lap, his tears dampening my jeans. I let him pull off my clothes and nestle his face between my legs. I closed my eyes and shut out any memory or knowledge of this roller-coaster relationship and let the waves of pleasure overtake me until I was screaming so loud, my throat grew raspy and raw.

But I couldn't let it go, so I told him more about the call with my parents, and the worry lines returned to his smooth forehead and his eyes darkened.

"If you tell them about every fight we have, they'll never accept me," he said.

His voice was calm. I watched for the telltale sign that he was about to flip into ice mode, but it didn't come. He grabbed my hands and hovered his face close to mine. I almost had to look away, he was so close.

"Do you want them to not accept me, to not accept us?"

I bit my lip. How stupid of me! I loved this man, and he loved me. Of course I wanted my family to accept him.

I shook my head.

"I'm so sorry," I said. "I didn't think about it."

He nodded.

"Of course you didn't," he said, and a knot formed in my stomach. I was supposed to believe in him, but he clearly didn't believe in me. Where was the fairness in that?

"Do they truly know you?" he went on. "Do they see who Charlie Tanner really is? Do they understand what you want in life?"

A little voice inside me wondered if he knew any of that, but I swatted it away and chose to focus on whether my parents understood me, saw me as a complete person separate from them.

I'd never thought about it. Did I even know what I wanted? I'd thought so when I came to Maine, but now I wasn't so sure. My parents loved me, that I knew. But did any parent truly understand their child, especially when grown? How could they possibly see me as an individual?

I wasn't going to be a mirror image of them—they couldn't expect me to be. But did anyone see the real me? James never even asked what I wanted for dinner, let alone what kind of career I had in mind or what my visions were for my life. I wanted to point this out, but I was afraid to send him into another funk.

He was saying things like, "Stick with me, honey. I'll guide you," and "You have me now. You don't need them."

And though a little voice in the back of my head was warning me to step away, to not believe him, I saw his mouth moving, the soft, pink lips, the white of his perfect teeth, the gleam in his golden-brown eyes and tried to tune out the little voice, focus only on James, my love.

He pressed his lips to mine then, and I sucked his tongue into my mouth. I breathed him in—the scent of pine and dirt and cold air—trailed my hands through his long, silky hair. In that moment, I needed him to prove that he could be my compass, that our relationship could be enough for me.

Our clothes came off quickly. His skin against mine was hot, searing, and he bore into me with force. I hissed an inhale. We'd made love so many times, but this time there was a tinge of pain when he entered me, as if he were piercing my soul, claiming it. But then the pain subsided, replaced with pleasure, and he thrust into me again and again, filling me up, the intensity of his body reaching deep into the crevices of my being. I rode the waves of passion until we gasped together at the height of it all, and he collapsed on top of me, our bodies sticky and wet, pressed together, our hearts racing in tandem.

He stroked my hair away from my face, planted a tender single kiss on my lips. His hands were on either side of my face, and he peered down at me. I could still feel him inside me.

"This is all that matters," he said, his gaze fixed on mine. "Nothing else."

I didn't sever ties with my family that day, nor in the days or weeks that followed. I didn't even realize I was pulling away or how subtly James was urging me to until months later. The school year was coming to a close, and my mother was pressing me to return to Michigan for the summer.

"We miss you," she pleaded. "You know how beautiful it is here in the summer. It'll be good for you to be home, reconnect with your high school friends, see your grandparents."

A part of me yearned for my grandmother's hug and the comfortable silence of sitting next to my father. But James was stamped all over my life. I'd become consumed by him, desperate for his approval, the strokes of his voice telling me I was okay.

"You can even bring James with you," my mother offered. "We'd love to meet him."

It was a generous offer and one that I knew didn't come easy for my mother. I flooded with warmth, wanting to believe her. But there was a hitch in her voice that told me she didn't trust him or this relationship. She'd even once said something that suggested I was losing myself.

Why did I stay with him? Was it because he was my first love or the incredible sex? It was heady, to be sure. I'd never felt pleasure like that before. But I had thought of myself as a strong woman. All these years later, I look back on those days and wonder how he took such complete hold of my sensibilities and why I let him.

One late afternoon after classes, we were in the library. I was studying for finals, and he was grading papers.

"I'm thinking about going home for a bit this summer," I said. "I don't have an internship, and it would be nice to see my family."

He looked up, lips pursed.

"You really want to go back there?"

Nearly every table of the library was filled with students in study-mode. Books splayed open, folders and loose papers scattered, headphones pumping tunes to help calm frazzled nerves. The tables were littered with energy drinks and paper cups half-filled with old coffee. We were off in a corner, a tall window above us shining late-day light along the gray carpet.

"I do," I said. "I miss my family. My home."

He looked at me pityingly, and I recoiled. What was

wrong about wanting time with family? Why didn't he? In all the time I'd known him, James had never visited his parents, nor had they come to campus for a visit. Whenever I asked about them, he winced and said, "You don't want to meet them, trust me."

But I did. I wanted to know everything about him, every dark secret, every funny childhood story, every quirk and fear. I was waiting for him to let me in. We'd only been together eight months by then, and I figured it would take time for him to feel comfortable opening up, but when would that happen, exactly?

"Why don't you come with me?"

He shook his head a little too quickly. "Can't get away," he said, chewing on the end of his pen.

"You can't?"

He glared at me. "You think I'm lying to you?"

"No," I sputtered. "Fine. It's fine. You don't have to come. I'll miss you, though."

I tried to smile at him, but he was looking down at a paper he had been grading, angrily gnawing on the pen.

Then he put the pen down and sighed, raking his fingers along his scalp and adjusting the bun atop his head.

"I'm sorry, Charlie." His eyes were big and round, like a puppy. "Forgive me? I didn't mean to snap at you."

"Of course," I said, reaching across to touch his hand.

He smiled back then said, "Why do you have to go? I'll miss you so much."

I loved being loved like that. I got drunk on it. Too often when I was a child, I was the last one waiting for my parents to pick me up from school as the aftercare teachers tapped their feet waiting to be set free from their long work day. And then, at home in the evenings, my father often headed back out to attend a performance or an athletic match at the high school. "The principal needs to have a presence," he'd explain, waving as he left.

Mom spent evenings creating craft projects for "her kids," as she called them. It confused me when I was little—wasn't I her kid? She'd laugh and say, "Of course you are—I always come home to you, sweetheart."

I'd watch my mother cut out construction paper angels for her classroom and sometimes even help run the glue stick over the paper to attach the wings, but I never got to keep any of the angels for myself. She'd bake batches of cookies and brownies to take for school events, letting me lick the bowl but never leaving any extra treats for my enjoyment. Everything was always for other children, the ones my mother spent her days with. I could help or I could watch it all, but that focused attention was never showered on me.

Hugs and kisses from my parents were plentiful, but their distractions left me lonely, and I yearned for a love that wouldn't make them look away or leave, all their energy trained on other people. Until I'd met James, I hadn't realized how hungry I was to be loved, how all-consuming

I needed it to be.

"Maybe I'll just go for a few days," I said.

He squeezed my hand. And then he reached his foot under the table up between my legs, wiggling his toes as he pressed against my thighs and inched higher. He always slid his shoes off when we studied, and his socked foot was surprisingly adept at finding just the right spots and pressing with just the right strength.

"James," I whispered sharply. "Stop that. We're in a public place."

"Makes it even hotter, don't you think?"

He kept going, ignoring my pleas to stop, and I tasted blood when I bit my lip to stifle my cries as his toes brought me to climax right there under the desk in the very public university library full of students agonizing over end-of-term exams.

I didn't go home that summer, and at some point, I stopped calling, too. My mother, my father, even my sister Willow, who was five years older and with whom I'd never been close, took to calling with urgent requests to return the calls, to come home, to respond in some way, and soon, *please*. I can't explain why I just faded away from family ties, from my hometown, from everything familiar before I arrived at College of the Atlantic. Even the studies I'd so eagerly anticipated took a back seat to the intoxicating attention James offered.

Before I knew it, months had passed, the calls became

less frequent then were replaced with letters, and I no longer entertained any thoughts of going home. It was odd that my parents never came to campus to see what was going on, to drag me home. I'd like to think, if I were the parent, I would've gone. But then, if they had come to campus, I wouldn't be here now.

At times, I missed my family. A familiar ache in the hollow of my belly that I'd learned to ignore. But by then, James had asked me to leave Maine with him and start real life as adults, as a couple, in a community on Cape Breton Island, a place where we could "live our values," he said again and again. I didn't know what that meant, but I loved the adventure of it all and that he wanted to do it with me. I'd go anywhere he'd take me, to stay in his orbit, and I loved the idea that we had shared values to live out together.

I read every letter that my mother wrote and mailed to me, her familiar cursive on the delicate, handmade envelope shooting pangs through my heart. She'd always enjoyed making her own paper, had taught me how from a young age. Another one of her craft projects for *her kids*. But I didn't respond. What would I say? Too much time had passed, too many questions gone unanswered, and I didn't have the energy, or the words, to start over. I tucked the letters into a shoebox and wedged it in the back of my closet where James wouldn't find it. I didn't want to risk another argument, and I didn't want to watch him tear my mother's voice to shreds.

When the semester ended that year, I packed my things into the Volvo my parents had gifted me when I graduated high school so I'd have an easy way to get back and forth from college to home without paying for expensive flights. James resigned his professor job, and we were off. I couldn't have known then that he was asked to leave, strung up on charges of assaulting a student who'd left the year before I came. The only thing I did before we left was sneak out to the post office to fill out a forwarding address card. I may not want to have the hard conversations or confront their judgment of my choices, but at least my mother's letters would find me. Someone in the world would know where I was. At the time, it felt like an important thing to do.

CHAPTER EIGHT

Ow I wished I'd finished my degree.

The whole nine-hour drive to Cape Breton, James had convinced me that I didn't need a degree to make a difference, to live a life of purpose, and I was desperate to believe him. But now, in Vermont at forty years old, I no longer did.

I'd be fine for a while thanks to the box of money I had stashed away, but it would go quickly, especially if I didn't have a way to replenish it. And, I'd had to convert it to American dollars from Canadian, which reduced its value with the current exchange rate. It wouldn't last especially long. What could I do to earn income?

I'd kept house. Been part of a collective community where I did all manner of jobs. I knew how to grow nourishing plants in difficult ground. As May thawed into June, the Vermont countryside bloomed with oak, birch and black cherry trees. Clover and wild bergamot grew in the meadow behind my cottage, bloodroot along forest paths. Blueberry bushes flushed with tiny green berries that fattened into a purply-blue in the growing warmth of longer days, and I got to know my new home.

Iris, peonies and poppies bloomed in the summer rain and constant sun. Woodpeckers balanced on the bark of a white birch in my yard, and I warmed my hands around a steaming mug of strong coffee as I stood very still and watched their tiny beaks tap into the flesh of my favorite tree. I fell in love with the flowering red maples, the first blooms in spring a beacon for early pollinators. I clipped some stems from a shrub willow down the road and arranged them in a vase on my table.

In April, Mary's sister had minded the store for a week so we could build a greenhouse beside my little abode. It was sturdy and beautiful and heavy with warmth; I loved looking at its opaque panels out the kitchen window, stepping through the little door that was just taller than my five-foot-five-inch frame. I wanted a cozy, productive space to nurture plants before the short growing season began. We ended up constructing an eight-foot-by-ten-foot aluminum structure with polycarbonate walls and roof. Come fall, I hoped to use it for hardy vegetables that could withstand the harsh winter—root veggies and hardy tubers, cold-weather greens and herbs.

When June hit, I carried my baby plants outside to nest in the warming ground. It didn't take long for me to till rows, press the seedlings with their fragile roots into the soil and surround the whole plot with fencing and chicken wire four feet in height. Every minute I spent with my hands in the dirt lifted my spirits. James faded from thought, and memories of Anam Cara grew distant, grainy in my mind. I breathed in the musty loam and turned my face to the brightening sun.

Some days when an employee stood watch at the store, Mary joined me; we were becoming good friends. She was at least a decade older than me and happily unattached. Her independence was infectious, as well as her disdain for being tied down. I needed that in a friend, the inspiration of a woman okay on her own and reveling in her own company. The kind of strong I'd always thought I was but had not yet achieved.

As an adult, Mary had always lived alone, but she never lacked for male company. In fact, she was the most sexually eager woman I'd ever met, and I admired that about her. The early and intense sexual relationship James and I had quickly calmed once we got to Anam Cara. Whenever we did make love, it was wonderful, but our times together in bed grew further apart. I felt like my sensual identity was just being awakened and then I spent the majority of my time waiting for James to come home to me, to stop sleeping with other women. Though it was common at Anam Cara to have multiple sexual partners, I couldn't imagine welcoming another human into my bed. And I didn't really want to. I wanted James.

I knew this about Mary because of the casual comments

she threw out when we were pawing in the dirt or patting soil around new seeds in the greenhouse. Things like, "Yeah, he was a crack." Or "Hoo-boy, that one was a live one. Stayed for three days, and I was dizzy when he left." I had no idea how she met these men; I was afraid to ask. But I admired her aplomb.

In the warmer months, she favored jeans and white T-shirts with long crocheted vests over top and dirt-streaked low boots. Her sister, Marisol, lived in Burlington, and their parents had long since left this earth. The store was their inheritance, and Mary treated it like a family member. I'd more than once broached the topic of helping out in the shop, part-time, to have something to do, to earn some money and be around her more. She'd only shrugged and cocked her head in a gesture that I read as "Maybe?" I'd revisit it when I was ready to take on another responsibility or when I really needed the money—whichever came first.

Leaves rustled with the skittering of frothy-tailed squirrels under the blanket of foliage bordering my land. I smiled at a gray squirrel bouncing across the grass. Sweat beaded on my face as I plunged the trowel into the earth and cupped dark soil up and out. In went one heirloom tomato seedling, and I patted the ground around it to bolster the plant. I stood, pressed a metal cage around the baby plant, and then repeated the effort two feet down with another seedling.

By the time I had transplanted all the tomatoes from the greenhouse, I was calm, happy and content. Dirt had furrowed into lines around my mouth and along my forehead and pressed beneath the nails I hadn't filed low enough. I shook out my gardening gloves and hung them over the fence post to dry in the sun then packed away my gardening implements in the quiet greenhouse. The shelves were empty, ready for the next batch of seedlings to start vegetables that wouldn't have a long enough outdoor season to really get going—I'd started a watermelon plant from seed in May on a lark and planned to transfer it to the outdoor garden soon. This was when I'd also plant slips of sweet potato root and leaves in the ground for a hopeful fall ripening. I had kale going in the greenhouse, also for a fall or even early winter harvest, and I was hoping to keep the greens going for most of the winter under a garden frost blanket.

After a long, needling shower, I pulled on a pair of navy linen pants and a loose-fitting beige sweatshirt, stepped into my well-worn sneakers and set off for a stroll. Two houses down, I waved to the young mother on the porch nursing her baby in a wooden rocking chair and smiled at her tow-headed toddler spinning circles in the yard. A variety of plastic trucks and shovels littered the lawn. I saw them often on my walks. She didn't cover up as she nursed the baby—there was no need; few people passed by, and besides, who would be offended? This was Vermont, home to earth mothers and quiet farmers. As the baby suckled, she patted her mother's flesh with one splayed fat hand, a tender and possessive gesture. A pang of envy speared my heart.

James had never wanted children, so I'd adjusted my dreams. We were together, and that would have to be enough. I'd upended my life for him and resigned myself to living just in our love. I'd never contemplated if it was enough for me. I just settled into that story and never looked back.

But now that I was alone and James was a memory, I'd peeled away so many layers to reveal the truth. I wished I'd had a chance to become a mother. Which made me miss my own mother more.

A month after I'd arrived in Vermont, I pulled out the box of letters and laid them on the floor. There were so many, they'd taken up the whole living room carpet in my small house. I spent a day and a half reading through them in order, from the very first pleading ones, begging me to respond, to come home, to leave James and that "crazy place on the edge of the continent" and return to my family, to my community, to my senses. The later letters were calmer, more carefully worded, and filled with love and longing. I could hear my mother's voice leap off the page as I read each one, fingered the paper, some of which was crisp with age.

How would she know where to find me now? I hadn't

left a forwarding address or even a note when I left Anam Cara. She'd be lost to me—unless I was prepared to do something about it.

I walked a mile down the road as the summer sun sank lower in the sky then turned to head back. My phone trilled just as I turned to return home.

"You up for a bottle between us and an old movie tonight?"

"Sure," I laughed and told Mary to come in time for dinner. I'd made a loaf of rye bread, and I would sauté onions, carrots and tomatoes in a skillet then add them to a pot with homemade vegetable broth, lentils, a chunk of local butter, salt, pepper, garlic and three whole cloves, and set it to simmer—just the kind of dinner I loved. I was gathering my courage to make an important call. I'd want a friend nearby to process afterwards.

While the stew was cooking, I dialed the familiar number that I hadn't called in nearly twenty years.

My mother's voice was honey to my ears. My breath caught in my throat, and tears stung my eyes.

"Hello?" Pause. Her voice inched up an octave. "Hello?"

I swallowed and hurried to answer before she hung up. "Mom?"

Quick intake of breath and a little cry when she recognized my voice. "Charlie? Is that really you?"

I was nodding as tears trailed from the corners of my eyes

down the sides of my face. I gulped and scrambled to regain composure, swiping at my eyes to staunch the tears. "Yes," I choked out.

"Oh, thank God," she muttered then muffled the phone with her hand and called for my father. "August! It's Charlie on the phone! It's our baby after all this time."

I heard a click and then my father's choked voice.

"Charlotte!" he exclaimed. "How we've missed you."

I was racked with sobs at the sound of their voices, as if I had arrived home just by hearing them. The voices of my youth, the voices in my head.

"Mom, Dad," I uttered in a breathless whisper. "I'm so sorry."

They were whimpering, too, on the other end of the line. We all sat there, crying into the phone, not saying anything, and my body shook with the sobs I'd held in for so many long and cold years.

Then my mother pulled herself together and said, "Never you mind, Charlie. The past is the past. It's done and gone, and we have now, and I'm so glad you've called us. Where are you?"

I licked my lips, which had grown dry and chapped from being in the sun all day. I reached for balm and slid it across my lips before responding.

"I'm living in Vermont, in a town called Present," I said. Calmer now, I settled into the couch and cradled the phone close. The stew was fragrant, filling the house with the scent of warmth and garlic.

"With James?" My father's voice was gruff, hesitant.

I swallowed. The pain of his death still hit me at the most unexpected moments.

"No," I said. "He's gone."

"You left him?" my mother asked, also hesitant but hopeful. I could practically see her holding her breath, waiting for my answer.

"He died," I said.

"Oh honey," my mother said. "I'm sorry to hear that." I knew she didn't mean it, but I appreciated the effort, and I no longer cared if they accepted the decisions of my past. There was nothing I could do about it anyway.

"You didn't want to come home?" my father jumped in.

I sighed. How could I explain why I'd landed here, rather than continue the drive all the way until I ended up in their arms? I was afraid to go back, worried they wouldn't welcome me in after so much time. It seemed crazy now but had made so much sense when I was driving west from the Canadian border.

And there was something else.

I was afraid to go back there. Afraid to confront the hidden truths of my childhood which had led me to choose James, to make Anam Cara my home.

My parents were quiet. Was it worry? Anger? Hurt? Outside, the sun slipped below the horizon, turning the sky a milky pink with the glow of oncoming sunset. I walked over to the stove and lifted the lid to peer in at the lentils. The stew was thickening nicely and bubbling. I gave it a stir and covered the pot. A few more minutes, and it would be perfect. As we talked, I sliced the bread, slathered each piece with butter and sprinkled crushed garlic and parmesan cheese on top and laid the slices on a baking sheet, which I slid into a hot oven. That's when Mary knocked at the door, which I'd left unlocked, and ambled inside the house.

"Charlie?" she called out.

I poked my head out of the kitchen, pointed to the phone at my ear and put a finger to my lips. Her eyes widened as she nodded.

Mom's voice grew strength, and volume, in my ear.

"Well, I'm sure you have a lot to tell us, and the phone just isn't ideal for catching up after so long. We'll come to you. Give us the address. We'll head out tomorrow. Too much time has passed. I need to see you, darling, hold you close. I've missed you so much. We've missed you."

Her voice trailed off into another sob, and I swallowed the lump in my throat at the sound of it.

I rattled off my address, surprised by the butterflies in my stomach at the thought of seeing my parents again. They were coming to me, no questions asked, no judgment offered. It had been twenty long years of being alone, twenty long years of following a man who had anything but my best interests at heart. A man who'd done what he'd wanted, leaving me as his plaything, wondering what my path was meant to be. Leaving me in our bed alone too many nights, wondering where he was.

That time was done, like a protected box I'd sealed myself inside. Now, it was a new era, and I was free to live according to my instincts, to welcome people I'd always loved back into my life.

I pulled the garlicky bread from the oven and turned off the heat then shut the flame under the stew. Mary hovered nearby, pulling bowls from the cupboard and spoons from the drawer. Just as she'd promised, a bottle of pinot noir stood on the counter, and she searched drawers for a corkscrew to open it. I was grateful to have a friend nearby just when I needed her. I was grateful to have a real friend, period.

Mary poured two glasses full of the dark-red liquid and handed me one. We clinked quietly as a smile spread across my face.

"How soon can you be here?" I said into the phone, warmth flushing my body and making me feel whole.

Chapter Nine

The moment we hung up the phone, my parents packed and headed out. The drive from Traverse City to Present took nearly fifteen hours without stops, crossing into and out of Canada. My parents were in their sixties, energetic and scrappy, nurtured by the white skies and cold winds of the far north, and while my father had wanted to drive straight until they arrived, my mother preferred to stop halfway for food and a few hours at a roadside hotel. They didn't sleep much, or soundly, they told me later. Only tossed in the bed sheets, hearts pounding with excitement at the thought of seeing me and having me back after so many years of distance. At four a.m., they headed out, arriving in the early afternoon.

I hadn't slept much either in anticipation of their arrival. I was up before dawn, baking blueberry muffins and a fresh sourdough loaf and running out to the village grocery as soon as it opened for fruit, cheese and a whole chicken to roast for dinner. I bought new potatoes and picked greens from my garden for a salad. If I could feed them well, I'd show them I hadn't wasted twenty years of my life. And prove it to myself, too.

Heartened by their quick acceptance of my call, I was still nervous about what it would be like between us. They had to be angry about my cutting them off. How long would it take for them to know me, the real me—the me now, not just the me they'd imagined all these years?

I flung open the door to watch them drive up. Their Ford truck puttered to a stop in the gravel outside the cottage. As soon as my father parked the truck, my mother leaped out the door and ran to me, her arms encircling me, her sobs muffled in my hair. She smelled of cinnamon. I closed my eyes and soaked in her warmth.

My father shuffled over, hands in pockets, clearing his throat. "Is there room in this mess for your old dad?" His voice was clipped with emotion.

I loosened my grip on my mother to let him in. The three of us held tight in a teepee of emotion, the insistent squeaks of birds cheering us on from the trees.

"Well, let's not make a scene outside," my mother said, wiping her eyes with her sleeve and straightening her shirt.

"The next house is a quarter mile down the road," I laughed, beckoning them inside.

"What a sweet little home," my mother said. "And it smells delicious in here."

I smiled proudly. "I've made blueberry muffins and sourdough bread. I figured you'd be hungry from the drive."

"You bet," my father said, ambling into the kitchen and grabbing a muffin. He took in half of it in one huge bite.

I giggled as my mother swatted him. "August, you animal," she said. "Where have your manners gone?"

"All this emotion makes a man hungry," he replied through a mouthful as he finished off the entire muffin with a second chomp.

I'd brewed coffee and filled a tiny pitcher with cream. Mugs were laid out on the counter, and I poured a cup for each of them and myself then joined them at the table. A pot of sweet butter sat beside the sourdough, along with fig jam and small plates. There was also a bowl filled with apples and bananas.

"You're here," I said timidly, another wave of regret and guilt washing over me. My heart pounded, and my stomach kept doing somersaults. Why was I so nervous?

My mother covered my hand with hers. "It's okay, honey. The past is past. Let's start from here."

I was grateful for her instant and ready forgiveness. My parents never held grudges and were quick to forgive, and I felt entirely responsible for the rift between us. How cruel to cut them out of my life entirely! Eternal optimists, they believed in the essential good of all people. I'd only begun to consider that this trait, which was baked into me and which I'd always seen as positive, might be to blame for my traipsing into James Grace's orbit and getting lost there for twenty years.

We ate and talked for an hour and a half, catching up on the surface of two decades of news. My sister, Willow, was married and a mother of four. Both of my grandfathers had passed on, but my grandmothers were alive and well and missing me. A pang of regret seared me at the thought of never seeing my grandfathers again.

The tears wouldn't abate, one or the other of us dissolving into a fit of emotion suddenly and without explanation. Relief at our reunion? Frustration and anger built up over time? Fear? Blame? It all came rushing forward as we ravaged the muffins, leaving just two of the dozen by the time we'd finished talking and hacking into the bread as if its airy flesh could sop up all the sadness we'd harbored during our time apart.

We danced around the questions in our minds but never broached the topic aloud. I didn't ask how they'd felt when I cut them off, and they didn't rail at me for doing so. But it had to happen sometime, didn't it?

"I'd like to show you my garden," I said, hoping to break out of the funk we'd settled into after so much stress-eating, and let the sweet summer air bolster us all.

Mom engulfed me in another spontaneous hug, pecked my cheek and looped her arm through mine. I smiled and led them outside.

The yard was bursting with color and energy, the grasses waving in a soft wind, the plants stoic and full-breasted. The tomatoes were inching skyward, having tripled in height from the day I'd planted them outdoors a month earlier. I swung the gate in the fence open for my parents to walk through. They followed the slate path I'd laid, a meandering trail that kept me from stepping on the young plants.

My dad looked around the garden slowly, kneeling to finger the velvety leaves of a young zucchini plant.

"Aw, Charlie, this is great," he muttered. He looked up at me, his face soft and eyes brimming yet again with tears. I couldn't remember a time in my childhood when he'd looked at me so intently or been so moved by something I had done. I swallowed over a lump that was growing in my throat and focused on the garden, letting pride fill my chest.

The garden took up the entirety of the yard, giving me a quarter-acre of growing space. All mine! The plants angled toward the sun, their eager heads drinking in the light.

There were gates at two ends, one close to the house and one a quick sprint from the greenhouse, which made transplanting easy.

My father nodded his chin at the greenhouse. I broke into a wide smile, still in awe of the little space I'd built to nurture new life, sustaining my own on the results. I was proud of what I could do, without following someone else's lead.

"My greenhouse," I said.

"You built that?"

"With some help from my friend, Mary," I said, nodding.

I held the door open as my father ducked inside. At six-two, he had to crouch to make it in, but once inside, he could rise to his full height with a few inches to spare. Shorter than me by four inches, my mother breezed inside with ease.

It was humid and thick, just how I liked it. A sauna infused with the scent of growing things. On the shelves, seedlings were rapidly ascending in height. Only mid-summer, we'd soon feel autumn's cooler breezes, and I couldn't wait to turn the garden over to a new crop and begin new plants once again in here. Most of the year, I'd live off the generosity of my land and the hard work of my hands.

My mother slurped the air. "I am beyond impressed."

My father nodded. "I can't believe you did all this." He pressed a firm hand on my shoulder.

Maybe the last twenty years hadn't been devoid of purpose or achievement after all. Fine silver strands threaded through my dark curls and the skin under my eyes wasn't as smooth as it used to be, but I was a forty-year-old woman starting over, and I had talents that I was putting to great use. I had new people in my life who saw the real me, who expected nothing but a smile and a conversation. And now I had my family back.

We settled on the porch as the sun dipped lower in the

sky. Insects came on in full song, fireflies winking in the coming dark.

I was happy, full, but sadness lurked around the perimeter of everything. I'd missed so much.

"So Willow is a mom."

Mom nodded vigorously. "And a good one."

A pang of envy rippled through me.

"What are her kids like?"

"Trevor is a rascal," Dad said. "He's the baby, and he has no fear. Also, gets everything he wants. She spoils him."

My mother swatted his hand. "You can't spoil a child, August."

"Humph," he replied. "Clementine is sweet as pie. Oliver's serious, always has his nose in a book, and Penny is talkative, outgoing, the life of any party. Also a little bossy."

Mom hit him again.

He pursed his lips. "What?"

"You can't say that. Chips away at her self-confidence. You wouldn't call a boy bossy."

"Right," Dad sighed. "It's not like she's listening. So many new rules." He sent a pleading look my way.

I smiled at him but silently cheered my mother's sensitive assertions, wishing she'd been this aware when I was a child.

"Who'd she marry?"

"Colton Broadman—you remember him," Mom said. "Grew up down the road, middle of five brothers. You know the Broadmans—they were boisterous and loud but a good family. She started dating him in college at U of M, though they'd practically grown up together. He's a lawyer now."

I nodded. I did remember Colton, though my sister and I had never been in each other's orbit. It was almost as if we'd been part of two different families. She left for college when I was in seventh grade. When I cut my family out of my life, I was nineteen to her twenty-four. Odd that I didn't remember any wedding chatter while I was still in touch with the family—was there more to that story than my parents were telling me? I guess it didn't matter now. They were married and parents and had been together the majority of their lives. I hoped she was happy.

Night was a cloak around us by now, with a cool breeze pimpling my skin. I shivered.

"Let's go inside," I said, ready to cook for them, to stay up late talking, anything just to keep hearing the music of their voices.

CHAPTER TEN

That night, long after a delicious home-cooked dinner where my parents once again praised my culinary skills, our eager conversation was replaced by huge yawns. We kissed and hugged goodnight, and I settled onto the couch with a blanket and a pillow so my parents could sleep in my bedroom. We were all exhausted and fell quickly into a deep and even sleep. So I was startled when the phone rang just after midnight.

"Boden?" I shook myself awake and sat up fully. "Why are you calling me so late?"

"I don't want anyone to know," he said, sounding muffled.

"Is your hand over the phone? I can't really hear you."

"Sorry, yeah," he said, and then he was clearer.

"What's up? God, it's good to hear your voice."

I'd been in Vermont four months with no contact from any of my Anam Cara friends. Although I'd wanted it that way, it had been too quiet, and I'd wondered what they thought of my sudden, middle-of-the-night departure, especially Boden. I hoped he wasn't angry that I hadn't told him, or hurt. But it was a relief that Armand had not found me. Or the money.

But if Boden could find me, so could anyone.

"Yeah, I miss you too, babe," he said, his voice sweet as homemade jelly.

Boden had come to Anam Cara five years after James and I arrived, a lanky college graduate a year younger than me with blond hair and green eyes. He'd grown up in Halifax and taken six years to finish a degree, working difficult jobs to earn tuition money. He spent summers on a lobstering boat off the northern tip of Cape Breton, the man of his family after growing up in Halifax with a single mother and quiet younger sister. He was sweet and alone, and I gravitated toward him in those early days after he'd arrived, unaware how desperate I was for companionship.

From the minute we'd arrived at the commune, James had charged forward, eager to make friends and work his way up to a leadership role in the community. He was always sidling up to the founders and their favorites, hoping to wedge his way into the bosom of Anam Cara. I only asked him about it once, and his response—"because you can't achieve anything if you're not in charge"—struck me like a slap across the face. I'd left it alone and focused on learning how to cultivate the land, making whatever friends I could among the people who seemed the least kooky and the most down-to-earth. It was the closest I could get to my earlier desire to contribute to sustainability and protect the environment.

It wasn't long before James was coming home later at night and leaving early most mornings. I waited for the schedule to right itself, for him to come home to me while there was still daylight, back to my bed before I was asleep. Just when I began to believe the situation was hopeless, he'd return, full of love and energy and attention, and we'd fall into each other as if our very lives depended on consuming each other in fits of passion. We'd stay in bed for days, full of laughter and stories, catching up like people who'd been unfairly pulled apart for too long, and I felt in those moments like I was back in the heart of the man I loved, the man who was my whole world. The contentment lasted for a few days after he'd inevitably disappear again, but eventually the loneliness would come slamming back stronger than before.

But when Boden arrived, his smiling presence and eager friendship revived me. We became close quickly, and James strangely didn't seem to mind.

"It's good for you to have someone to pal around with when I'm busy," he reasoned.

So I did. Boden was what I missed most after leaving Anam Cara.

"There are some strange rumors going around," he whispered into the phone.

"Rumors about what?" A zing of unease zapped

through me. I didn't want to be pulled back into the drama. I wanted it erased from my memory, and me from the memories of the people there, except for those I could trust.

"About James. About how he died."

I went cold, and my breath hitched in my throat, recalling Indira's words at the memorial.

"He died of a heart attack. They call it a widow-maker. It's that sudden and powerful," I said, reciting what Armand had said.

"Maybe not," Boden said. "Shit, I can't talk. Gotta go. I'll call you again." And the line went dead.

Though I was beyond tired, my racing heart wouldn't let me ease back into sleep. Suddenly, the darkness outside my windows seemed thick and ominous. My parents were in the next room and the front door was bolted, but chills rippled through me as I contemplated what a different story about James's death might mean. *Please, let him be wrong*, I thought, but in my gut, I knew that he probably wasn't.

CHAPTER ELEVEN

I woke up to the sound of sizzling and bright sun cascading through the window. I arched my back and stretched before glancing at the clock on the mantle. Ten in the morning! I hadn't slept that late in years.

I leapt off the couch and wandered into the kitchen. My mother was frying eggs in a skillet, and my father was eating a thick slice of toast.

"Why didn't you wake me?"

My mother put down the spatula, wiped her hands on a kitchen towel, and came over to hug me. "You needed the sleep, obviously," she said. "And there's no rush. We're here for as long as you want us."

My father nodded in my direction with a half-smile. They'd tuned the kitchen speaker low to a classical playlist. The window over the sink was cracked, and a warm breeze sifted through the screen.

"I can't believe I slept that long," I muttered, heading for the bathroom to wash up. After changing into denim shorts, a tank top and a zip-up hoodie, I padded back into the kitchen and poured a cup of coffee, swirling in the cream and trying to wake up.

"Maybe the late-night phone call interrupted your sleep?" Mom slid a plate of over-easy eggs and two slices of golden toast in front of me.

I smiled my thanks and looked at her. Had I imagined all the loneliness of my childhood? Or were they different now in their golden years? Regardless, I couldn't get enough of having them this close to me. I never wanted them to leave.

"You heard that? Sorry," I said, dragging a corner of toast through the runny yolk and crunching into it. "I didn't mean to wake you."

"It's not a big house, love," my mother said.

"No, it's not." I ate breakfast quickly, suddenly starving. The eggs had come from a local farmer, Layton Spelman, whom I'd met at Mary's store. When I was bored or in need of some earth-bound wisdom, I ambled over to his land and offered to help in the fields. He always said yes and then paid me in cartons of eggs still warm from the chickens or a package of sausages made from his latest herd. It was the way I was used to being, after twenty years of living broke—I would do something and get paid in items I could use. Money had no resonance for me.

"Who was it?" my father asked. "Who called so late? I assumed everything was okay because you didn't fly out of here on some urgent matter."

I nodded, considering my words. "It was my friend Boden, from Anam Cara," I said. "My best friend there."

I hesitated, not wanting to worry them that I might miss the place or that life. Their silence was thick.

"I miss him," I said, hoping to soften the sudden tension.

My mother nodded, but I could see hesitation in her eyes.

"I haven't made many friends here yet," I said by way of explanation. "And he was my closest confidant there for a lot of years."

She nodded again then asked, "Why did he call so late?"

I decided to be honest, to put all my cards on the metaphorical table. Two decades of distance were behind us; I'd only go forward with total honesty and complete transparency. A new leaf. My new approach to life in general.

"He said there are rumors about how James died," I said slowly.

My father put down the newspaper and looked at me. "I thought you said it was a heart attack."

"That's what I was told. A widow-maker. Instant and final."

Mom swallowed, put down her coffee cup. "Now they don't think so?"

I shrugged. "We didn't talk for long. He had to go quicky."

I hadn't realized I'd been twisting my fingers together. As soon as I saw it, I stopped and hid my hands on my lap. "I don't honestly want to know," I said, attempting to sound light but failing. I gulped some coffee.

My parents were staring at me, waiting for me to say more.

"I've left all that behind me. I don't want to get swept up in the drama there again."

Mom's shoulders relaxed at my words. "I'm so relieved, honey," she said, reaching for me. She glanced at my dad, and they held a meaningful glance. "We don't want to lose you again."

Relief flooded through me. "I don't want that either, Mom, Dad." I looked from one to the other. "It's all my fault anyway. I won't let that happen again."

They shared another meaningful look that had words behind it I wasn't privy to.

"What is it?"

My mother shot a pleading look at my father, and he nodded and patted her hand. "It's okay, Mellie. You can say it," he said.

My mother swallowed and looked at me. "Have you ever considered talking to someone about, um, what you went through?"

I blinked. "What I went through?"

"Well, you followed James to a commune and cut off your family and friends for twenty years, darling," she said.

Her voice shook as she spoke, and though I felt defensive, I shoved it down because I knew how hard it was for her to say this. "It's not like you. Or at least not like we thought you were back then." She swallowed again and added hastily, "Or now."

I smiled, though my heart was racing. Had they ever really known me, how I felt? It took decades for me to figure out myself—I was still just at the beginning of getting clear—and they'd always been too busy to really focus on me.

But I swallowed down my defensiveness so I could speak with a calm and even voice. "I appreciate your concern, Mom," I said. "I'll consider it."

Though really, I had no plans to talk to anyone about my past. It was dead and gone, and that's exactly where I wanted it.

CHAPTER TWELVE

We spent the morning in the garden, freeing the soil of weeds, carefully digging out the dandelion greens that had grown deep in the soil, around roots that wouldn't give up easily. The fanning leaves looked like a medieval royal collar in a rich shade of green. I loved the taste of the bitter leaves, sauteed in butter and garlic and sprinkled with a little lemon zest. This weed, while considered a pest in so many gardens, was a happy byproduct in mine, a sudden gift that sprung from the ground as if to say, "Take me! I'm full of nutrients and free." That old miserly instinct from Anam Cara—use everything you possibly can—was deeply embedded in my soul. But I didn't mind it when it brought me nourishment from the land.

The truth was, I didn't mind a lot of what I'd learned there; much of it had shaped me, connected me to the earth in a calm and beautiful way. Of course, I was glad for the box of money I'd found, but I didn't need much to live a happy life. I was good with my hands, confident in my independence—mostly because I'd been forced to not rely on James or anyone else to get by. For all the faults of that twisted place, the control and kooky philosophies, living off the land and relying only on myself were not bad things.

Mom had tied a red bandana at the top of her forehead and looped it under her dark bob. "To catch the sweat," she claimed, but she was always finding ways to keep her hair out of her eyes. It was shorter than when I was young but still shone with the glossy darkness I remembered, although now it was threaded with white. She sat on one of the paving stones, her light-blue baggy jeans rolled at the ankles and the sleeves of her pink cotton shirt rolled up to her elbows.

Dad wore work pants and a battered, navy blue University of Michigan T-shirt. He kept mopping the top of his head, where the gray curls were thinning most, with a kerchief he looped through the waist of his pants.

"I have sunscreen, if you want it," I said, but they both shook their heads. Though the sun was bright, it never got too hot, and though I was well aware of the damage even a northern sun could do on pale skin, all of us tended toward more olive tones and rarely burned. Still, I worried about Dad's thinning pate.

I watched my mother plunge the trowel into the earth and pluck out the weeds with her fist. I watched my father level the soil along the garden's perimeter and smooth it over with a hoe, humming as he worked.

We took a break on the shaded porch for lemonade and granola bars before showering and heading north for an afternoon exploring Burlington, an hour and a half from Present.

"You know, honey, Dad and I were thinking, it might be nice to go to Shabbat services while we're here," Mom said between sips of lemonade. We were on the porch, the late-morning haze warming the wood.

I huffed, thinking it was a joke. While our family had Jewish roots, we'd never been remotely observant. I couldn't remember going to synagogue even once when I was a child. The most Jewish we'd ever gotten was when my grandparents invited us over for Hanukkah, and my parents seemed to go begrudgingly, out of obligation.

But Mom's eyes were serious, and Dad watched my re-action with a curiosity that caused his eyebrows to rise.

"Oh, you're serious," I said soberly. "Um, why?"

Mom glanced to Dad and back to me.

"The thing is, Charlie," Dad said, "since you've been gone, we've found a Jewish community back home that we really like. We're pretty active members now, going to services almost every week."

"Since you retired," Mom huffed.

"I couldn't miss the Friday night football games at the high school, Mel," he reasoned.

Mom turned to me then. "I'd go when he couldn't." She

thumbed in Dad's direction. "People know us. And we feel good, proud, about being Jewish now."

"Really?" I chewed a piece of ice just to have something to do. Why did this annoy me?

They nodded slowly, as if waiting for me to shoot down the idea. I wasn't going to, though this news triggered a discomfort in me that I wished I could shed. I'd had enough of communities built on rules and strictures. But I held my ground, breathed evenly, listening to them and hoping I'd get the time I needed to ponder why the idea of a strong Jewish identity bothered me.

"I guess it's fine." I shrugged. "I'm not sure I can be much help, though. I don't even know where to look for a synagogue in Vermont."

I laughed nervously. Were there Jews here? Maybe some old hippies, I thought, careful not to roll my eyes. And I'd had enough of old hippies already at Anam Cara.

"Well, we've already looked into it, actually, and there's a cute little congregation in town," Mom offered. "They meet in a congregational church, in the basement."

I swallowed. The ice nearly lodged in my throat, but I slowed my breath, and it slid down. They'd already looked into it? Was this subterfuge? And why did I care? I could go with them, humor them, and never go back. Or just let them go on their own. They were free to do what they wanted.

As was I.

I nodded and took a deep breath, exhaling audibly. "Okey doke, so you'll go to religious services!" I smiled thinly.

They looked at each other but didn't respond.

"Why don't you come with us, honey?" Mom said gently.

My heartbeat increased. The familiar resistance to other people telling me what to do reared up. A gate was closing, separating me from them. My gut told me to move back, create some distance, but I couldn't do that, not now, when we were back together after so many years.

"Why do you need me to go with you?" I said quietly.

Mom laid a hand on my arm. Her eyes were shining. Was she about to cry again? I knew my face was steely, stoic. I couldn't help it. Every muscle in my body tensed up, my fingers going rigid.

"Honey…" Her voice was low, soft, slow. "When you cut us off, we were devastated. I don't know what prompted us to seek out the Jewish community, but it helped. Really, it did. The rabbi helped us weather your absence. He guided us through what was, essentially, mourning. It was as if you had died—we lost you, and we were bereft."

She didn't seem to be laying the blame at my feet, but I couldn't help but feel a jolt of defensiveness anyway.

"Your father took a leave of absence from work in those first months," Mom continued. I was shocked. I couldn't remember my father ever even calling in sick when I was young. His job was everything to him.

Dad shifted in his chair. He couldn't look at me.

"I cried every day at school and almost lost my job," she said. "I was scaring the children."

I sucked on my bottom lip, my heartbeat pulsing at my temples. The voice in my head was screaming, a child throwing a tantrum: *They're putting this all on me, blaming me for ruining their lives. How dare they! Don't they understand I, too, had pain and anguish?* The past twenty years hadn't been easy, though I'd taken it on myself.

Implied in my mother's "the past is in the past" statement was a deliberate turning their backs on any of my experiences. It was rather one-sided, about how my choices affected them, and that fact started to grate on me. I wanted them to ask how it had been for me, why I'd chosen to follow James, why I'd severed ties. The thing was, I didn't really want to answer.

"The Jewish community helped us, Charlotte," Dad said simply, still not looking in my direction. "They picked us up off the ground. They got us going again. Living again."

I got up from my chair and paced the length of the porch.

"So you want me to go to synagogue out of guilt for ruining your lives?"

My mother looked stricken. My father scowled. From the forest, birds twittered and called. Life as usual for them. No big drama among the trees.

"I'm sorry," I said quickly. "I don't want to get into it, but the past twenty years haven't been the easiest for me, either."

My mother's mouth softened, her eyes becoming kind. My dad exhaled audibly.

"Maybe we'll get to it in time," I said, resting a hand on my mother's arm. "Just understand that I have scars from being in a rigid community for so long. I know it was my choice. But any mention of religion makes me recoil."

It was then that Mary called with news of some heirloom seeds that had just arrived for mustard greens that I could pot in my greenhouse to transplant in later September and harvest in the very late fall. I motioned to my parents that I'd take the call and escaped into the house.

"Really?" The door bumped me on the behind as it slammed shut behind me. "I can plant in the ground that late up here?"

"Yeah, it's really cool," she said. "People don't understand how far you can extend the growing season this far north. Oh, and I've got these cold frames you can put around them once you plant them outdoors to extend the season. Did you ever use those in Nova Scotia?"

We hadn't. Which amazed me since Anam Cara was known for its agricultural prowess.

"Unbelievably, no," I said. "I'm excited to try it."

"I can bring them over tonight if you want, and a bottle

of red?"

I sighed. "Wish I could, Mary. Rain check?"

"'Course, honey. What you got going on?"

I laughed. "My parents are here. We're heading to Burlington in a bit, and then tomorrow, they want to go to synagogue services."

Mary sucked in air between her teeth and said, "Yeah, the temple in the church with the cute rabbi. Poor guy."

I was shocked that Mary Hobson of the long gray braids who rode a motorcycle like it was built expressly for her would know anything about the local Jewish community.

"They're being really weird about it," I said. "Saying the Jewish community back home saved them when I cut them out. Nice guilt trip. So fun."

"Aw, honey, go easy on them. They're your parents," she said.

Her soothing voice brought my boiling blood to room temperature.

"You're probably right," I sighed. "What's sad about the rabbi? And how'd you cross paths with a rabbi?"

"His wife used to come in here for her summer garden," she said wistfully. "She died."

"Oh." Mary was full of surprises. Who knew the local garden-store proprietor was actually the town crier.

"She was sweet," Mary said. "He is, too. Poor guy, alone these two years. Loved her so much. You could see it in his eyes. But he doesn't seem haunted, just continues on in his duty. Steward of the community. Everyone loves him."

I'd never heard Mary ramble like this. The rabbi must be one hell of a guy. I wondered if he'd been among her many conquests.

"Okay, kid, see ya later. Lemme know when you want those seeds. And the wine." She chuckled before hanging up.

I went to the door and pried it open. They looked pensive on the porch, and regret washed over me.

"Okay, we'll all go check out the local synagogue," I said quickly before I could regret it.

Mom looked up with relief. "Are you sure?"

I nodded. "I'm going to shower and change. Let's head to Burlington soon, yeah?"

Dad nodded. A light had returned to his eyes, and he looked straight at me with a relieved smile.

I smiled, then headed into the cottage, the door thwacking closed behind me.

I didn't stop to eavesdrop on their chatter. I wanted the stinging pelt of the shower and the slow strokes of a comb through my wet hair to calm me. It had always been like this for me when people broached the topic of Judaism. Visions of my strong, proud college roommate Sivan hovered in my mind—so proud of her Jewish and Israeli identity, even when the far-left faction got in her face. She didn't stand down, didn't cower in their wake. She knew who she was and wouldn't let anyone steer her

away from it. Why had I? And why did my ancestral identity rising from the ashes and claiming my family cause
insecurity to ripple through me?

Chapter Thirteen

Traipsing around Burlington was fun, and exhausting, and we returned home late at night, only to collapse into sleep without even washing up. I slept late again the next morning and when I woke, I almost thought the whole plan to attend Shabbat services had been a dream. At the breakfast table, I learned it was anything but—our Friday night plans were solid. There was no going back.

Mom was all abuzz with excitement. She'd been on the synagogue website and was rattling off all the details she'd learned.

"It's a fairly small congregation, but they have a regular rabbi," she said, her voice ending in a little exclamation. "Can you imagine that? Most small towns have rabbis who travel in once a month from a bigger city. It looks like he also does other work to cobble together a couple salaries, which makes sense. What an innovative man! And he looks very handsome." She blushed and glanced in my dad's direction.

"It's okay, Mel," he said, patting her hand. "I'm not

threatened by a little rabbi crush."

"Parker Mizrahi—what a dreamy name." She was like a teenage girl drooling over the captain of the football team. "He's been with the temple for more than ten years! That's a long time for a rabbi to stay with a congregation, especially a small town one," she said, looking at me.

I shrugged. What did I know—or care—about synagogue politics?

I dug into the stack of fluffy pancakes Mom set before me—buttermilk with local blueberries we'd picked up at a store in the city. I loved having someone cook for me, especially after so many years of being on hand for James, making his life easy—setting his table, cooking his favorite foods, being available for his spontaneous requests, then waiting for him when he disappeared. If he came back at any moment and I wasn't ready to wait on him, I'd hear about it. I'd had nothing else to do other than my farm shifts. And I was starting to realize that I did it out of desperation, and a belief that it was the best situation I could get. Which made me incredibly sad.

I drizzled maple syrup over the pancakes and sank my fork in to spear a bite-sized piece. Mom was humming as she washed dishes.

"So what's the plan for our religious excursion," I asked.

My father sipped coffee and looked up from the newspaper.

"We're not religious, Charlie," he said with a hitch in his

voice. "We just like being Jewish."

"Okay," I chortled. "It's just a surprise. It'll take time to get used to it. It never mattered before, and I need to get used to this new version of my family."

Mom turned off the faucet, wiped her hands and turned to me in a defiant stance. "You've been gone a long time," she said rather strongly. "Didn't you consider that your cutting us off might cause us to change?"

In fact, I hadn't. I swallowed a gummy bite of pancakes and washed it down with a swig of coffee.

Anger brimmed at the surface for all of us. I wished they'd consider what prompted me to leave in the first place. I wish I understood why I hadn't been stronger, why I'd been willing to cut my family off completely. But we hadn't been the perfect family they imagined. Maybe they had realized this over the intervening years but as yet, I hadn't heard anything to that effect. Did they know I'd felt lonely and ignored as a child? We had a lot to work through, to open up about, and we were only just finding our way back to comfort with one another. But I was anxious to heal the gaps.

"Why are you being like this, Charlotte?" My father's voice was coaxing. I couldn't avoid his penetrating gaze.

It stung to hear his stern voice directed only at me. I laid my fork against the plate, pressed my napkin to my lips and took a big breath.

"I'm sorry. I just don't like being blamed for everything.

There's a lot we need to understand about each other, and I know it will take time. I guess I'm just impatient to get everything out in the open."

Silence. Mom looked down at the floor. Dad gazed out the window. The classical music on the speaker plinked a lilting tune. I wanted to throw the damn thing against the wall.

Though my voice was measured, anger bubbled up inside me, and it felt surprisingly good. Cleansing. It was easier to be angry than to take responsibility for the misguided actions of my youth. I don't even think I was angry at them entirely. I was sick of sitting quiet in a corner and tending to the needs of everyone but me. Deep down, I recognized that I'd gone willingly—James hadn't kidnapped me or held me against my will. Still, it was easier to look outside myself for answers than straight in the mirror.

They couldn't know how triggering it was when they spoke of going to synagogue, that visions of the Great Hall at Anam Cara flashed bright in my mind. I opened my throat to let air in. I felt suffocated, as if I were back there, yearning to tear out of the big double doors and run as fast as I could, as far away as possible, from the control of group-think. It was the first time I considered that I might suffer from PTSD after twenty years of living there. I would need to tell them all of this, but I just wasn't ready. And I wasn't sure they were ready to hear it all, either.

"There's not blame here," Mom said slowly. "If anything, we should be thanking you. We're happy to be re-connected to our Jewish roots. Your grandparents were thrilled, and it brought us closer to our parents. Grandma Lucy joins us often for services. I think it's a good thing that we have a community and a faith."

Dad got up and stood next to Mom, his arm around her shoulders pulling her close to his side.

"You don't have to come with us," Mom said.

I looked at them, a unit pressed together. Them against me. As it had always been. My stomach fell as I thought of being forgotten at elementary school, the secretary waiting for them to pick me up so she could go home and grumbling about their tardiness. Memories of all the kids they made time for, and then I got the tired, overworked versions of them instead of the fun people I imagined them to be at work. I hated those kids, and I resented my parents for not seeing what their absences did to me. What would they say if they knew I turned to James because I was so desperate to be loved? And what a disaster that was anyway.

I heaved a huge sigh.

"I'll go to services," I said. "But there's going to come a time when we have to talk about uncomfortable things if we want to move forward with total honesty and no barriers." I swallowed.

"I want that," I said quietly. "And I hope you do, too."

I resumed eating, suddenly starving.

Mom came over and sat beside me, inching her chair close. "Did you think time stood still for us when you cut us out?" I could feel her breath against my cheek, she was that close. It was warm and sour-sweet.

"No," I said quickly, only then realizing that, in fact, I had. I'd traveled into a life and world of my own, all the time thinking that what I'd left behind was frozen in time and space. I knew they'd be older, but I hadn't expected them to look it. I knew they'd lived a life without me, but I felt left out nonetheless. And yes, it was my choice, my doing, but the effects of the last twenty years ravaged me, thinking of the time I'd lost, the moments I'd missed. It was curious that I wasn't angry at James. Or myself.

I placed a hand softly over Mom's and turned to face her.

"I'm sorry," I said. "I guess I did expect time to stand still. Even though it hasn't for me. I guess I thought that I could come back to all of you as I had left you, even though I'm drastically different than I was then. That isn't fair, but it wasn't conscious."

She leaned closer and kissed my cheek then pressed her forehead to mine and closed her eyes.

Before we left for services, I snipped some herbs from the garden—long stalks of parsley and fragrant lemon thyme—tied them with twine and laid them in a wicker basket I often took to the farmers market. I pulled out some beets and carrots, rinsed them with the hose and dried them to lay beside the herbs, and then I lifted a head of butter lettuce from the soil, shook off the excess dirt and fitted it beside the other vegetables in the basket. Finally, I snipped some lavender stalks and tied a twine bow around the stems and laid it on top of everything.

At Anam Cara, communal meditations weren't necessarily a religious experience, but each member was expected to bring a gift to the gatherings, our version of tithing. While we all tended the communal gardens by obligation, many of us had our own window-box herbs and backyard plots, and it was understood that we'd bring a donation from anything grown on our personal property to the leaders whenever they called a gathering. After, we'd use whatever was brought to create a communal meal with singing that lasted well into the night. It was one of my nicer memories of the place.

I slung the basket over my arm and called to my parents that I was ready to leave.

Mom came out of the bedroom in a long denim skirt and loose silk top with layers of beaded necklaces. She looked sun-kissed and radiant, her hair sleek, her eyes shining.

"Well don't you look nice," I said, leaning in for a kiss. She smelled of cinnamon and the sweet assurance of earth.

"As do you," she said.

I was wearing navy blue linen pants, a flowing cream silk sweater and a multicolored scarf in earth tones draped around my neck. I'd fished out small gold dangling earrings with little amber stones and swept my thick mane into a wispy bun.

"Thanks, Mom." I smiled.

Dad came out of the bathroom in khakis and a polo shirt with a crocheted yarmulke clipped to his hair. I'd never seen my father wear a head covering before. It was like he'd stepped out of a foreign film, looking like my father, but I wasn't entirely sure it was him.

"Wipe that look off your face," he said with a smile.

"Sorry, Dad. I've just never seen you looking like a rabbi."

He harumphed and then whistled when he got a glimpse of Mom. They were so symbiotic and in love, after more than four decades together. My parents had met in high school and dated for six years before they married at twenty-two. Willow came along a year later and me five years after that. They'd always been energetic and in sync. Now, having been through so many years with James and beginning to understand how not-ideal that relationship had been, I envied their easy love and their continued connection so many years in.

"Both of you look stunning," Dad said, kissing Mom full on the lips and then pecking my cheek.

We trooped out to their truck, Dad behind the wheel, me pressed between them, the basket on my lap. It was only a couple miles down the road from the cottage, an easy and quick drive, and we pulled up to the church with ten minutes to spare before services began. I hadn't expected to feel nervous, but butterflies fluttered in my stomach.

The church was a two-story traditional white clapboard New England structure with Greek Revival columns on either side of the double doors. It had stood in this spot for a hundred years, congregations cycling in and out of the space until the Congregational Church took it over in 1983.

The late afternoon was still, punctuated by the sound of crickets chirping in the long grasses. Behind the building was a stand of paper birch trees with Hostas and lady ferns beneath them. Someone had landscaped the perimeter well and with care. A wide, open meadow extended beyond the property, and I couldn't help conjuring ideas of what I might do with so much fertile ground.

The door creaked open, and we stepped inside the echoing hall. We'd entered right into a shallow lobby behind the sanctuary, where dark wooden pews filled the belly of the space leading up to a little stage down front. A brass cross was mounted on the white wall behind the lectern. There were red cushions on the pews and tall, colorful stained-glass windows with biblical scenes in great detail.

A table of pamphlets stood near the door, and a room off the lobby held the church's small library. There were signs pointing to the parish office down one hall, restrooms down another, classrooms up a carpeted staircase and the communal kitchen and gathering space down another set of stairs.

"This way," Mom said, pointing downstairs.

I followed her and Dad down a lit staircase, which was wide enough for them to walk side-by-side. I trailed behind. The low hum of chatter vibrated up toward us as we neared the bottom, voices in warm conversation volleying back and forth. We entered the big room to find a couple dozen people gathered in small groups, talking, gesturing, smiling. Chairs had been arranged in six rows, facing a lectern and a wooden cart on wheels with a golden Star of David on sliding doors.

The basket hung heavy over my forearm, and I felt ridiculous for bringing produce to a religious service. What had I been thinking? I looked for a place to stash it out of sight, but before I could find one, a beautiful man with sandy-brown hair, sparkling hazel eyes and pressed jeans approached us. His green sweater made his eyes shine; it matched the little yarmulke that sat atop his thick and glossy hair.

He was gorgeous.

"Shabbat Shalom, Rabbi," Mom chirped. He held out a hand, and she shook it, smiling bigger than I'd ever seen.

This was the rabbi?

Dad pumped his hand next, and then the man trained his stunning smile on me. "You must be Charlie," he said, enveloping my fingers in his warm hand. I stood mute, gaping, unable to form words.

He didn't look like a rabbi. He looked like a man I'd meet in a library under soft lighting, who might lay down a towel over a muddy puddle so that I could walk over it. A man from a fairy tale, a prince with no flaws.

What the hell?

"It seems our daughter has lost her ability to speak," Mom said. "I'm so sorry. She's never been to a synagogue before."

I shook out of my trance and held the basket out to him.

"I brought this," I said, stumbling over the words. "It seems silly now, but I thought it would be nice to bring a gift, since I'm new."

My face flushed with warmth, and I wished I could run out of the room, never to return.

He took the basket, crooked it over his arm and pulled out the lavender bundle, lifting it to his nose. He closed his eyes and breathed in the scent.

"I love the calming effect of lavender," he said, directing those shining eyes back at me. A dimple appeared in his cheek as he smiled. "This is the most thoughtful gift I've ever received from a congregant," he continued. "Thank you so much."

"It's all from Charlie's garden," my mother crooned.

"Impressive. Welcome to you all," the rabbi said. "I'm so glad you came."

He walked away with the basket, and the rest of the people left their conversations to find seats. People filled the first rows, eager to be close to the rabbi. I'd wanted to disappear into the last seat in the last row, but Mom tugged my arm and headed for the closest open seats she could find. We ended up in the middle of the second row, in full view of the lectern and the box on wheels.

The service was interesting and not too long. The rabbi strummed a guitar and hummed tunes that everyone could join in with. We stood, we sat, he called out page numbers and we read aloud the responsive lines in an easy back-and-forth cadence. At one point, the people sang together and then stood to face the back of the room, bowing at the door.

"It's Kabbalat Shabbat," Mom whispered. "Welcoming the Sabbath bride."

I didn't understand any of it, but I quite enjoyed the mystery and pomp of it all. The double doors on the wooden box never opened, and I wondered what was kept inside it. After, two congregants brought out plates of cookies and pitchers of lemonade and everyone stood around two tables at the back of the room, snacking and talking.

I went up to the rabbi. "What's in the box?"

He swallowed some lemonade and smiled. "The box?"

I pointed to the wooden cart with a metallic Star of David on the front.

"It's the Aron, the Holy Ark, where we keep the Torah."

I nodded as if I knew what he was saying. He saw the

confusion in my eyes, but he didn't look like he was judging me.

"The holy scrolls, the Five Books of Moses," he explained in an even tone.

I nodded again. "And why didn't you open it during the service?"

"We only take out the Torah to read it in the morning, on Mondays, Thursdays and Saturday, if we have a minyan, a quorum of Jews," he said.

There it was, that word. *Jews.* Like a grimace, a spit. I must've made a face, because he quirked his head and looked at me questioningly.

I shook my head. I wouldn't go into an explanation because I didn't have an easy one. Organized religion, or anything that came close to it, gave me the willies. It reminded me of the group-think of Anam Cara. It wasn't a distant-enough memory. Not yet. I would not be dragged into another blind-faith community.

Jews. Was I one? By birth perhaps, but I didn't embrace that aspect of my identity. It was someone else telling me who to be, what to believe, and I bristled at the thought.

I scanned the room for my parents, eager to make my escape. They stood in a small group of people, in avid conversation, smiles dancing in their eyes. They looked so at home here. How had that happened, such a complete and total transformation? What did they gain from being an active part of a Jewish community?

I was about to head in their direction, when the rabbi reached out and put a hand on my arm.

"It was so nice to meet you, Charlie," he said. The warmth of his body hovered beside me, pulling me into its orbit. Like a sun around which everyone in this room revolved, a beacon.

A buzz of electricity hummed through my body at his touch. His eyes sparkled even more than they had initially, if that were possible. I traced the outline of his full lips with my eyes. Could he hear the fast pace of my heart?

I hadn't expected to be attracted to anyone so soon, let alone a rabbi. I was not looking for love.

I smiled as a dismissal, trying to expel the images of our naked bodies that were dancing in my head. I needed to leave, and fast.

"It was nice to meet you, too," I said then sauntered off to find my parents.

Chapter Fourteen

"You didn't tell me how hot he was," I said, leaning on the store counter. It was a slow morning for Mary, and I'd escaped the cottage to give my parents—and myself—a little space. I'd always thought I'd minded James leaving me alone, but with my parents in the house round-the-clock, I was realizing how much I enjoyed the solitude.

Plus, I wanted to process the whole Shabbat experience with my friend.

She licked her lips and whistled. "I tried," she snickered.

"I mean, it's not like I'm looking to hook up, and certainly not with a rabbi," I said, stumbling over my words. "I wouldn't even know how. I was with James for a long time. He's the only man I've ever been with, and that was a complete mess." I rolled my eyes. "I'm not sure I'd be good at a relationship anyway."

"We're already at the relationship stage, are we? I think the lady doth protest too much," Mary said, popping a stick of gum into her mouth and chomping down.

The door rang as a customer entered, and our conversation hushed. But I couldn't silence my thoughts.

"Might be good for you to go out with someone new," she said quietly.

"Ya think?"

She shrugged.

How would I know when I was ready? Desire vibrated through my body, but I was scarred from everything I'd been through. How could I ensure I'd be different with a new man, that I wouldn't repeat old patterns? Of course, the rabbi might not be as controlling as James. At least, I hoped he wasn't. Mary was right; I *was* getting ahead of myself.

"Let me know if you need any help, love," Mary called down the aisle to the older gentleman who was scanning the shelves in search of something.

"Will do," he called back.

"It might be good for you," Mary said in a half-whisper, smacking her gum. Then she spit it out into the trash.

"I don't like chewing for long," she said in response to my questioning glance. "Just a spark of minty freshness will do." She winked.

I laughed, saluted, and headed out.

My parents stayed for ten days, attending services a second time the following Friday and dragging me with them. And while my small cottage was cozy, to say the least, with two more bodies in it, I was sad to see them go. There was no way we could cram twenty years of missed hugs, long talks, crying on shoulders and homemade meals sparking laughter and connection into a few days, weeks or even months. I'd never get back the time I'd so callously thrown away.

"Seriously, let's not lament the mistakes of the past," Mom said as she hugged me tight, reading the regret on my face. "There's no point. We can't go back. So we'll go forward. Together. I'm just a phone call away."

I bit my tongue to staunch the tears that threatened to pour out. Dad hung back, leaning against the truck, his arms crossed, his eyes cast down at the ground. He looked caught up in emotion, too, and I threw my arms around his big frame and pressed my cheek against the softness of his well-worn flannel.

He cleared his throat and thumped my back. He, too, smelled familiar. God, how I'd missed the scent and sound of my parents! I swung between regret at cutting them out of my life to anger at them for not seeing me enough to understand what I'd needed back then. On the same emotional pendulum was grief over James's death and emptiness at the realization that he'd never truly loved me. He'd only loved the control he had over me.

Mom climbed up into the truck. Dad carefully closed the door after her then walked around to the driver's side and got in. They waved fiercely as he backed the car down the gravel drive and turned out onto the country lane.

I waved back, watching until the truck was a dot in the distance.

The afternoon seemed strangely quiet, though a slow wind whistled through the grasses. The birds were busy in the trees, as if nothing had changed.

I retreated to the house, wishing I had something else to do to distract my focus. I was feeling sorry for myself, seething with loneliness. My mind reeled with ideas of packing up everything I owned and following my parents west, back home to start over again, safe in the bosom of family and friends who might just remember me. I was frantic with discontent, itching for something to do, when the phone rang.

"I need to return your basket," he said. Parker. The rabbi. Calling me. His voice went down an octave as he said huskily, "I've been thinking about you since we met."

My face went warm at the sound of his voice, all sultry and soothing.

"Perfect timing," I said with a laugh.

"Oh?"

I could almost hear his smile, see those even teeth and endearing single dimple.

I nodded then remembered he couldn't hear my head moving.

"Yes. My parents just left, and I'm melancholy and dangerously close to hopping into my car and following them back to Michigan."

He hesitated a moment before responding, and I wondered if I'd been too blunt.

"That's hard," he finally said, and his voice sounded genuine, like he meant it. Maybe that was part of being a rabbi, convincing anyone you connected with that you truly cared about them and their issues.

"Yes," I said, carefully considering whether I should say more. Then I figured, why not? I had nothing to lose.

"It's an even bigger deal for us, though," I said, wandering into spill-my-story-on-the-table territory.

"Oh? Why is that?"

I chewed on a fingernail as I thought about how to word it. Outside my kitchen window, a red-breasted robin stood sentry on a tree limb. I watched its puffed chest, its unblinking tiny eyes, the sharp tip of its beak, before it suddenly took off, fluttering to another resting place.

"This was the first time I'd seen them in twenty years," I said quietly.

He was quiet too, maybe processing my words, maybe waiting for me to say more. He was a really good listener.

"It was my fault," I went on in a torrent, "and I know I can't turn back time, can't undo the past, but still, I feel terrible for shutting them out of my life for so long." I hiccupped a sob, trying to contain my emotions. Boy, I was really showing my ugly to this refined man whom I'd just met, who had it all together and would soon regret calling me.

"Hey, Charlotte, do you want to go for a walk in the woods?"

I laughed. "I don't think anyone has ever asked me on that kind of date before," I said, then bit my lip, hoping he'd intended it to be a date. "I mean, I haven't dated in years. Or maybe at all. You did intend to ask me on a date?" I was spiraling.

Parker laughed. "Yes, that was my intent. And I had a plan all set when I dialed your number, but then I thought, why wait? Let's just meet up now and you can tell me the whole story." He paused. "If you want to."

I laughed again, relief flooding my body, making me feel lighter, less burdened and definitely less sad. "I want to," I said. "You're easy to talk to."

"Part of the job description," he said, and this time I could hear him smiling.

"Okay, what woods are we walking in?"

"I'll pick you up, and we can drive together to my favorite forest trail," he said confidently, as if he already knew where I lived and this was not the first time we would be alone together, two strangers who felt a spark but otherwise knew nothing about each other. I doubted we had much in common.

I gave him my address, and he said he'd be by in a half hour and to bring a sweater because it often felt cooler under the canopy.

Ask and you shall receive... I'd wanted a distraction, and

one arrived in the form of a very hot rabbi.

Chapter Fifteen

It took a while to get to Lye Brook Falls Trail, but the drive was easy, as was the conversation. Parker was funny, kind, calm and fun to be with. He was adorable in his hiking pants, T-shirt with 0.2 on the front—"The percentage of Jews in the world," he explained—and un-buttoned flannel over it. The little crocheted yarmulke perched atop his hair matched the T-shirt. I wondered if he had a drawer full of them in every color. His hiking boots looked well-worn, like they'd tromped over many miles. I kept stealing glances at him from the passenger seat of his Jeep Cherokee. He was beautiful in a classic sense—chis-eled jaw, perfectly even eyes and teeth that glinted in the light. He took my breath away, which surprised me and made me not a little uncomfortable.

Since I hadn't known any rabbis in my life, I didn't know what to expect from one, but this definitely wasn't it. Still stunned by my parents' new interest and involve-ment in our Jewish heritage, I had no idea how to form opinions or expectations about what a Jewish community, or its representatives, should be like. More formal, I guess, than your average person. Judgmental, even.

Demanding, like the leaders at Anam Cara. Congregations filled with blind followers and power-hungry leaders like I'd known for the past two decades.

Parker was none of that—at least as far as I could tell. Of course, James and Armand had been charming and charismatic at first, too, but never this calm or kind.

He was easy to talk to, easy to be with, and my body buzzed with attraction sitting so close to him. I tried to recall if I'd felt like this when James and I were first together. It had been exciting, yes, but looking back, I think it was more the pull of his power on campus that drew me. We'd only just met, but I felt like Parker and I stood on equal terrain. I'd let James control me. I had the feeling Parker would never want to.

Since it was the middle of the afternoon on a Tuesday, the trailhead parking lot wasn't full. There were three cars already there when we pulled in. Parker shut off the engine, ambled out of the Jeep and pulled a backpack from the trunk, along with two filled reusable water bottles.

"I brought snacks," he said, hoisting the straps over his shoulders.

"Thanks." I smiled at him.

He locked the car, and we started off.

Though I loved being in nature and meandering along forest trails, I'd done surprisingly little of it since I'd arrived in Vermont. I'd needed time alone in my little cottage to heal from James's death and my hasty departure from Anam Cara. Time to process leaving everything I'd known. I hadn't been ready to explore on my own further than a mile or two down the road or into the woods behind my field.

Until now.

The climb was easy at first, and we settled in to the calm, tree-lined path, walking in silence, our only music the whisper of leaves waving and our boots crunching on uneven ground. We found a rhythm and started talking.

"So, are rabbis even allowed to date?"

His laugh came from deep in his throat and echoed against the trees. My face flushed with embarrassment, and when he glanced up, he quickly got serious.

"You really don't know anything about Judaism?"

I stared at him. "That's what I've been telling you."

He reached out a hand. "That came out harsher than I meant. I apologize."

I stared at his hand on my arm, unsure how to respond.

"Your parents are so involved and knowledgeable."

I pursed my lips and stared at him in annoyance. "That's new," I said. "At least to me. I grew up with nothing Jewish in my life."

His eyes softened. "Yes, rabbis are allowed to date," he said with a smile. "It's not only allowed, it's encouraged. The Jewish community is all about marriage and family and raising future generations of proud Jews to carry the spark of identity forward."

It was almost like a sermon, all passion and pride in his voice. He blushed then, and I softened, relieved to see him as human and not just some gorgeous, pious demi-god who had it all together.

"Not like priests, who are married to the church and celibate?"

"God forbid," he said a little too quickly. He blushed so deeply, the redness reached the tips of his ears. "I mean, it works for them. Some of my best friends are priests."

I laughed.

The ground was damp from recent rains. Halfway in, the climb rose steadily uphill, and we leaned into it, breathing heavier. My heartbeat pounded in my temples. Parker stopped, pulled out the water bottles and handed one over. I flashed a smile of thanks and gulped down the cool water.

For a time, we followed Lye Brook, the water copper-colored under the sun, with little white caps where the stream leaped over rocks.

"Most of this trail is an old logging railroad from a century ago," Parker narrated, pointing to railbed remains.

There were tiny waterfalls gurgling where the stream spilled over rocks that had grown furry with moss. In the distance, I heard the falls and couldn't wait to get closer, to see them and feel the spray of the charging water.

"I've never really dated, though." His sudden words broke the quiet between us. "I was married for a long time," he said quietly, his eyes cast down at the fragrant ground.

Something about the tone of his voice told me to wait for him to speak again, not to press him further or probe deeper. I kept walking, letting him lead, gazing up at the treetops, the sunlight boring down through the leaves and casting a yellow-green glow on the ground. I felt protected, and quiet, in the forest's embrace and content beside Parker.

Two miles in, we came to a wide, open space from a landslide during Tropical Storm Irene. We stood inches apart, surveying the damage and the power of the forest to heal itself over time.

"I lost Sylvie two years ago," he finally said. He turned to me, trying to read my eyes. I hoped my gaze beamed compassion.

"Breast cancer," he said. He held walking poles and stabbed at the ground as if to emphasize each word.

I put a hand on his shoulder. "Parker, I'm so sorry."

He nodded and tried for a smile but failed. The pain was vivid in his expression, his eyes shimmering. His cheeks strained with effort, the lines in his forehead deeper than what age can do to a face.

In the last leg, up to the base of Lye Brook Falls, which spilled down over 125 feet of rock, there were a few slick stretches. Parker offered a hand, and I clasped it. We stepped slowly, until we stood at the base of the waterfall, staring up at smooth, glossy tiers of rocks and the white water cascading over it, like fingers clawing their way down.

I closed my eyes, and the rushing water grew louder, more forceful. I swayed in its spray.

It was magnificent. Shelves of rock jutted all the way down, water tripping over each level and making for a truly spectacular sight.

Parker slipped his backpack off and sat on a flat rock across from the cascade, with a perfect view of the tumbling water. I sat beside him. He pulled out grapes, a hunk of cheese and a bag of nuts. I popped a grape into my mouth and savored the sweet burst as my teeth snapped it in half.

"We met at summer camp," he said, chewing on a handful of nuts. "We were teenagers, both counselors. We just fit together. We married young, before I went to rabbinical school."

I nodded, wondering how old that would make him today. I didn't see any strands of silver threading through his thick brown hair.

"We have two children—Alice and Ethan," he continued.

I popped another grape in my mouth, nodding. It was tangy-sweet, refreshing. He broke off a piece of cheese and handed it over.

"They're grown now. Alice is a sophomore at Bennington, studying history. Ethan is a journalist in New York City. I grew up there, New York," he said, glancing at me.

I smiled, urging him on.

My heart melted at the anguish in his eyes. I was mere months out from the loss of my life partner, the man I'd thought I'd spend my life with, and my whole sense of things was unraveling as I realized what a mistake my relationship had been. Here was a man who had met his match and lost her, and the pain seemed not to abate two years out. I laid my hand over his.

He looked up, and the breath hitched in my throat. My heart beat faster. We locked eyes. It would be weird to kiss for the first time after talking about his late wife. But he was leaning in. I could feel his breath on my face, warm and sweet. I closed my eyes, the rush of the waterfall a long, unending sigh. And then his lips were on mine, firm, soft, pressing. I pressed back. Salty from the nuts, tangy from the taste of him.

It was just one kiss, but a zinger, and I sat back after, silent, staring at the falls, my thoughts a jumble.

He squeezed my hand.

"Your turn," he said.

I cocked my head. "For?"

"You're going to tell me why you didn't see or speak to your parents for twenty years, remember?"

I exhaled loudly and leaned back on my hands.

"You tell me this incredibly romantic, tragic story, and it makes me feel all sorts of emotions for you and about you, and now I have to tell you how I royally messed up?"

His eyebrows rose.

"Fine," I sighed. I turned to face him, crossing my legs and looking at him head on. "I hope it doesn't change what you think of me."

"How do you know what I think of you?"

I swallowed. "Well. You just kissed me in front of a waterfall after talking about the love of your life. You called me after meeting me twice at religious services that I really did not want to attend and invited me on a difficult but romantic hike in Green Mountain National Forest. I'd say right now, before I reveal everything, you're rather fond of me—but sending very mixed messages."

He smiled and reached out a hand, cupping the side of my face. "You're adorable, Charlotte," he said.

"No one calls me that," I said quietly.

His eyes were a question. "Do you want me to call you something else?"

I was silent for a minute. It was nice to hear my full name. James had never said it. But the only times someone called me Charlotte was as a reprimand. It felt stern, referring to a distant, misbehaving version of myself.

"Call me Charlie," I said. "That's the name of someone who gets her hands dirty. Someone who is down to earth and real."

He was nodding, trailing his fingers along my face, tangling in my hair.

"You're adorable, Charlie," he said, his thumb on my bottom lip, pressing into the soft skin there, and sending my heartbeat into fits of intensity.

"I don't think I can have a serious conversation when you're doing that," I said coyly.

He nodded and withdrew his thumb.

"I'm not saying I wanted you to stop," I said with a coy smile.

He smiled back and waved his hand, an invitation to speak.

"Okay," I said with a big breath. "Here goes. I went to College of the Atlantic to get away and find my path. My parents were well-known in Traverse City, and I was always in their shadows. I wanted to be known for me. Then I met James Grace. He was my professor, and I fell for him, hard. I fell under his spell and forgot all about my desire to be seen. Pretty much gave up everything about myself to follow him."

I swallowed. The words sounded worse when I spoke them aloud. I was embarrassed.

Parker laid a hand on my knee, his warmth penetrating through the fabric to my pulsing skin, a reassuring pressure. I'd lay my story at his feet, and he'd either take me as I was or I'd never hear from him again. I'd be no worse off.

Except I really hoped he'd kiss me again.

I told him everything—how I'd fallen for James and believed he'd fallen for me, how we'd left for Anam Cara, me dropping out of college and cutting ties with everyone who knew me before, including my family, when they objected to my plans. How it had made sense at the time, how I'd believed they were trying to stop me from fully realizing myself, how it was always James's voice in my ear, how I'd let his voice course through me until it became my voice and I heard no others. How I'd never really known myself and forgot about wanting to until James died, and I landed in Vermont to try to figure out who I want to be at forty.

I didn't even realize I was crying until Parker raised a hand to wipe away the tears that silently trickled down my cheeks. I told him how James had died suddenly, how I'd snuck away in the middle of the cold night, how I'd lost my voice from the moment of his death until I reached the border, and how, back in the United States, I'd felt free after too many years of not noticing that I hadn't been.

When I stopped talking, he scooched closer and wrapped me in his arms. I laid my head against his chest and cried new tears, which I didn't even think was possible.

"You're a very brave girl," he murmured into my hair, stroking the back of my head, his lips pressed to my forehead.

I pulled back to look at him, swiping a sleeve across my

eyes.

"Am I? I feel stupid and gullible, with loads of regret." I sniffed. "I've wasted so much of my life." The words rang hollow, which was how I felt on the inside.

He shook his head. "In Judaism, we have a chance to start over every single day. There's a morning prayer, *Modeh Ani*, which thanks God for returning our souls each morning, for giving us a new day to start over. It's a daily second chance. Each day, your life begins. Every single day."

I raised my eyebrows at him. "I hate to disappoint you, but I don't believe in God. And I'm not really Jewish. My parents might be, but I've never done a thing in my life remotely connected to my heritage. And we've already established that I know nothing whatsoever about it."

He shook his head. "Reform Judaism believes that you're Jewish if one of your parents is Jewish. And you'll be happy to know Judaism encourages questioning. It's pretty much the only universal thing among all Jews."

I winced. That word again. *Jews.* It sounded like a slur.

But Parker looked so eager, so happy, that I began to consider it was only me who had a problem with that word.

I ran my tongue over my lips. I was parched. As if he could read my mind, Parker handed me a water bottle, and I drained it.

"What I'm saying, and you should know this from the

start, before we get in too deep, is that I don't know if I want any of it. I've never been interested in religion, and after living at Anam Cara, with all its group-think and demanding rituals, well, I may not have the capacity to consider any faith or organized community."

"I hear you," he said, nodding. "I've been warned."

But I didn't believe him. I could see in his eyes that he relished the chance to lure me in, that he actually believed it was a possibility. I didn't want to end up breaking his heart. Or letting him break mine.

He quirked his head. "What does Anam Cara mean?"

I chuckled. "It's Gaelic. *Soul friend*. Though that place is anything but." I rolled my eyes.

He smiled funnily.

"What?"

"We're getting in deep?"

God, he listened well. I hadn't even remembered saying it until he brought it back up. I blushed and looked away. "Feels like it," I said, nodding. "I mean, this isn't a normal first date, is it?"

He was quiet but still smiling.

We headed back, completing the nearly five-mile round trip before the sun set. By the time we reached the car, we were both exhausted, but calmly so. The stress had seeped out of my body and into the forest, and I felt freer than ever and content. Plus, I was starving.

"I know a great place that does a mean baked haddock,"

Parker said.

"Is that kosher?" I asked.

"Do you even know what kosher means?" he replied.

I shook my head and laughed. "But I'm assuming you do," I said.

Chapter Sixteen

By the time Parker dropped me off at home, it was late. He was romantic and respectful, walking me to the door but not coming inside. I didn't invite him in, though I wanted to. We stood in the shadow of the porch light, moths buzzing around the bulb, kissing, his hands in my hair, pulling me closer to him, my hands on his soft, smooth cheeks as I pressed my tongue inside his mouth. Our breathing was heavy, fast, and I wanted to undress him, to make love to him in slow, sure strokes, but we both held back. It was well after midnight when he retreated to his car, and I watched him drive away with longing.

I bolted the door behind me and stepped out of my hiking boots, dropping my clothes on the floor of my bedroom. I'd shower the next morning. All I wanted now was sleep.

And I would've rested soundly if it hadn't been for the phone ringing me awake as the first fingers of dawn were lighting the sky outside my window.

"Boden, you can't keep doing this," I whispered into the

phone when I heard his voice. "Please call me at a normal time."

"Charlie—you have to listen to me," he pleaded.

I turned over in bed, cupping a pillow against my body. I set the phone on speaker and laid it flat. Eyes closed, I could hear panic in my friend's voice.

"I'm listening," I said. Through the cracked window, the first birds were singing to the rising sun.

"I was right about James," he said. "He didn't have a heart attack. Someone killed him."

I gnawed on my bottom lip. It took a lot for Boden to be afraid. Why didn't he just leave Anam Cara if he was so scared? And why hadn't I thought to bring him with me when I left?

"Why do you think that?"

"I've found evidence," he said, his voice going lower.

"Who would want to kill James?"

"That's the thing—there might be a lot of people who would," he said.

Something twisted in my chest, and I felt queasy. So many things I'd never considered, never seen before James died, were clear as the coming day to me now. I had a sick feeling that Boden was onto something, and I wanted no part of it.

"Listen, of course I'm curious about what you found, but I don't want to get involved," I said. "I've put Anam Cara behind me, and that's where I want it to stay."

I softened my tone. "Why don't you just leave, Bo? Come to me. Start over like I did. What's done is done. We can't bring him back, and honestly, I don't know if I'd want to anyway."

"But if it's murder, someone has to pay for it," Boden pleaded. "Don't you want justice for James?"

I sighed. "What good would that do now?"

If I could have James back, would I want him? My gut lurched as I admitted to myself that I would not.

"And besides, who are we to search out the truth? We have no power to do anything about it, even if we can confirm that it was murder," I said, fully awake now and pissed about it. I wanted to return to warm, pulsing dreams of Parker, focus only on my new life in the safety of the Vermont trees, pretend that James and Anam Cara had never existed.

"We're not law enforcement," I said. "And I don't feel the need to avenge James's death. After all I'm realizing about those years, I honestly want to forget they ever happened."

He was quiet. "I'm thrilled to hear you say that and only wish you'd had that realization years ago."

I sucked on my bottom lip. Had everyone but me seen what a jerk James had been? Why did so many women lust after him, in full sight of me? Was I just a sucker?

Boden went on. "We can't turn back time. And it's not just justice for James. I mean, what if someone else gets killed because we did nothing, Charlie? Do you want that on your conscience?"

He had a point. But I still didn't want to be involved.

"Look, I love you, and I think it's time for you to leave that place. Bring whatever you found to me, and we'll talk about what to do with it. Turn it over to proper authorities. Put it in someone's more capable hands."

He whistled through his teeth. "You think we can have any sway with Cape Breton law enforcement from Vermont?"

"Do you have any sway with them while you're there?"

He was quiet for a while, and I closed my eyes, almost drifting into sleep. Then he spoke again, and my eyes fluttered open. The birds were louder, the wind whistling through the window screen.

"Why do you call so late each time," I asked.

"Because they're watching me," he said.

"Who?"

He paused before answering then whispered, "Armand and his goons."

Arrogant, egotistical, self-impressed Armand Villencourt. I'd never liked him but had no beef with him personally. I'd stayed out of his way and focused on James as the center of my world. I'd heard rumblings about Armand and his so-called bully-leadership. More like thug tactics, harassing the poor peacemakers who called Anam Cara home. People who were drawn there envisioned a better world, where everyone got their fair share and justice prevailed. A society that depended only on itself, where every member earned an equal share and everyone was taken care of.

Armand didn't exactly embody that ethos, but he talked a good game, and somehow he'd won the head honcho spot on the shores of Bras d'Or Lake, a big fish in a very small remote sea.

"Even more reason why you need to leave," I hissed. "Start over. Think of yourself."

"When did you get so selfish? I'll call you again, Charlie," he said. "I miss you. I love you."

"Love you too," I said before hanging up.

Was I selfish to look out for myself? Fuck him. I loved Boden, but he was still brainwashed and under Armand's thumb. I'd been gullible for too long, and I wasn't going back there now.

I lay back on the pillows and set the phone on the nightstand. What if he was right? What if James *had* been murdered? And what if keeping the truth silent led to someone else getting killed?

But what could I, Charlie Tanner, hapless follower, do about it anyway? No one would listen to me, and I did not want to confront anyone from that community ever again. James was gone, and he wasn't coming back. I was in a better place now than I had been my whole adult life. I didn't want to go back to the drama and control of Anam

Cara, a place I'd blindly called home for far too long. I needed only to come home to myself and stay there.

Chapter Seventeen

I loved Anam Cara from the moment James and I arrived. I didn't want to. I wanted to hate it and feel out of place so I could rationalize fleeing and persuading James to leave with me. Back then, I still held dreams of happily ever after, of James as my soulmate, and I even believed I held some sway over the man. We hadn't discussed marriage or children or any of the traditional next steps that I assumed we were headed for. We were still in the riotous, we-can-do-anything spell of early love, before we showed our true selves and revealed our secrets. Or so I thought.

We drove up on the quiet community and through the gates. The Bras d'Or gleamed under the golden beams of setting sun. The saltwater tidal lake in the center of Cape Breton Island was huge, more than four-hundred square miles in area, forty-four miles long and up to twenty miles across at its widest and connecting to the fierce North Atlantic in two places.

Many people thought Bras d'Or was French for "arm of gold," but it was actually a Labrador word, meaning farmer or laborer. The founders of Anam Cara loved the layers of metaphor and inspiration when they built the community there.

I'd come to love the deep-blue tones of the lake under a full sun and its toiling grays in harshest winter. Sometimes, in serene sunset or sunrise moments, it was a glassy gold, the sky streaked in constantly changing light.

In an instant, I fell in love with the natural landscape. I think James knew I would. He knew me better than I knew myself. The evening we arrived, the community was quiet, most of the members gathered in the Great Hall of the Lodge for service. I'd come to learn that there were times every day when the community leaders sounded the ram's horn to pull everyone together, whether to hear an important discourse from one of the leaders, or to meditate together, or sometimes to dance.

James and I got out of the car and wandered around the dusty paths. We came upon the Lodge, the interior lights casting an orange hue in the windows as if a real fire burned inside. James pulled open one of the heavy doors; I walked in, and he followed behind. There were at least two hundred people sitting on floor mats and round brocade pillows. Small children ran and played with toys and nursed at their mother's breasts. Older children either sat at the feet of the speaker on the stage, their heads craned to gaze up as they listened, mesmerized, or they sat near their parents reading books quietly.

I had been afraid of what I'd find when we arrived, but it just looked like a community of hippies in denim skirts and overalls, their long hair braided and ribboned, some with hair shorn short and spiky. Many featured tattoos of Celtic crosses and Celtic knots, often on their left bicep or the back of their left hand. In time, I'd come to learn that this was a commitment to the communal ideals, a step many members took to more fully immerse in the ways of Anam Cara. James got one of each within a year of our arrival, though I never did. I wasn't comfortable with the idea of emblazoning my flesh forever with a brand.

We settled in at the back of the room, perching on a bench close to the wall. The person speaking from the podium was an older woman with a thick bun of white hair, wind-reddened skin and a long white skirt that trailed along the floor.

"That's Edith," James whispered. "She rarely speaks. This is a rare treat."

I nodded, but I didn't yet know what a big deal it actually was. Edith and Eamon Andrews had founded Anam Cara in 1967 after fleeing to Canada to avoid the Vietnam War draft. They were young lovers, unmarried, unbelieving in the institution of marriage, in fact, and devout peace-activists. Eamon descended from Scottish ancestry, Edith from proper English blueblood, and they'd both grown up in Boston, Eamon in a working-class family and Edith from the Episcopalian upper crust. I knew so little back then, not even how James had come to know about Anam Cara or what drew him there. Turns out, he'd known Edith's family growing up. Like his, they were Boston elites, and he'd heard rumors of Edith as the consummate rebel, rejecting every gift and privilege she'd been handed to march for peace and be with Eamon. James's family regarded Eamon as the worst kind of low-class trash: a poser, thinking he deserved to rise in the economic hierarchy, that he knew some secret about how society was meant to be. Edith's family disowned her when she fled with Eamon, and James admired her confidence and brazen independence.

In the back of the Great Hall, I was mesmerized by her strong words, her lilting voice.

"They said this land was unworkable, and we've cultivated every crop you can imagine in this dark, hard soil," she sang out. "Now, agricultural experts come to Anam Cara from around the globe to study what we do. We are a beacon to the living world."

I picked up a pamphlet from the floor titled *Our Story: The Spirit of Anam Cara*. Eamon and Edith had come alone, bought land by dipping into Edith's trust fund before her parents severed ties and cut off access. Their aim was to live sustainably without need of government, and they vowed to not be beholden to the laws of the land. Instead, they would follow the laws of the spirit world, listen to "the true voice within." The pair insisted they received guidance from an inner source that told them how to connect with the divine and cultivate the hard, rocky land. It was a bit kooky, but Anam Cara had indeed become an agricultural star, a stunning example of what was possible with hard work, determination and unyielding belief. They'd succeeded in growing crops that had never before flourished that far north.

I found it inspiring. Edith seemed to glow, backlit by carefully arranged lights, and the people in the hall watched and listened and held her in their unflinching gaze.

Of course, I didn't know that their pictures were on the wall in American post offices as "wanted" by the FBI for border corruption. I didn't know that before they properly bought land on the Bras d'Or, they squatted, illegally planting crops on public lands and sleeping in tents to avoid the authorities ripping out their rapidly growing vegetables and trees. I didn't know that they weren't married because they believed in a perverted concept of free love, which meant flowing in and out of the beds of anyone and everyone, regardless of their relationship status, and never looking back at the trouble they sowed. I didn't know that Eamon had fathered dozens of children he took no responsibility for and that many of the children at Anam Cara were unknowingly related to their friends and neighbors, which would create an incestuous mess for those who stayed in the commune, grew up there and partnered with other community members.

That first night, I was merely in awe of the smiles, the generous handshakes, the friendly hugs. It was the kind of welcoming love I'd always wanted. Edith finished speaking and seemed to levitate down from the stage and through the crowd, kissing and hugging anyone who approached her. Eamon followed in her wake, a wizened, skinny old man with a halo of white hair and a frizzy salt-and-pepper beard that ended in a tight, tiny braid. He, too, wore white—trim pants and sandals though the night was cool outside.

Years later, when new members would arrive at a gathering, I'd shake my head at their easy innocence. They had no idea what they were in for. I always wondered what drew new people to Anam Cara but never approached any of them to ask. I didn't want to risk breaking the mystery for them by sharing the harsh, cold truth of what it was like to live there. I feared they'd read in my face the loneliness that had taken root in my bones, see the cracked skin of my hands and know that it wasn't as idyllic as that first gathering made any of us believe it would be.

Chapter Eighteen

"You're going where?" my mother had shrieked into the phone when I'd told her of our plans to leave Maine and head to the Canadian Maritime provinces.

"You're not leaving college," my father had insisted on another handset.

I'd tried to stay calm, to explain why this made sense for me, that I was an adult and I knew what I was doing, and if I didn't like it, I could always return to college and finish my degree. But they'd refused to listen.

"I knew that boy was trouble the first time you mentioned him," my father had muttered.

"James is not a boy," I'd said, calmly and evenly.

"Even worse," Dad had said. "He should know better, ten years older than you, a professor corrupting an undergrad. It's not right! It's probably against the college code of conduct."

I'd bitten my lip because I'd had the same concern when James first asked me out, and I'd chosen not to check. I didn't want to find out that dating him was off-limits. I'd wanted the adventure of an older man who desired me. And I'd gotten it—along with everything that came with it.

That conversation had ended with my mother in tears, my father boiling over and me not knowing what to say.

"I hope you can accept my life choices," I'd ended with, thinking I was so brave and independent, believing my plan made great sense. "And if you can't, well, I'm sorry for you because this is what I'm doing, and you'll miss having me in your life."

I'd hung up the phone, my heart racing.

Sivan had heard the whole thing, her arms crossed in front of her, a look of disdain on her face.

"I've never heard anything so stupid," she said.

I felt about as low and piercing as the look on her face.

It was a juvenile, impulsive decision that I regretted the moment I ended the call. I was about to call them back when James knocked on our door.

"You don't have to go to him, you know," Sivan said, shooting me a defiant look. I wanted to be as strong as she was, but I loved him, I wanted his adoring attention, and I believed my life was braided up in his. And now, without my family, I needed someone to be my emotional rudder.

I stepped around my roommate and opened the door.

He pulled me to him. "Did you do it?"

I nodded, tears trickling down my face. He kissed away

the wetness, brushed my eyes with his lips and then kissed the top of my head. Sivan threw up her hands and stormed out. On James's face was a satisfied smile.

I reached for the phone. "I can't leave things like that. I have to call them back."

He put a hand on my shoulder and a hand on the phone. "You don't want to do that," he said softly. He turned me to face him, both hands on my shoulders. "Stay strong, Charlie. My love. My everything."

He knew exactly what to say and what to do. He'd traced the contours of my face with two fingers then leaned in for a deep and probing kiss. I'd fallen into his trance, let him lead me out of my dorm and away from my friends to his bed, where I'd stayed until we drove off the next day. Sivan had been at class when I'd ducked back into the dorm to grab my things and pack my car with everything we both owned. I'd used the credit card my parents had given me for our expenses on the road and in those first weeks at Anam Cara until my father had finally canceled the card.

Most of the time, one look sideways at James, and I'd felt bolstered by my decision. But in the quiet moments, as the long and open road extended in front of us, thoughts had collided in my head, second-guessing, lamenting, crying with regret without making a sound. We'd crossed the border into Canada with James at the wheel, and I'd turned to look back, but I couldn't find anything familiar in the landscape.

CHAPTER NINETEEN

Parker called the morning after our hike, and I answered on the first ring.

"Is it crazy that I miss you?" he said.

I breathed through my teeth as emotion swirled within me. "Yes, but I feel the same."

He sighed with relief. "Can I see you today? A small-town rabbi doesn't have a full calendar in the summer, and especially not on a Wednesday. And my other job—providing kosher supervision for maple syrup companies—doesn't require a lot of my attention in the warmer months."

"Hmmm," I said.

"What?"

"I don't know much about what makes something kosher, but I would think that maple syrup would be a no-brainer," I said.

He chuckled. "You'd think that," he said. "But there used to be a practice of using lard during the curing of the sap into syrup, and of course lard is not kosher, so the rabbis insist it is a product that must be supervised to be approved as kosher." The words just slipped off his tongue. He knew the Jewish world so well; I couldn't think of one world that I'd inhabited and seen clearly.

"Wow, who'da thought it?" I laughed. "Glad they have you to approve the process." I pictured Parker peering into vats of swirling, sweet-scented syrup, strolling through a smoky factory made of rough wood. It sounded like an easy and interesting job. There was so much I wanted to learn about him and his world.

I had no demands on my time either, other than tending to the garden. I'd been considering looking for work to replenish my finances and also to keep a little busier, especially now that I was comfortable in my surroundings and could breathe easy. I was reasonably sure no one from Anam Cara cared that I had left. I had only heard from Boden, and I had expected that. After all, I'd slipped a note with my contact info into the secret place where we used to meet to trash-talk those we didn't like at the commune, where we were reasonably sure no one would overhear. It was a small rocky area down by the lakeshore, with a few little hidey-holes in old, thick trees.

James hadn't minded my friendship with Boden; he didn't consider him a threat, and he never imagined I'd cheat on him. Which I wouldn't. It just wasn't my style. I'm a one-partner-at-a-time kind of person. And even if I had, I'm not sure James would have cared. Or noticed.

Still, there were times I wanted to unload without anyone judging me or casting doubt on my relationship, and Boden was the person I turned to—even though I believed at first that he harbored romantic feelings for me. We'd found a private place where we could be alone and talk freely. Those were some of my best memories of Anam Cara.

Boden had been on my mind since our pre-dawn call. I wanted to tell Parker about it, but I didn't want to be that woman who brought a boatload of problems into a new relationship, especially since I had dumped all my mistakes at his feet on our first date. Somehow I knew there'd be time to share everything down the road.

"I'm free as a bird," I breezed cheerily into the phone.

"Great. How about I bring lunch, and we make it an easy day at your place," he said.

"Sounds lovely. I'll bake muffins. When will you be here?"

I heard a knock at the door. "You're kidding. You're here now?"

I hung up and whipped open the door to see a smiling Parker on my doorstep in jeans, a polo shirt and that ever-present yarmulke pinned to the top of his head. He wore shiny loafers and no socks.

"Oh, you're one of those men who goes without socks?" I scrunched my nose as if to judge him, but I didn't really care.

He shrugged and walked inside, pocketing his phone.

He deposited two reusable shopping bags on my kitchen table and started pulling out containers of prepared salads, a half of a watermelon, and a growler full of beer from Long Trail Brewing Co. He held it up and smiled. "Summer ale—refreshing, local and consciously produced," he said, setting it down with a thud.

"You're amazing," I giggled, picking up and inspecting the salads—tuna pasta, corn, tomato and black bean, and mozzarella-wheatberry.

"You like?"

I nodded. I felt warm, safe and excited that he was standing in my house.

"May I," Parker asked, pointing to the refrigerator, and I nodded eagerly, prompting him to put the food and beer away for later. When he was done, I threw my arms around his neck and kissed him loud on the mouth.

"You know, I was thinking, our names—Charlie and Parker. It's like the worst joke possible," I said, trailing a finger along the back of his neck.

His eyes narrowed and peered at me intently, and I knew I was turning him on. Good. I was already there. Had been since he left me alone at my front door.

"I've already thought of that," he said. "Do you like jazz?"

"Sure," I said in a noncommittal way.

"So that's a *not really*, then," he corrected me, and I nodded.

"I don't really know it that well," I said. "I've been on another planet for twenty years. Jazz wasn't a popular choice at Anam Cara, and my parents were more the classical music types. Give me a traditional Scottish session anytime, and I can clap and dance along with the best of them, though!"

He laughed, the skin around his eyes crinkling. "Good to know," he said. "You can teach me a Scottish jig, and I'll teach you about jazz."

I nodded, my smile growing melancholy. "That sounds nice," I said, settling into the couch.

"What?" He sat beside me.

"I don't think I realized until just now how much I have to learn. Or relearn, I guess. The way things are at Anam Cara, it's not normal. And that's where I've spent my adult years so far."

He reached for my hand, and I clasped his as if we had always been here, in this spot together. It was so natural, so familiar.

I sighed. "I'm assuming you like jazz?"

His grin was wide and immediate. "Growing up in New York City with very liberal artistic parents, it was all we listened to. They dragged me to a jazz club the first time when I was four years old! I fell asleep under the table on a sticky floor, and they didn't even notice until one of their tapping feet accidently jabbed me and I wailed. That taught them to keep me on their laps from then on. It didn't teach them to leave me at home." He laughed.

"I like the idea of us taking our cues from jazz," he continued. "I feel like we have to, given our names."

"What do you mean?"

"Make it up as we go. Improvise. Feel the music and let it come out on its own in an utterly original way."

He scooted close to me, a hand on my arm, as he leaned in for a long, slow kiss. I closed my eyes to feel the hum of his body next to mine and let him kiss me. It was warm, sweet, buzzing. He smelled of the woods and campfire and fresh-baked bread, all the things I loved most.

I broke away and nuzzled into his neck, planting little kisses along his smooth skin. He responded immediately and fully, grabbing a handful of my hair and tilting my face up so he could plant another long, deep kiss on my lips.

"Charlie, I want you," he hummed into my ear, his tongue darting along the sensitive skin of my neck.

Chills shivered through my body. I nodded.

It felt amazing to come alive after such a dormant stretch. The windows of my house were open, the curtains waving in the breeze. A symphony of birds and insects sailed in, the business of the natural world intense and constant. The summer air was warm, fresh.

I stood up and offered him a hand. He smiled as he took it, rose and followed me to my bedroom.

The queen-sized bed was covered in a cream quilt decorated with tiny flowers. A warm blanket draped over the edge, which I often pulled up over the quilt at night. I'd arrived in winter and used soft flannel sheets to start, but when spring turned to summer, I packed the flannels into an old trunk at the foot of the bed and dressed the mattress in light, airy sheets the palest shade of pink. My bedroom had become my haven, my refuge, a space all my own that, until my parents came to visit, no other soul had penetrated.

Parker was mere inches behind me, his warm, pulsing body looming. I dropped his hand, and he came as close as he could, the front of his body pressing against the back of mine. I felt him, rock-hard, against the base of my spine, and thrills shot like needles to the ends of every nerve.

I was about to turn and face him when he stopped me, his strong hand planted on my shoulder, keeping me where I was. He lifted my hair and nuzzled underneath it, kissing, biting, licking at my skin. I wore only a tank top and sweatpants. I hadn't been expecting company, and I'd had no plans until he called, but then he was there and I hadn't had time to put on real clothes or even check my hair in the mirror.

"You're gorgeous," he said as if reading my mind. He continued nibbling on my neck, my ears, my shoulders, while one hand snaked around to the front of my body and found my breasts. With two fingers, he rolled my nipple, pressed it tighter, sending sparks to every corner of my being. I laid my head back on his shoulder and closed my eyes, a moan escaping from my mouth.

"Oh Charlie," he growled, spinning me around and lifting me up then laying me back on the bed. He covered me with his body, and we rocked together, our hands everywhere, exploring each other's curves and bends, unyielding hardness and soft, pliable invitations.

The curtains flapped as the breeze picked up. A cloud covered the sunlight, and the room grew close, darker, and then the sun was bright again as the cloud moved on, bathing us in light.

I shimmied out of my sweatpants, pulled my tank top over my head and threw it on the floor. He dropped his clothes at the base of the bed and climbed up next to me. I got my first look at this beautiful man and loved what I saw.

He was all muscle and sinew, the broad expanse of his chest covered with only a flutter of soft curls sprinkled with silver, his skin smooth and bare. I trailed a hand through the fur of his chest, rolled over his nipples, and he closed his eyes and gasped. My hands explored further, dipping between his legs, where he was rock hard and not small in any way. He brushed my hands away and plunged his fingers between my legs, where I was wet and waiting.

He circled a fingertip around my lips, delicately over the nub of pleasure. I arched into his hand, biting my lip.

"Let me hear you," he cooed.

He kept pressing, touching, circling, softer, then harder,

slipping two fingers inside me then sliding those wet fingers simultaneously along every pressure point at the heart of my being. I couldn't keep still, and I couldn't move. I wanted nothing but his touch.

"Let me hear you," he said, louder.

I moaned as his fingers brought me to the swell of one wave and then another.

"Yes, like that," he cooed. "Charlie, you're so incredibly beautiful."

He kept stroking me, and the waves built bigger, stronger, then came crashing down as he mixed it up, slipped a finger inside me. I arched in protest and in welcome. Just when I was on the brink of orgasm, Parker pulled away.

My breath came in heavy, tortured gasps. "Why did you stop?"

"Because I want to join you," he said, reaching into the pocket of his jeans and pulling out a condom. He tore off the edge of the wrapper with his teeth and slid it over his hard shaft then climbed onto the bed, nudged my knees wider, and eased into me.

"Oh!" I exclaimed.

He was big and throbbing and warm, and he filled me just perfectly. God, how I wanted him! I clutched at his backside to pull him deeper into me. His voice was in my ear, his face pressed against my face, soft satisfied grunts coming from his throat.

He withdrew, and I gasped as he danced the tip against my opening. I wanted more of him, all of him, everything he could give me. Then he plunged into me hard and hot and pulsing, and I saw the mountaintop. I saw stars dancing in a vast night sky. He withdrew again, teased me for a desperate moment, then rammed right in, and I held him against me as the earth spun around me, and I was blinded by the searing sunlight of a gorgeous day.

The more he penetrated me, the more I climaxed, over and over again, in ways that I'd never felt at any time with James. And we'd had good sex. Great, even. But with Parker, it was mind-blowing, and this was only our first time together.

Finally, he hit his release with a gasp and a grunt and collapsed on top of me, his slick skin slapping against mine. We were bathed in mingling sweat, and I couldn't tell where he ended and I began.

He rolled off and lay on his back next to me.

"Well. That was something," he said.

I nodded as my hand feathered over my belly. So many thoughts swirled in my head, and I didn't know which one to pluck from the morass of second-guesses and anxieties. Tears threatened to spill, and I had no idea why, nor how to stop them.

He turned onto his side, propped up on an elbow and looking at me with concern.

"Charlie, what is it?" His finger caressed my face as quiet

tears spilled hot against my cheeks.

I couldn't find the words, any words at all, to explain what I was feeling. I tried to smile, but my lip quivered, and I collapsed into heaving sobs, which I muffled by turning into his chest.

His arm came around me, and he held me until my sobs quietened. Then, he clambered off the bed, handed me my clothes, and pulled on his own.

When we were dressed, he pulled me to sitting and propped the pillows behind me against the headboard. He sat cross-legged in front of me and clasped his hands almost in a prayer tent.

"Tell me," he said.

What could I say? That he was only the second man I'd ever slept with and the one who came before him had rendered me half a person? That I wished I'd found this kind of tender and intense love twenty years earlier, so I could erase all the mistakes of my past and just have smooth sailing in a relationship of equals? But then, he was with the love of his life back then, so he wouldn't have looked twice at me. How could I say that I was so grateful to know him now, and I wished I'd known a better love, sooner in my life?

This was our second date, if you could even call it a date. I couldn't say any of this.

Suddenly, memories of when I'd fallen mute after James had died, when I couldn't find any words or any crumb of a voice, when I drifted quietly from room to room at his memorial, without a word to anyone around me, and no one cared enough to coax me back to life, memories of all that came crashing down. I shivered. I didn't want to go back there. I didn't want to be alone again.

He scooped me into his arms and cradled me against him. I lay my head in his lap and let him stroke my hair.

"You'll tell me when you're ready," he said.

I closed my eyes and let sleep overtake me.

Chapter Twenty

I awoke in the dark. Lying on my side, Parker's arms around me, the blanket pulled over us both. He snored softly in my ear, his sour-sweet breath a comfort.

I slid out from under his arm and sat at the edge of the bed, staring out at the full moon. Finally, I pulled on clothes and ambled into the kitchen.

I flicked the kettle on and pulled a mug from the cupboard along with a lemon-mint tea bag. Then, ravenous, I opened the fridge, grabbed the salads Parker had brought and ate right out of the containers. The kettle screamed, and I doused the tea bag.

It was then that Parker appeared, smiling. Was he always happy? I both wanted to be that way and didn't trust that it was possible.

"Scowling? I thought that was pretty damn good." He snickered and pulled out a chair to sit with me. "Got a fork for me?"

I reached into the drawer and handed one over. "Are you always happy?"

He thought about it as he chewed a forkful of tuna pasta then nodded. "I try to be."

I envied him.

He took another bite then got up, opened the fridge and pulled out the growler. "Glasses?"

I pointed to the cupboard, and he helped himself. I liked that he was comfortable in my home, and it also scared the hell out of me.

"So what happened back there?" he asked as he poured golden-hued beer into a glass.

I rolled my lips and thought about how to word it, grateful that I'd only been mute for a short time.

"Look, I loved that, and I like being with you, but it's early and I'm scared..." I hesitated. He was watching me, waiting, so patiently. I really wanted to trust it.

"I was in a relationship for twenty years that I thought was the love of my life," I started. His eyes never left me, even as he sipped, even as he chewed. Parker watched me, hanging on every word, giving me space to think, to process, to find my way. Through the open window over the sink, the night seethed with crickets. I never grew tired of that sound.

"And when he died, I didn't know how I'd go on. Except..." I paused, trying to slow my breathing, to calm myself, even as my stomach knotted and my heart raced.

"Except...when he died, after he died, it all became clear to me. It wasn't love—I see that now. It was control. And apparently I loved it. I chose it. Or at least, something about it drew me and kept me. For a very long time." I shook my head and stood, pacing near the sink. "Geez, I don't know if I'm making any sense."

Parker came to me and softly gripped my shoulders. "Shhhh," he soothed in my ear. "We have all the time in the world. You're safe with me."

I ached at his words. What was safe, really? I had believed I was safe with James, and he broke every tie I had to anyone who mattered, crushed me until I was no one without him. I couldn't enter into a relationship until I understood if it was James alone who caused that or if there was something in me that allowed him to take such total control. And if it was me, then I'd either have to make peace with who I was or pull it out at the root.

I stepped away and looked straight-on at Parker. "In there"—I thumbed in the direction of the bedroom—"it was beautiful and intense and passionate, and God I loved it, but..." I swallowed, ran my tongue over my lips. "When you told me you wanted to hear me..." My face flushed with warmth as I remembered submitting to him on the bed, how doing so sent thrills throughout my body. "When you said that, it turned me on so much. Your demands. Which scared me."

His face changed then. His eyes went wide, almost sad, and lines of concern furrowed his forehead.

"I'm so sorry," he breathed, reaching for me, but I

shrank back.

"Let me finish," I said. "This isn't easy."

He nodded and leaned back against the counter, giving me space.

"I need to understand why I stayed with James," I said. "Even when he was mean to me. Even when he cheated on me."

I wiped a tear from the corner of my eye.

"I don't want to be in that place ever again."

He was shaking his head and covering the distance between us to press me against his chest and close his arms around me in a tight and reassuring embrace. This time I let him. I melted into the warmth of his body, his scents that drew me, the thunder of his heartbeat in my ear.

"I would never want to control you," he whispered into my hair. "And I would never hurt you, Charlie."

I nodded, pulled away and sat down at the table to sip my cooled tea. Parker joined me. The air had calmed, and we were both breathing easier.

"I know you wouldn't," I said. "It's not a you thing. It's entirely me. I feel like I'm just waking up, discovering myself for the first time, at forty years old. Most people learn about themselves much younger. I have a lot of catching up to do."

He was nodding and sipping beer.

"How old are you?" I asked.

"Forty-seven." He smiled.

We ate quietly for a while in an easy silence.

"James was ten years older than me and my professor," I said. I looked for the gleam in Parker's eyes. "It would be easy to say that he took advantage, a man in a position of power, and me, an eager and naïve coed. Maybe that's all it was."

I sighed. "But for twenty years? You'd think I would've woken up sooner."

Parker laid a hand on my forearm and gave a soft squeeze. "Or maybe this is exactly how it's meant to go. I'm in no rush, Charlie. I promise, you're safe with me. You always will be."

I wanted to believe him. I loved not only the sound of his voice, but the truth of his words.

Chapter Twenty-One

Memories came racing back at the strangest times. I was in the garden the next day, legs stretched wide on the warm soil, trimming leaves and pulling weeds, when James danced back into my mind.

His hair was long on his back, his beard fluffier than usual since he hadn't trimmed it in weeks. He'd come flying through the door, scooped me up and spun me around. I'd giggled until I'd recognized the scent on him: the scent of sex.

I'd stepped back, recoiled, grimaced.

"What now?" he'd said, rolling his eyes.

It was early in our time at Anam Cara, maybe a year in, and I was spending most of my time in the greenhouses. We were approaching our second summer in Cape Breton, and I was grateful for the thawing of the ground and the longer days of light.

But I'd been melancholy, missing family, missing the pace and challenge of college, missing my friends. James waved it away whenever I mentioned it, and I wondered why he didn't care more about how I was faring in our new life together. It was *our* life together after all, I thought. We had a little house on the commune, and we were making friends, James more than me.

Most nights, we went to bed together, and we had sex often. It felt very free. James had come alive at Anam Cara. It was like something had been holding him back, a horse in a bridle and saddle that were both removed the minute he arrived, and now, he could run free, his amber mane flying in the wind.

I'd broached the topic of exclusivity when we were at the college, but on the drive to Anam Cara, I'd pressed harder. He'd shushed me, gawked at the idea of labels and restrictions. "I'm into free love," he'd said. I didn't know what he meant, but he didn't give me a chance to ask about it, and he certainly didn't explain.

I'd planned to bring it up again when we were settled, but things were so frenetic once we arrived, so intense, that I never did. And then, in April of that first year, I finally broached the topic over breakfast on a Sunday. There was snow on the ground and hot air hissed from the radiators, but the windows were laced with ice. The structures at Anam Cara were primitive, solid enough to keep us safe from frostbite but not entirely insulated.

I shrugged into a sweater, grabbing a throw from the couch and wrapping it around me like a shawl. I held a mug of tea between both hands to warm them.

"Sweetheart," I said. "There's something I've been wondering."

"Hmmm?" He looked up from the book he was reading, his coffee steaming on the table.

"I'd really like to be exclusive. I mean, I assume we are, living together here, me leaving college to be with you... I know you'd mentioned free love on the drive here, but I figured after all this time, we could commit to just each other?"

I waited for a response. A flicker of light from the window sparkled in his brown eyes.

"We've talked about this, hon," he said. "I told you, I'm into free love. I've always been clear about that."

It was difficult to swallow, and I considered my response carefully.

"Yes, I remember, but what does that mean exactly? And why won't you agree to only be with me?"

He flicked at his hair, which tilted in a sloppy bun atop his head, and sighed.

"Look, you know I love you, right?"

I nodded, watching him, wary of what he'd say next.

"That won't change, no matter what," he continued. "I just don't think I'm the kind of man to commit to one woman for my entire life. I mean, you are my partner, and I don't want to live with anyone else, but that's all I can promise."

I warmed at those words, waiting for the catch.

"But..."

He smiled. It wasn't a warm smile.

"From time to time, I might want sex with someone else," he said.

I suddenly realized my nose was cold, icy, and I covered it with two fingers to warm up.

"Sex with another woman," I said, making sure I'd heard him correctly.

"Sex with someone else," he said slyly. "I didn't say woman."

"You're bisexual?"

He just grinned. I had a sudden image of James as the Cheshire Cat in *Alice in Wonderland*. Cunning, mysterious, speaking in riddles.

Except sitting in my garden in Vermont nineteen years later, I didn't see any riddles. He'd been clear as the white day with me, and I'd chosen to believe his statements were layered with meaning and metaphor.

James had wanted what he'd wanted. He'd taken it and satisfied himself, and I'd stayed behind in our shared house and let him, feeling sorry for myself, waiting for him to change his mind.

That day when he'd scooped me up and I'd recoiled from the recognition of sex on him, sex with someone else, I was disgusted. And hurt. And afraid.

What if he left me? Where would I go? Crawl home to my parents in shame?

"I told you, Charlie," he'd said forcefully.

"Yeah, free love, I get it," I'd said, but there was an edge to my voice, perhaps for the first time in our relationship.

He'd inched closer, gotten up in my face and gripped my elbows, lifting me inches above the ground.

"Got a problem with that?"

His breath had been sour, and for the first time, I'd been truly afraid of him. He'd never physically hurt me, never threatened me, but now he was too close. I'd tried to slow my breathing, searched for words that would soothe him and calm the situation.

He'd set me down and stepped back.

"If you don't like the way things are, you're free to leave," he'd said.

My stomach had fallen.

In that moment, I'd panicked. I'd only wanted to win back his favor. I'd given up everything to be with him, gone so far away from everything familiar, and starting over seemed too hard, too humiliating. I had no money, not even a credit card. I had nothing of my own except some threadbare clothing and a few new skills.

How would I leave? I couldn't afford to fill my car with gas to drive home. I was so far from everyone and everything. And too embarrassed to call my parents and admit to my mistakes.

I went to him, reached for him. "James," I said. His head whipped around to stare at me with an icy glare. "I'm sorry."

I didn't know what I was sorry for, only that those words would calm him and bring him back to me, and I was right. He pulled me to him, kissed me deeply in the way that set me spinning, and before long, we were beneath the sheets of our bed, skin to skin, and he was touching all the right spots and I was pretending he hadn't just been with someone else, our scents mingling on his fingers. But I couldn't climax. I couldn't get lost in the passion.

"What's with you?" he said.

"I'm sorry, James." I bit back tears, my breath coming in panicked waves.

He narrowed his eyes at me for just a second then huffed and leaped out of bed. "Forget it," he said, stalking to the bathroom.

The shower hissed on, and he shut the bathroom door.

I begged my mind to quiet. I wanted the fantasy. It was so much easier to live there than in the real world.

Chapter Twenty-Two

Parker and I were in the garden, dead-heading spring plants, harvesting the last early lettuces so the fall vegetables—squash, pumpkin, broccoli and Russian kale—could grow big. I wanted as much of a year-round crop of fresh produce as I could grow, like I'd had at Anam Cara. One good thing about that place.

I was telling him about Boden and his frantic late-night calls, and Parker was visibly concerned. The sleeves of his flannel were rolled up past his elbows, and a trail of dirt mingled with sweat along the side of his face. He was adorable like that, steeped in soil from my garden, leaning on a shovel. My very own rabbi-farmer.

"Why doesn't he just leave?"

I shrugged, wiping sweat from my forehead with the back of my arm. I wore a big floppy sun hat, baggy pants and a torn T-shirt speckled with dirt. I still found it hard to buy new things, to use the money that I finally had. Too many years of counting pennies and trying to make it all work on nothing.

"I've asked him, begged him, to come here," I said, patting the earth around the broccoli. I never got tired of the fresh scent of soil. I was tempted to lean my nose right down to the ground and breathe in the heady, close scent.

"Wait, what? You invited him here? Is that a good idea?"

I looked up at him backlit by a bright sun. His silhouette looked larger than life, a broad, strong man standing on terra firma. We were two months in to our intense and almost ordinary romance, and it felt like I'd always known him. He was at my house, or I was at his, every day, and I missed him in the hours between, when he visited congregants in the hospital, did a round of kosher supervising duties, or tutored bar mitzvah students. ("There are exactly three this year in the congregation," he'd joked.)

Every Friday night, I sat in the back of the church basement, watching him preside over Shabbat services. It was becoming familiar, and with each passing week, I became more comfortable with the idea of religion and the possibility of participating in a heritage—my ancestry—that weaved back through centuries. I knew I'd have to if I wanted to be with Parker. Judaism swirled around him. He ate only vegetarian food or fish when he was out of the house and shipped kosher meat in from New York every three months to keep in a freezer in his garage. That damned yarmulke followed him everywhere he went; I often found it wedged between the headboard and the mattress in the morning after he'd slept in my bed. He practically levitated off the ground when he spoke poetically about the Torah, the traditions and stories he'd carried with him since childhood. If I wanted to be with him, I'd need to want Judaism in my life, too. And I was trying to get there.

"Why wouldn't it be a good idea for Boden to come here?"

I was done gardening and ready for a shower and a tall glass of cold tea swirled with honey and mint. I got up, tucked my tools into a linen basket I kept in the greenhouse, pulled out my snipping scissors and headed for the pots at the edge of the garden, where the herbs leaned toward the light. I cut several stalks of mint as Parker responded.

"Well, if he thinks James was murdered, and if he has evidence of this, then isn't he a walking target? Which would make you, by association, another target?"

I scowled and shook my head, but wondered if he had a point. Probably why I waited for Boden to ring me instead of pursuing him. Definitely why I didn't want to know anything about what he'd found.

"I hope these plants take root," I said, shaking the dirt from my gloves. He did the same, and we tucked the gloves and tools inside the greenhouse and fastened the latch. I didn't like spending daytime hours in the greenhouse in summer. The brightness and heat magnified the humidity, making it stifling and hard to be in there for too long.

Inside the house, Parker reached for a slim paper bag that he'd brought with him and left on the table when we'd headed outside. "This is for you," he said, handing the bag over. He was always bringing me little gifts, listening intently to what I said and quoting me thoughtfully at just the right time. If this was love, I was all in. It was so much easier than what I'd known with James.

I peered into the bag and pulled out a slim wooden item with a Hebrew letter painted near the top.

"A mezuzah," he said.

I shook my head. "For…"

"You," he said, taking it from me and turning it over to reveal a rolled-up parchment scroll pressed into a slot on the back. "Jews fasten these to their front doors—it's a blessing for the home."

He was smiling. I knew he meant well, but my throat was closing at the site of the little artistic item in my hand. On the one hand, he was just responding to my regular attendance at services and the comments I'd made about how beautiful the singing was, how I'd felt at home in his Friday night rituals.

On the other hand, a voice inside me was screaming, *It's too much! Don't let him change you! He's trying to make you into what he wants. Hold firm! Don't let another man control you.* I wasn't ready for a Jewish branding on my home.

On me.

"Too soon?" he said, reading my face.

I smiled an apology. "Maybe?"

"I'm sorry," he said, grabbing it back and stuffing it in the bag. "I'll hold on to it. If you want it at some point, let me know."

His face burned red, and he looked away from my gaze. I hated to hurt him. I walked over, closing the gap between us, and stroked his chin. He hadn't shaved in two days, and the dark stubble was dotted with white.

I stroked his face. "You need a partner who wants what you want."

He smiled kindly and closed his eyes. "Yes," he said, and it sounded like a question. "I didn't think I wanted a new partner at all. Until I met you."

He swallowed, his Adam's apple bobbing in his throat. I kissed it and turned my face up to meet his gaze.

"We didn't even have one of those on my house growing up," I said softly. "Maybe they do now? I wouldn't even know. I meant it when I said being Jewish was never part of my identity. I'm warming to the idea, but I can't promise anything. It's a little sudden for me."

I laced my hand under his hair. He leaned his head back and closed his eyes.

Something shifted then between us. My feelings for Parker-the-man were strong, but I recoiled often when I thought of him as Parker-the-rabbi. I'd been singed by the fire of strong beliefs, of communal-think, and I wasn't ready to get too close to another fire anytime soon.

But I kissed him anyway, long and deep, taking my time, tasting the man who was becoming a central focus of my life. I wanted him, but I wasn't sure I wanted any of what came with him. How would I reconcile all the parts of him with all the parts of me?

Chapter Twenty-Three

The next morning, Parker left with a travel carafe of hot coffee and six fresh-baked carrot muffins to take to his morning Torah study. Not many people attended, but he showed up eagerly for those who did—usually a few old ladies who had crushes on the handsome widower, or a divorcee with two small children who hoped he might consider becoming husband number two.

I wrapped a thin cotton robe around me. The mornings were growing chilly. Parker had been talking about preparations for the High Holidays, which sounded daunting and intimidating. I wanted to be there for him, but I wasn't sure long, serious services were my thing. Funny that I'd immersed in half-day intensive meditations at Anam Cara without question. Was it because I had nothing else to do then? Or was I trying to please James, stay close to him, keep an eye out for my competition?

I kept revisiting that time and the choices I'd made, hoping I'd arrive at an understanding. I didn't want to be that person ever again. And while things were good with

Parker, a little voice inside me warned against getting too close, too soon, lest I fall into familiar patterns.

I settled onto the couch with a book and a mug of steaming tea swirled with honey and tuned the speaker to a meditative Spotify channel. I was five pages in when there was a knock at the door.

I wrapped the robe tighter as I peered out the window to see who was there then whipped the door open.

"Boden!"

He fell into me, his whole body shaking, kicking the door closed behind him.

My heart swelled to see him, his sandy hair flopping over his green eyes, his worn jeans held up with a rope-belt and a hoodie that was fraying at the sleeves.

"You've seen better days," I said, drawing him to the couch. "I'll make you a cup of tea."

He shook his head. "Something stronger," he said, striding to the kitchen and opening cupboards to look for a bottle of something.

I pointed to the top of the refrigerator, and he darted for it, uncapping the bourbon and taking a swig.

"I guess you don't want a glass," I chuckled, settling at the table.

He plopped into a chair, placed the bottle on the table and exhaled.

"Why are you so spooked?"

"I've been telling you, Charlie, every time I call."

I nodded. "But you left there. You're free now. Far away and safe. It's behind you!"

He was shaking his head. His energy was agitated, nervous. He got up and paced then grabbed the bottle and downed another swig without bothering to pour it into a glass.

"Bo, talk to me," I said, taking his hand and leading him to the couch. "Sit. Breathe. Talk."

He sank onto the plaid cushions and leaned back, closing his eyes. He scraped his hands through his hair, feathered it out behind him and laid his head against the wall behind the couch.

"Charlie, you don't understand how serious this is," he said. It was almost a wail.

"I want to," I said.

He looked around as if he expected to find a dark figure in the corner, waiting to pounce. I placed a hand on his thigh, and he jumped.

"Hey," I said, hovering in front of his eyes. "Hey. It's me. You're here. Just breathe. You're safe."

"I don't know if I'll ever be safe," he whimpered. "Or if you will be."

He looked me dead-on, his serious eyes scaring me.

Boden was a year younger than me, and when we first met I'd thought he'd wanted something more between us. But two years into our friendship, he came out to me, and that put to rest any hint of romantic love between us. As long as I'd known him, though, he'd never had a lover—at least not one he'd told me about. I loved him like a favorite sibling. We were pals, confidantes, soulmates of a sort. I'd missed him greatly, and I hated to see him so wound up.

He closed his eyes and settled into the breathing we'd done in meditation at Anam Cara. In one nostril, hold, out the other nostril, then switch. After a few minutes, he opened his eyes, which were calmer.

"Okay, now tell me what you're so scared of," I said.

He'd dropped a bag at the door when he arrived. Now, he got up and grabbed it, bringing it back to the couch. He pulled out an old laptop and pressed the power button. "I took this from the computer room," he said quietly. "Took two, actually, and hocked the other one for cash so I could hop a bus and make my way here." He exhaled audibly. "It was a really long journey."

I patted his shoulder and pulled him close, as the computer dinged to attention. He waited for it to load then typed in a password, clicked a few times on the track pad and then inched closer to me so we could both look at the screen.

"There." He pointed to a spreadsheet. It was a roster of Anam Cara members with a grid of family connections. He'd landed on James's name and scrolled over to the column where blood relations were listed; there were sixteen names.

"What?" I blinked and took a second look.

Other than his family in Boston, James had no relatives that I knew of, and certainly none at Anam Cara.

"Read the names, Charlie," Boden insisted, thrusting the laptop closer to my face.

I leaned in, my breath catching in my chest, and scanned the list. They were, indeed, all Anam Cara members, but the names were of the youngest residents, babies up to teens.

As the truth hit me hard, I turned to Boden, who was nodding.

"All his," he confirmed.

That bastard.

It had never occurred to me that all of James's hookups could result in children. I knew there'd been other women. And maybe men, from what he'd said. But never imagined there would be this many or that he'd be so careless. That fucking jerk.

"There's more," Boden said, reclaiming the computer and clicking over to a new series of documents. He handed it back to let me read.

One was a letter from Armand to Edith, sharing concerns about James attempting to wrest the leadership from him. Another was between Edith and Eamon, detailing the characteristics that make for a good leader at Anam Cara, among them a person they could control and a person who believed in their version of history and events. A third letter, from Eamon to Armand, hinted that things were getting too difficult to contain and they'd have to take action.

"This is horrifying," I said. "But how does it add up to murder?"

"I haven't shown you everything." He closed the laptop and placed it on the coffee table. "And I won't. I don't want you to have information that could put you in danger. This is enough for now."

I shook my head. "We've never had secrets, Bo, and I won't start now. I'm fine here. I'm safe. I have a new life. They won't get me—they can't. I have nothing to do with any of this, other than being involved with James." I huffed. "And apparently, I was not alone in that."

He put a hand on my arm. "It wasn't your fault."

I closed my eyes, the names swirling in my head.

"I know," I said softly.

"Do you?"

I looked at my friend, relieved by his presence, warmed by his smoky scent. I nodded. "I do," I said. "It's all become clear since I left."

He smiled and squeezed my arm. "Good. It's about time. I wished for years you'd come to your senses and leave him."

I shrugged and leaned against him. He pulled me close until we were lying together on the couch. He kissed the top of my head and sighed.

"I wanted you to love someone who could fully love you

back." His breath was warm on my cheek. "You deserve so much more than James Grace."

"I know, honey," I said, patting his arm. "Too bad we couldn't be an item." I chuckled. "I love you that much."

He sighed again and lifted his arms behind his head. I rested my cheek on his chest. His heartbeat thumped in my ear. "Yeah," he said. "If only you were a slightly pudgy, round-faced man. Then you'd be my type."

I laughed. "How come I've never met your type in the flesh?"

He pulled me closer. "Because I keep my liaisons quiet and out of sight," he said, chuckling.

"Any particular reason why?"

He shrugged. "I just don't like anyone knowing my business. Even my best girl."

A few minutes later, I stood, pulled the robe around me and carried my cold tea to the kitchen.

"I'm going to shower," I called out. "Get settled. You can stay as long as you want. We'll figure out what to do—or not do—about all of this."

In the bedroom, I texted Parker. *Boden's here. Can you meet up later? I want to introduce you.*

I wouldn't share anything over text about the evidence Boden brought or his shattered nerves. Something bigger was scaring him, and it had to be serious if he wouldn't share it with me. I wasn't sure I wanted to know. I was still determined not to get sucked in to the Anam Cara drama ever again. Perhaps Vermont hadn't been far enough away to make sure that stayed true.

Chapter Twenty-Four

On the day James died, I was canning tomatoes from the greenhouse cooked down into sauce with sprigs of basil and fresh garlic. The kitchen was a steamy mess, and classical music played on the old transistor radio that sat atop our refrigerator. The apron I'd stitched from old scraps of T-shirts was tied around my waist, and my knotty hair was pulled into a bun at the base of my neck. Two cuts on my fingers stung from the acid in the tomatoes, but I ignored the pain as I filled jars, fastened lids and boiled them to seal them. I couldn't wait to line the pantry with jewel-toned jars of sauce that would fill my house with warmth when the wind howled bitterly across the lake.

There was banging at the door. I turned down the music, wiped my hands on a towel and went to see who it was.

Indira burst into the house as if pushed by the wind.

"He's gone!" she wailed, falling into my arms.

Indira and I were not friends. At Anam Cara, there was a myth that we were all a family, a community of kindred spirits, and we were supposed to be accepting, warm and friendly, even when times were hard, and personalities clashed. Most people feigned some amount of friendliness, and in truth, I got along with almost everyone. Even before I got to Anam Cara, I'd never been one to pick a fight or judge people too harshly. I took everyone at face value, trusted what they offered, and only when I'd been greatly wronged did I turn my back on someone I'd once called friend.

I had no real problem with Indira as a person, but her obvious love for James—and her brazen lack of hiding it—pissed me off. Did she have to flaunt her feelings in front of me? James would never turn away from a beautiful young woman who so clearly desired him, so I was sidelined, watching their flirtation up close with neither of them caring how it made me feel.

But aside from her attempts to claim my partner, she was nice enough. She'd grown up at Anam Cara, the daughter of hippies who were in the first wave of followers to land at the commune. They adored Edith and Eamon, and they'd raised their children to know nothing different than this open, welcoming, bed-hopping community.

It didn't help that Indira was beautiful. Ink-black hair and mesmerizing blue eyes, skin pale as the morning light. She was petite, barely five feet tall, but a force, with a hearty laugh and a surprisingly deep voice. Everyone in a room knew when she was there. It was hard to look away, her magnetic energy occupying all the space.

A decade younger than me and the mother of a five-year-old, she burst through my door on that fateful day.

"Who's gone where?" I asked, shepherding her into the house and urging her into a soft living room chair. The kitchen was the warmest place, but every surface there was covered in jars or splatter-painted in sauce. A chill rippled through the living room. I pulled a blanket from a chest and draped it over her legs.

Sitting across from her, I asked again, "Who's gone?"

She sniffled.

"And who's with Lacey?"

She swallowed and looked at me. "She was at the nursery for a few hours."

She looked away, her cheeks reddening. It wasn't unusual for young children to be dropped off at the commune's nursery, a de facto day care staffed by a rotation of community members so the children's parents could work. I'd opted out of my turn there, offering to work longer greenhouse shifts or drive sales routes in the towns. I didn't want to fall in love with the children. I'd long since made peace with the idea that I'd never be a mother, but I was wistful about it and often sad. Especially in my thirties, my body screamed to hold a tiny new soul to my breast, to lie beside a child whose blood matched mine. James was adamant that it wasn't part of our story to become parents, so I gave up hoping, but that didn't make me want a child any less.

But while it wasn't unusual that Indira's daughter would be at the nursery, her shifty eyes and red cheeks told me there was more to this story.

"What is going on, Indira," I pushed.

She licked her lips and twisted her hands.

"I was with James," she said.

I flushed with warmth—anger or humiliation? Possibly both.

"That's why Lacey was at the nursery."

I quirked an eyebrow, prodding her to continue.

"And he died."

I tilted my head and narrowed my eyes. What she'd said was as believable as if she'd insisted the sun had fallen from the sky. James wasn't dead. He was fifty years old, strong, energetic, in great health.

"What?"

I practically spat the word.

It was ludicrous. James was strong, confident, a gale wind. He'd be around for decades.

"James and I were together," Indira repeated. "In bed. Everything was fine, and then he seized up and then went still." She swallowed. "I checked for a pulse." Another pause, her ice-blue eyes piercing into mine.

"There wasn't one."

Coldness coursed through my veins. I was imprisoned in my body, stuck to the seat, my hands gripping the thin wood armrests. I stared at the icy patterns on the windows, the white day outside angry with clouds.

James was dead?

She hopped up, looked around for my coat and held it out. I slipped my arms into it, stepped into my snow boots at the door, the apron still tied around my waist, warm and damp with splatters of sauce. She ushered me out, led me along the cold, snowy path to her house, a quarter mile from mine. The door was open wide. Outside, a crowd was gathering, commune members drifting from their houses to see what was going on, whispering questions behind their hands. Someone had called for an ambulance. Soon, the bright-yellow lights would swirl in the white air.

I tore into the house to Indira's bedroom at the back of the abode. I wanted to see him. His skin had turned gray, and his lifeless eyes stared at the ceiling. I climbed onto the bed and lay beside him. His skin was clammy and cold. I lay my head next to his shoulder and wept.

I didn't lie there for long, though, before paramedics marched in. One man knelt over James and started pumping his chest. The man glanced at me, cleared his throat, then looked away. I knew he wanted me to move, but I couldn't let go of James. Silent tears trailed down my face, the only warmth in this cold house. Winter air blew through the room from the open door, and I could hear the low thrum of conversation. Why were people gathered? Why did they care what was happening to my James?

Why couldn't they just leave well enough alone?

"Ma'am?" The paramedic's voice startled me.

I sniffled, dragged a finger under my running nose. He reached out a hand and gently placed it on my forearm. "I'm going to need you to move away from the body, ma'am," he said, almost apologetically. He was just doing his job, but I resented his presence.

"Just one moment longer, please," I whispered.

He nodded, squeezed my forearm and stepped back from the bed.

Indira hovered just beyond the bedroom, crying in awful, loud wails. Why was she so distraught, so undone, when I had no words? I was a shell of a person, a ghost in a body. I got off the bed and stood beside it, staring at the body that had once been James. *My* man, gone. On *her* bed. It was a slap in the face to die like this, in someone else's private chamber. His red-brown hair fanned around his head on a white pillowcase, a fire of color when all hue had drained from his skin. The paramedic brushed a hand over James's eyes, closing the lids. I shut mine, trying to remember his shining brown eyes, the way they sparkled with the light of adventure, the way they'd drawn me in and held me for so many years.

Just one night earlier, we'd lain together in our bed, laughing as our hands reached for the familiar places. We'd rolled into each other, couldn't get close enough, and he'd whispered in my ear, "My Charlie-girl, my whole world, I love you from the depths of my soul."

And then this morning, he came here, to her.

He'd talked like that more as he'd grown older, perhaps glimpsing an end closing in. I told myself he regretted the brazen distance of our early years, but that he'd died in Indira's bed was evidence that nothing had changed, and I was only telling myself a sad story. Clearly his turn of emotion at midlife didn't stop him from seeking warmth elsewhere. I'd given up caring, accepted his wandering, made a choice to stay, to ignore the pangs of jealousy and regret and loss that reverberated like a drum. That didn't mean I liked it. It still hurt.

But I reasoned that I had more than so many—a good life, with a good man in a place that did meaningful work, a place that welcomed me and gave me purpose. James loved me, always came home to me, and sometimes he knew me better than I knew myself. At least, he'd made me believe that.

And now he was gone from this world. Indira gulped, edging closer to me, her sobs slowing, her body shuddering with sadness. I stared at the body on the bed, watched it shrink into death.

The paramedics lifted James onto a stretcher and covered him with a white sheet. One of them caught my eye, and my silent gaze implored him to tell me what had happened. I couldn't form the words. I opened my mouth, but no sound came out. I combed the air for just one word but found none within reach.

After they'd wheeled the stretcher out to the ambulance and shut the body up inside it, the paramedic came over to me.

"Are you the wife?"

Indira was nodding, clutching my arm as if she were my best friend. I wanted to clarify—*we never married, we were life partners, he didn't believe in institutions that pen you in*—but I couldn't find the words, couldn't get my voice to make any sound.

It didn't occur to me then, that, as a life partner without a legal tie to James, I'd have no say in what happened next, no claim on his body or his earthly possessions. But by the time his family swooped in with all their wealth and might, I no longer cared. I didn't need a trinket to remind me of what we'd had. Besides, I wasn't thinking clearly, wrapped in a cloak of grief and disbelief, and couldn't have made a decision if I'd had the opportunity to. Which, frankly, may have saved me.

But in the moment, in that frantic, fraught moment, the paramedic stood before me, believing me to be James's wife, and he said in a solemn and apologetic voice, "I'm so sorry for your loss, ma'am. It looks like a heart attack, but we'll know more after the post-mortem. How old was he?"

"Fifty," Indira answered for me.

The paramedic looked from her to me and nodded.

"It looks like she's in shock." He reached his hand out

to me again and patted my arm. Indira inched closer, her arm looped through mine. "Take her home and keep her warm. Tea, blankets. Be there for her." She nodded at him, flashing her famous smile.

The paramedic nodded at me with sympathetic eyes and retreated to the ambulance, which whirred away into the wind.

Suddenly, Armand was at my side. Indira fell silent.

"Charlie," he said, a hand to my shoulder. "How are you doing?"

He pulled me to him, breaking the link with Indira. My nose to his chest, he pressed me close, his strong arms wrapping around me, his warmth seeping into me. He smelled of smoke and sweat. One hand patted my back in a soothing rhythm. I closed my eyes.

"We'll take care of you. Don't worry," he whispered into my ear.

Then he pulled back and released me from the embrace, clucked his tongue against his teeth and beckoned to an older auntie in the crowd.

"Stella, take her home, won't you? Get her warm. Stay with her for the night."

The woman came close, nodding, her arm snaking around my shoulders. I let her shuffle me off as Armand called, "I'll take care of everything, don't you worry. We're here for you, Charlie. We are your family. You won't be alone."

His words were intended as a comfort, but they sounded hollow. What someone was supposed to say. There was no heart there.

The next few days were a blur. Stella stayed by my side the whole time, tucking me into bed at night, helping me out of it at dawn, stirring porridge for me in the morning, making soup to ladle out at lunchtime, and boiling copious cups of tea throughout the days. I assumed it was Stella who'd cleaned up all the jars of tomato sauce, lined them up neatly in my pantry, washed the pots, scrubbed the spatter off the floor and counter and walls.

James was cremated, I was told. The coroner's report confirmed a heart attack, I was told. A widow maker, the kind that is sudden and total and fierce, I was told. He stood no chance. It was a tragedy, I was told again and again. So young. So strong. Such a force in our community. A future leader, perhaps. What a shame.

His ashes came home to me in an urn, and the community remembered him in the Great Hall, member after member taking turns at the podium to say nice things about James Grace. And when it came to my turn, I shook my head and kept to the shadows off to the side, and people looked at me with pity, shaking their heads, tsking their tongues. *So sad*, they murmured. *Such a lovely young woman. Has her whole life ahead of her. What will she do now?*

All good questions, and for which I had no answers. I

heard them, but I could not respond even if I'd wanted to.

James's family came to Anam Cara. Flew in on a private jet to the Sydney airport then hired a car service to cart them to us and whisk them away with nearly all of James's possessions. I couldn't imagine who operated a private car service on Cape Breton Island. The people who lived there were hardy and independent and certainly didn't have the kind of money that blew in on the wings of American wealth.

His family were beautiful and well-appointed, with fur coats and gleaming jewels, wearing all black and navy blue and arguing with Armand and Edith and Eamon about what to do with their son and his few earthly holdings. In the end, they retreated as quickly as they came, returning to their posh lives with a few boxes of stuff that held the tiniest of clues about their son and brother. They'd never know the full story of James because he hadn't wanted them to know anything about him. But I could tell that he hadn't known them, either. Such distance in a family.

I knew it all too well. He'd molded me in his image, and I hated him for it.

That might've been the moment when I realized I'd been duped, become James's pathetic puppet. I could live a different story. Retrieve the love of my family, reconnect with those who wished I'd been in their midst all this time, make amends for past mistakes and write a new chapter for the time that stretched out ahead of me. I had a chance to make things right.

Even before the memorial reception, I'd started packing. There was nothing left for me at Anam Cara. Though Armand insisted they were my family, that I was loved, that the community was my true home, once James was gone, my tether was cut and I felt like I was sailing on the wind.

CHAPTER TWENTY-FIVE

And now Boden was here.

We settled into a rhythm. I was so glad to have him close by, my puppy-dog best friend. I knew that sounded harsh, but he was loyal and loving, and I thought the comparison was a good one. We didn't speak again about the evidence, or the rumors, didn't even mention Anam Cara for the next three days. He met Parker, and after, we dished late at night about my new relationship. He could see it was real between us, and he said he was happy for me. He watched me pull on a long flowy skirt and bell-sleeved tunic for Shabbat and clucked his tongue when he learned it was for a Jewish service.

"Don't start," I said, rolling my eyes.

"I'd never have predicted the great Charlie Tanner turning all religious," he quipped.

I swatted him, but I was smiling.

"I am not religious, and I don't plan to be," I said, fluffing my hair. "I'll admit, there's something nice about it. Grounding. I can't explain it better. But I've had enough of following."

"I can explain it for you," he said, popping a handful of potato chips into his mouth. "Rabbi Hottie."

I giggled. He wasn't wrong. I'd never pursue this type of communal involvement without Parker at the center of it. Still, I wasn't as resistant as I had been when my parents visited. I was making friends with nice people, and the weekly services were stabilizing in a way I'd never experienced at Anam Cara, or anywhere for that matter. I felt a part of something real.

You'd think I would have felt that way at Anam Cara, and I guess I did a little bit, for a short while. But I'd always retained an air of skepticism, caution, held a part of myself back. Probably to protect from heartbreak. James had his hand in every corner of the community, so there was no space for me to carve out my own niche. Maybe I hadn't wanted to.

On the fourth day after he arrived at my doorstep, I came in from the garden to find Boden pale and pacing.

"They keep calling me," he muttered, looking frantic.

"Who?" I pulled him to the couch. "Bo, talk to me."

He was shaking his head. "They're going to find me," he said, shaking.

I turned his face to mine. "Bo—who?"

"Armand's people," he muttered.

"Armand has people?"

He shook his head and closed his eyes. "God, I can't

believe how oblivious you are. You literally know nothing about Anam Cara."

I recoiled. "What do you mean? I lived there for twenty years. I lived there longer than you did!"

He raked his fingers through his hair until it stood up wild. "It's true, though I don't honestly know how," he said, almost as if he were mad at me. "How can you be ignorant about how things work? How can you not see what's right in front of you?"

I sucked in my breath, recoiling.

"Bo, this isn't my fault," I said slowly. "I want to help. Who is calling you?"

He held out his ancient flip phone and showed me the call log—twenty-seven calls in the last thirty-six hours, all with 902 and 782 area codes, Cape Breton.

"Do you recognize any of the numbers?"

He shook his head violently then buried his face in his hands.

"They say things like, 'We're coming for you,' or 'You won't get away with this,' or they just breathe into the phone until I yell at them or hang up," he said.

My heart raced. It was a cloudy day in Vermont, turning cool with autumn. I was busy harvesting the huge vegetables that I couldn't keep up with and planning to winterize the garden so the soil would be fragrant and ready come spring. Boden knew this time of year was chaotic with garden work. He'd lived it like I had. And until today, he'd been helping me. It was a relief to have a second set of hands, though I liked to lose myself in the garden, didn't mind the long hours of hard, solitary work. Parker would've been there if he hadn't been bogged down with High Holiday prep. We were seeing him that night at a bistro twenty minutes away. I'd been looking forward to it.

"Why don't you block those numbers?"

He turned to me with wild eyes.

I took a deep breath, like a mother trying to show a strong front to a scared child.

"You're not alone in this, Bo," I crooned. "We'll take care of it."

"How?" His eyes were big, his voice a high-pitched squeak.

"We need to take the evidence and the phone calls to the police," I said.

He shook his head. "Think they'll do anything? They'll laugh us out of there. And besides, Armand has a long reach."

"You think he has cronies in Vermont?" I scoffed. It was a ridiculous idea. Armand Villencourt might have weight in the small, remote community of Bras d'Or, maybe even in the fingers of local law enforcement around Cape Breton, but beyond that, I doubted anyone knew him or cared about some little commune in the remotest corner of North America.

"You have no idea," Boden said, all serious.

He had to be inflating things. I was confident American law enforcement would be able to help or at least keep us safe. That was their job.

"Let's talk to Parker about it tonight," I suggested. "I've told him what you told me already anyway."

He looked scared. "Why did you tell him?"

"I tell him everything, Bo," I said.

"You always were too trusting," he spat.

I shot him a stern look. "That's not fair, and it's not nice. I don't deserve it."

He shook his head and stood up. "No, you don't. I'm sorry. But this is serious, Charlie, and it's not going to go away."

I hoped he was wrong, but a spark in my gut told me he wasn't. I'd been sleeping through my life for decades, unaware of the evil machinations of the people around me. I tended to look for the sunshine in any situation—kind of like Parker.

Dinner that night would've been lovely if Boden hadn't been so wound up. We met Parker and Mary at the bistro, settled into a corner table. The lights in the restaurant were low, the tables covered in gingham tablecloths. Mary ordered a bottle of red wine for the table, and Parker ordered a whiskey for himself, since he didn't drink non-kosher wine, shooting me a questioning glance when he saw Boden's stricken face.

The server rattled off specials and took our orders then returned with the bottle and poured our glasses three-quarters full. Boden downed the wine and signaled to the server for another bottle. "Hope you're paying," Mary said to Boden through her teeth. Parker's eyes went wide.

"Okay, enough. What's going on here?"

He was in rabbi-mode, ready to solve a challenging situation, help people in need. I'd seen that look before, and I loved him for it. To believe that you had the power to save someone's day or fix a problem in their life? I wished for that kind of calming confidence.

Boden told him everything, and Parker and Mary listened, Parker's expression never changing. He had a great talent for maintaining a straight face no matter what news was dropped on him. I didn't know how he did it. I'd never had a good poker face; people could always read my emotions, sometimes even before I knew what they were. But Parker had a knack for listening, caring and calming everyone around him, no matter how dire the crisis. It made him a great rabbi.

Mary, on the other hand, was an open book.

"You both were fools to live there for so long," she said, draining her glass and pouring another. I loved her frankness. It was refreshing.

Parker shot her a stern look.

"We can't change the past," he said. "The only thing to

do is move forward, and I happen to agree with Charlie on this."

We were halfway through our entrées by then and well into a third bottle, which calmed Boden's hysteria.

"This is a matter for the police," Parker said.

Boden looked pityingly at the rest of us. "You're naïve," he said. "I'll go, but it will not end. You don't understand the reach of these people," he insisted. "I'm in danger."

Boden turned to me. "And as long as I'm here with you, so are you." His eyes swept the table. "And the rest of you, too."

I shrugged. "What do they want with me? I'm not part of this. I never was."

"Oh, really? What about the money?"

I froze. How did he know?

"Everyone knows," he said, as if reading my mind. "That's the part I didn't want to show you."

Parker turned to me with a question in his eyes, but I looked away. I hadn't wanted to tell him about the shoebox that was funding my new life.

"Yeah, and they don't want to mess with me," Mary barked. Her Harley was parked outside, and her tough motorcycle friends were never too far from her reach. They'd come the second she called.

If only Boden and I had a protective posse like that.

Parker laid a hand over mine and squeezed. "It'll all work out," he said, sounding the most like a calming, confident pastor that I'd ever heard from him.

"That's what you think." Boden shook his head, gulping the last of his wine and emptying the third bottle into his glass.

Chapter Twenty-Six

My parents were understandably concerned when I told them everything. Since their visit, my mother had taken to calling daily, and I looked forward to those conversations with great eagerness. Several times, I burst into spontaneous tears over how long we'd been apart, and each time my mother shushed me and said, "It's history. Don't ruin now by looking back."

The last time I did it, her voice grew stern. "Enough of this, Charlotte," she said. "I forgive you. Now, forgive yourself. And don't ever mention it again."

I was finding my way to settling into the love she and Dad had to offer. They kept urging me to call my sister, and I was working up the courage to do so. I had no idea what I'd find when I did, but the idea of a close sibling relationship dangled in front of me like candy before a child. But I had my hands full with Boden.

I hadn't told them about the money, and I was surprised they never asked how I afforded my life. Parker had asked about it after the dinner, but I put him off, saying I'd explain it later. I wasn't ready to yet. Surprisingly, he let it go.

"Have you gone to the police yet?" Mom asked. Dad, as usual, was on another handset, listening in.

"Yes, Parker and I went with Boden, and he shared all the evidence he's gathered," I said. Boden was outside working the garden to calm his nerves, and I was grateful for the help, and the momentary reprieve.

"Honestly, I think he's onto something. I want to help him, but I don't want to be involved with anything related to Anam Cara."

"We understand, and we agree," my father said gruffly. "Stay as far away from those people as you can."

"I so wish you'd come home," Mom pleaded. "Vermont is lovely, but this is where you belong."

It would be easier, and I'd considered it, but since Parker had come into my life, I didn't want to go anywhere—not while things were going so well between us. They were ecstatic about our burgeoning relationship and my participation in the Jewish community, but that didn't stop them from begging me to move back to Michigan.

There was something else holding me back, too. It would be going back in time, returning to the person I'd been decades earlier, stuck in the shadows of others, desperate for a love that ended up crushing me. In Vermont, I could start fresh, decide who I wanted to be now.

"Maybe your friend needs to find another place to

crash?" Mom suggested.

The thought had crossed my mind, but I felt guilty even considering banishing Boden. I'd discussed it with Parker the night before.

"I know a place," he'd said. We were lying in his bed, giving Boden my cottage to himself. Parker and I had made love slowly then curled into each other against the pillows. Earlier, we'd started to make pizza—the dough had been rising all afternoon—and lost focus when he started kissing my neck.

I was always starving after sex and as he spoke, I pulled on sweats, a hoodie and thick socks to head to the kitchen and finish what we'd started. He followed me and kept talking.

"I have a friend who is the rabbi of a community near Toronto, and I bet he'd take Boden in."

I snickered. "He's not even Jewish, honey," I said, licking tomato sauce from his fingers.

Parker shook his head. "Doesn't matter," he said. "It's a very liberal community. More of a commune, though not cultish." He snickered. "But he'd feel at home there. The residents are peace-seeking and welcoming, not like that place you two called home." It was the closest I'd seen Parker come to judgmental.

Would Boden go for it? If he was right that Armand was out to get him, it wouldn't matter where he went. But, if he got farther away and hid in a community where no one would expect to find him, he might have a chance.

I finished shredding cheese over the top of the pizza and shoved it into the oven.

"I like it," I said. "Let's see if he'll go for it."

Twenty minutes later, the pizza was puffy and golden, the crust crispy, the cheese just starting to brown. We pulled it out, ran a knife through the soft crust and slipped gooey slices on two plates. Parker flipped the radio to a local country station and poured beer into glasses.

"A rabbi who likes jazz and also country twang," I joked. "You are a lovely contradiction in terms."

We slept late the next morning, the sunlight shining into our windows a little later each day. He came with me back to the house to talk to Boden, who was calmly poring over papers spread across my kitchen table.

"What's all this?" I leaned on his shoulder and peered down at the documents. My breath hitched in my throat as I read one, then another, and my knees gave out from under me.

Parker caught me before I tumbled to the floor. Boden jumped up and swept the papers into a bin.

"I hadn't expected you to walk in," Boden quipped.

Parker led me to the couch and steadied me on the cushions. Then he turned to Boden, glaring.

"What do you have there?" he demanded.

Boden brought the bin of papers over and sat with us, sighing.

"I didn't want you to see any of this," he said apologetically, handing the box to Parker, who sifted through the pages.

All I could recall was James's name, the word "rape," and the names of several men in the community previously thought to be the fathers of children who were now biologically attributed to James. The men had been working up a collective action against James just before he died, with a possible punishment of banishing him from Anam Cara.

"Are you serious?" Parker was astounded, fuming. He threw the pages back into the bin and shoved it at Boden. "You think this helps?"

Boden winced. "I didn't want her to see it, man, but she already knows."

Parker regained his cool and swallowed. "Yeah, she told me about all the babies." He glanced at me, and I tried to staunch the tears welling in my eyes.

"All those years he said he didn't want children," I said to no one in particular. "He knew I did—desperately!"

"You know, honey, I love you, but I am sick to death of hearing you whine about all that you missed because of James," Boden said.

He was angry—really angry—at me. How could he be angry at me? I wasn't to blame here! I was the victim.

I didn't know how to respond, but he didn't give me time to anyway. Parker sat next to me on the couch, slipped his hand in mine and stroked my palm as Boden gathered steam.

"It might've been like that in the beginning, Charlie, but we're talking twenty years—*TWENTY FUCKING YEARS*! You gave him your whole life. You. Gave. Him." He raked at his blond hair, his green eyes electric with emotion. "I get it that a controlling partner can play with your mind and convince you not to believe yourself or that you have no power or whatever. That's what Anam Cara was all *about*! And you were the perfect target."

He was shouting now. He'd moved from blaming me for my situation to blaming the community for everything in his. I saw the parallels. He wasn't wrong.

I swallowed and found my voice. "You're right," I said calmly, shaking off the malaise that was all too familiar. "It's time I take control of my story."

Boden was nodding. "That's more like it," he cheered. "That's the Charlie I knew was inside you. Bring her out. Let her take charge."

And actually, it felt freeing. James was gone. The person I'd been was history. The past was done. None of it mattered. Only today. And I could make tomorrow anything I wanted.

Energy surged through me, and suddenly I was smiling. Parker looked at me strangely, and it was my turn to pat his hand with reassurance.

"Tell him," I urged Parker, pointing at Boden.

He laid out the plan to scuttle him off to a Jewish commune in Ontario, to hide him there until everything could settle down. At first, Boden was perplexed, but he quickly warmed to the idea, and by the time we went to bed that night, we'd settled on a plan that both of us felt confident would buy time...and perhaps his freedom.

Parker headed home. We had three days left before the Jewish new year, and I wouldn't see much of him over the next month, at least not the two of us alone. I'd go to services, join him for meals, maybe sleep at his house a few nights here or there. I was eager to experience everything and a little nervous, too. But Boden would leave in a couple of days, and I wanted time with my friend before I sent him off.

That night, Boden lay in the bed beside me, a calm settling over us both. We were closer than ever. I couldn't wait to visit him at his new home. Who could've expected that both of us would find our way into the bosom of Jewish enclaves? Maybe he'd even fall for a nice Jewish guy, and we'd raise children in the footsteps of my ancestors, who I was only just beginning to know and grow comfortable with.

"You could become a mama now," Boden crooned as the moonlight sparkled in the night sky.

"God, I hope so," I said. "I hope it's not too late for me. I'm not young." I laughed and looked at him, propping up on my elbow. "But Parker might not want that, you know. I mean, we've only been dating a few months, and he has two grown kids. Plus, I don't know if he wants to be married again." I sighed. "It would be weird for Alice and Ethan, who are in their twenties, to have a baby sibling."

He laughed. "It is kinda crazy," he said. "But I like that for you." He stroked a stray hair away from my face. "You'd make a great mother, honey."

The possibility rippled through me.

"First things first," I said, desperate to change the subject so I wouldn't get too hopeful. "Let's get you to safety, and let's get me through this bizarre month of holidays. I have no idea what to expect. I hope I don't implode in the middle of it and give Parker a reason to break up with me."

I laughed, but I was truly worried about all the religious observance to come in the days ahead. Boden could see through my bravado.

He sat up and pulled me to sit facing him. Staring straight into my eyes, he said, "You deserve a real love, Charlie. Don't look for reasons to walk away. And don't doubt that you are entirely worthy of a lasting love."

I licked my lips and swallowed nervously. "I won't," I promised.

CHAPTER TWENTY-SEVEN

From the shoebox, I gave Boden enough money to buy an old clunker that would get him as far as Toronto. It was strange to have money after so many years of having none. I didn't know if I'd ever get used to the freedom that money brought. It still felt best when I gave it away.

He promised to repay me, but I shook it off, clasping his hands. "Please don't," I said. "This was found money. It means nothing to me other than to give me—us—a second chance."

His eyes shone with emotion.

I squeezed his hands. "You're going to be fine."

I looked at him and said, "Bo, do me a favor. Destroy all the evidence. Let it go. Trash the files, burn the papers. Move on. You deserve a fresh start, just like me. It's not our business whatever havoc James wreaked back at Anam Cara."

I wrapped my arms around him, standing on my tiptoes to lay my head against his chest. "I love you," I mumbled into his sweater.

He squeezed my shoulders, kissed me full on the lips then pulled away, swiping at his eyes. "Call you when I arrive," he said with a backward wave and hastily folded into the car and backed away from the cottage.

As I closed the door behind me, my phone buzzed.

"You ready?" Parker's voice was eager, like a little boy before his birthday. I loved his enthusiasm but for the life of me couldn't figure out what, exactly, excited him about these holidays.

I'd been researching the Jewish High Holidays, and the seriousness of it all weighed heavily on me. I'd always been a carefree, go-with-the-flow kind of person. I didn't know if I had it in me to sit in services that lasted for hours or spend a full day atoning for my sins. Hadn't I been doing that for months? Years, even?

But Parker had reassured me that his congregation was liberal, that the services were inspiring and not too long. I wanted to believe him. Desperately. This was a hurdle in our relationship, and I wanted to leap over it with ease. He was becoming too important to me to consider what would happen if I didn't.

"No," I laughed, "but I'll be there."

His voice turned caring, concerned. "C'mon, Charlie. Trust me. I think you'll love it."

"You want me to love it," I said, cradling the phone against my shoulder as I flipped through my closet at the few garments that hung there. I'd made the rounds of all the thrift stores within an hour radius in search of something nice for services, and all I'd come up with was a long denim skirt, a soft sweater set and a floral blouse. I didn't love any of them, but they'd have to do.

"I do," he said eagerly, and I could almost hear him nodding. "But I'm not worried. So you shouldn't be. I'll just be glad to see you there among the congregation. And if you don't love it, don't worry. I'll still love you."

I stopped cold. We hadn't said that to each other yet, and he was blurting it out over the phone, in a conversation about religion?

The flush crawled up my face and out to the ends of my ears. Even my hair was hot. I didn't know what to say.

"Say something, Charlie," he urged.

"So that wasn't a slip?"

"No." His voice was strong, calm, confident.

"I don't know whether to smile or scream," I admitted, sitting on the edge of the bed. "I mean, I love you, too. It's just, I hadn't imagined saying it like this."

I forced a small laugh into the silence.

His voice grew husky. "I mean it," he said. "I love you, Charlie Tanner."

My voice was weak. I gulped. "It's not too soon? Are we moving too fast?" I wished he were there beside me to steady me so I could look into his eyes and know the truth.

"I'm surprised by the intensity of this, too, but it feels right," he said, now in his rabbi voice, trying to calm me, to soothe.

It *did* feel right. And I'd waited too long for right.

Chapter Twenty-Eight

Services the first night of Rosh Hashanah were short and uplifting, just like Parker promised. I was more nervous about meeting his kids, who'd come home for the holiday.

But that was easy, and nice, too. They definitely gave me the once-over when we met before services started, but they seemed kind and friendly and not at all offended that their father was dating someone two years after their mother's death.

After, at his house, we ate a delicious meal of roast chicken, carrot souffle and salad. Parker had kept it simple, so we'd have time to talk and get to know each other. The other holiday meals—two lunches and another dinner—would include congregants and friends around his dining room table. He promised culinary surprises at every meal. "Foods that have symbolism for the holiday." He'd winked.

He dipped apple slices in honey, for a sweet new year. The carrots were for physical and spiritual abundance, but also to sharpen our eyesight so we could see clearly in the year ahead. There were two huge round challah breads that he'd made himself—which really impressed me—and he drizzled honey over the cut slices, again for a sweet year. There was a star fruit cut into beautifully-shaped slices, and he said it was important to have a new fruit at the meal so we could have a reason to say a special prayer of gratitude, the *Shechechiyanu*. And there was a sad-looking fish head on the table, meant to inspire us to be like the head, and not the tail. I found it all fascinating and poetic.

Alice was talkative and beautiful, with Parker's shiny brown hair, worn long down her back, and the same sparkling hazel eyes. Ethan resembled his mother more, judging from the family photos strewn around their home. He was a serious, reserved young man with thick brown curls and light-blue eyes, taller than his father.

"It's quite an accomplishment to land a reporting job at the *New York Times* right out of college," I said.

Ethan nodded. "I'm mostly making calls, fetching coffee, and writing obituaries—and not about the important or noteworthy people who've died. But, since losing Mom, it feels like a meaningful mission to honor the recently departed." He scooped some souffle into his mouth.

"Did you write your mother's obituary?" Why not get it all out in the open, show them I wasn't there to replace their mother, that I knew I never could.

He gave me a grateful smile. "Yeah. It was the hardest

assignment I've ever had."

I nodded as Parker shot me a thankful grin.

I asked Alice what she was studying, which was a far easier conversation. She went deep into the importance of resurrecting indigenous history and how she wanted to fill in the huge gaps in academic writings about the people who were on this land before the colonists took it all for themselves. Her voice brimmed with purpose, similar to the way the Anam Cara leaders railed on about the reasons the community was so important—not just to the region, but to the world.

To be fair, their agricultural prowess *was* impressive and groundbreaking. But the commune's success cultivating crops in difficult soil didn't justify the self-importance that puffed up its leaders, inflating them to superhuman status. Of course, Alice wasn't anything like that, just young, passionate, and energetic about her studies, which I admired with a sense of longing. I'd been like that once. Why the hell had I let it go so easily?

Parker and I had agreed that I wouldn't spend the night while his kids were home. "I'm not hiding you," he'd assured me. "I just want to ease them into the idea of a woman in my home and in my bed."

He'd paused before continuing.

"In their mother's place."

I understood. Though our feelings for each other were intense and strong, we'd only been together a few months.

Sure, at our ages, things moved faster. We didn't have all the time in the world to explore and do the coy dance, and besides, we were both people who'd experienced great loss. We knew how fleeting life could be. We didn't want to wait or play games.

But Alice and Ethan wouldn't understand that. I thought back to myself at twenty, when life was a wide, open invitation and I believed I had all the time in the world to explore, to do, to become. At twenty-three—Ethan's age—I was already in the fog of James Grace, squirreled away in a commune on Cape Breton Island. I chose to cut myself off from everything I knew; they hadn't. They'd lost their mother to a cruel disease, and I was sure it imprinted on the adults they were becoming. At least they had Parker's kind, generous love to guide them. It was enough that they welcomed me into their father's life and into their home.

I said my goodbyes, and Parker followed me out to my car. Glancing back to make sure his children weren't watching out the windows, he leaned into me, pressing me up against the car and planting a long, soft kiss on my mouth. Then he pulled me in for a tight, warm embrace.

"Hmmmmm," he hummed into my hair. "What I wouldn't give to have you naked in my bed right now."

I swatted him on the back as I pulled him closer. "Soon," I whispered into his ear.

He kissed me again. "See you tomorrow, bright and

early!" He smiled as he said it, and I tried to mirror his enthusiasm.

"My parents are so thrilled with all of this," I said.

He was nodding. "Of course they are! Not only are you back in their life, but now you're in love with a rabbi and discovering your Jewish roots." He practically sang the words.

"You are far too happy about this," I laughed, pushing him away.

He edged closer, his nose nudging against my cheek. "I am," he said. "Very happy."

I settled behind the steering wheel, and he closed the door softly, smiling and waving as I drove away.

It was a quiet drive home, and I rolled down the window to feel the night. It was pure black, the moon hidden from view in a vast sky. I felt like I was driving through a tunnel, the country roads huddled in darkness from the tall trees on either side of the two lanes.

Chapter Twenty-Nine

Although I fell into a quick and deep sleep, I slept fitfully that night, awakened three times out of terrifying dreams, my heart racing.

In the first, James was alive and grabbing at me. I yelled at him to let go, to leave me alone, that I was done with him, but he wouldn't release me and I couldn't get away. The second dream disappeared the moment I opened my eyes, but I knew he hovered in the periphery, and I yelled into the darkness of my echoing house, "James Grace—I don't love you anymore!" My voice reverberated back to me, and I shook with sobs, wanting to be free from the fear that had inhabited my core for far too long. If it hadn't been two in the morning, I'd have dialed Parker just to hear his voice. But I couldn't do that to him, especially not with his kids at home and services beginning seven hours later.

I got up, drank some water and peered outside into the darkness. I thought I saw something in the shadows near the greenhouse but reasoned that any manner of night creatures lurked out there, in their natural habitat, and

I was the interloper on their land. I pulled the curtains closed and got back into bed, clutching the blanket under my chin.

The third dream happened just before dawn, and it was a perplexing one. James was there again, but he didn't speak to me, wouldn't make eye contact. Boden, Armand, and my Anam Cara friends Lily and Charmaine all gathered around me. I was supine on the ground, and they all stood around me, staring down. I tried to speak, but my voice caught in my throat, so they spoke for me, charting my course, deciding how I would move forward in my own life.

I wanted to shout at them that I was right there, that I could decide for myself, that I was sick of someone else taking charge for me, but I couldn't manage even a squeak. And then Armand sent them all away and they went willingly, waving back at me, and I knew I'd never see them again and I was at the mercy of this towering man with a wicked gleam in his eye. What did he want with me? Why couldn't I fend him off? And why couldn't I get up from the ground, stand tall, defiant, before him?

I woke up in a cold sweat, my breath in gasps. I sat upright in bed. The sun was just beginning to color the horizon in pinks and lavenders. The clock read five fifteen. I didn't want to descend into yet another unsettling sleep, so I padded into the kitchen for tea.

My phone buzzed a half hour later.

"Is this Charlie Tanner?" It was a man's voice, formal and unfamiliar.

"Yes," I said as my heartbeat quickened.

"Ma'am, we found your phone number as an emergency contact in the wallet of Boden Trillium."

My stomach fell. I waited for the man to continue, to tell me what I already knew.

His car had gone into a ravine outside Montreal. Dead on impact. Skid marks on the road suggested he'd veered to avoid a collision. Probably an accident, but they'd investigate.

It was no accident. But I couldn't tell them that. I had no proof. Just a hunch. And after so many years of ignoring my instincts and waiting for someone else to tell me what was right, I was finally getting good at knowing what the still, small voice inside me was saying. It was nearly always right, and this time was no exception.

I thanked the officer for calling and gave him Boden's mother's information. He'd inform her of her son's passing. He'd take it from there.

I tried to imagine what it had been like. Boden driving along, ready for a new start, happy, maybe singing along to music on the radio. Leaning into the curves and bends of the road. Watching the sun set behind the trees.

Then, headlights coming at him, blinding his view. His heartbeat rising as he waits for the oncoming car to veer, to move away from his lane, and then the realization that no, it wasn't going to move, it was coming straight for him, and in that split-second, he'd need to do something to protect himself, to move out of the speeding car's path, so he swerved, jerked the steering wheel to the side, and the car lurched. He couldn't know how close he was to the rail, how easily it would bend on impact, how forceful an automobile at great speed, with momentum, could tear apart that ribbon of metal meant to protect drivers from the dangers of the undulating land, how quickly the car would go over the side and, in the few seconds that he was airborne, how eerily still it was, how beautiful to be leaping through the air, weightless and free. I hoped his death was immediate, painless. I hoped he didn't have time to realize that it was the end, that he'd never make it to his new home, that he'd never find a love that made life more colorful, the air sweeter.

I ended the call and sat at the kitchen table, stunned. If they knew where he was, if they could chart his course along the backroads from Vermont on the way to Toronto, they could absolutely find me. They were probably watching me already.

I shuddered and got ready for services, hoping I could pretend everything was okay at least until the end of the holiday, until I could share it all with the man I loved. I couldn't distract him when he had to lead the congregation through one of the most important days of the Jewish year. I hoped I could stay safe until then...until I could figure out how to ground myself in the strength it would take to face this threat head-on.

Chapter Thirty

It was really hard not to tell Parker anything about Boden's death for two more days, but the minute second-day lunch ended and all the guests drove away, I pulled him outside for a private conversation.

He was stunned but also angry.

"Why did you wait to tell me, Charlie?" His voice swelled, and he grabbed at his hair with a wild look in his eyes. "You're in danger now! You shouldn't have waited. I don't want anything to happen to you!"

His gaze bore into me, and I remembered suddenly that this was a man who had had a great love and lost her. I hadn't realized the true depths of his feelings for me until now. I reached out a hand, and he took it, clasping mine in both of his then lifting my hand to his chest.

"You—I can't lose you," he said almost in a gasp.

I stepped closer until there were mere inches between us, our hearts beating in tandem. I planted a soft, lingering kiss on his lips. He sucked in air.

"God, you smell good," he whispered, his fingers in my

hair.

Then I remembered his kids were inside the house and stepped back.

He was calmer now, with a half-smile on his face and a hand combing through his hair.

"Don't worry," he said. "They're lost in their technology."

I hadn't slept the night before out of fear, just sat upright on the couch, scrolling through old movies on my laptop and eyeing the bolted door. No one came. I was fine. But I couldn't sustain this level of emotional stress much longer, and I was glad to be able to share my fear with someone. I wouldn't dare tell my parents until I had a plan.

He paced the patio, eyes wide, fear written all over his face. His kids would leave the next morning, Ethan to return to his job in New York and Alice to her college dorm.

"You're staying here tonight," he insisted.

"But the kids..."

He shook his head. A cool breeze sifted through the birch tree beyond the patio.

"I don't care," he said. "I need to keep you safe. They'll have to understand."

I folded my lips, not wanting to ask what he'd tell them. I didn't want to cause trouble, to intrude on their family life, but I was relieved to not have to return to that house, where someone could be watching me at any time.

"We'll go to the police," he said, glancing at his watch. It was after five. He shook his head. "Someone will be at the precinct. Maybe not the chief, but at least we can start the conversation."

I reached for him, clamped a hand on his arm to calm his tirade. "Maybe we should wait until morning, after the kids have left?"

He sucked in a breath and nodded. "You're right. It's a better idea. I don't want to scare them."

We migrated inside and sat on the couch. I leaned my head on his shoulder and closed my eyes, desperately wanting sleep.

"Dad!" Alice called from the kitchen. "What's the plan for dinner?"

"I can't believe they're hungry," he said. "After all the food of the past forty-eight hours." He snickered then called back to his daughter. "Leftovers—whatever you can find in the fridge, sweetheart. And there's a pizza in the freezer, too."

His arm snaked around me, and I leaned closer. He squeezed my arm. "We'll figure this out, Charlie," he said. "I have no doubt."

But I did.

Parker had no idea what we were up against. I'd told him about Anam Cara and James, opened my life and my soul to this man. But it's one thing to hear the stories and another to live them.

At Anam Cara, there'd been mandatory fasting, once a month, sometimes more often. It seemed that the spiritual leaders chose the time and day on a whim then announced to the community at a gathering what was coming. It was strictly enforced, and I still couldn't understand exactly how. We all had our own houses, with doors that locked. There weren't cameras watching our every move, at least not that I knew of. But there were door-to-door checks during those fasts, which they insisted were for a soul cleansing, to give us clear focus so we could tap into spiritual wisdom. Except the only people imparting spiritual wisdom at Anam Cara were those who spoke from the stage in the Great Hall, those who set the rules and enforced them.

The door checks were carried out by tall, menacing men with thick beards and thick biceps, who came thundering at each door to see who had kept the fast and who had snuck a sip of water or a palmful of nuts. I don't know how they knew; they just did. And the guilty parties were sent off to commune with Armand in a closed chamber off the side of his abode. Thankfully, I'd been too obedient back then and never transgressed, but the stories were legendary and frightening. One or two community members ended up hospitalized after it was all done, and yet no one left the community, no one called authorities on our stranger, or more dangerous, practices. The power of the community, the power of communal silence, prevailed.

I was glad to be free of their claws. I just hoped I could stay that way.

Evening turned into night, and Alice put her schoolwork away and came to sit with us. Ethan meandered downstairs for a late snack and joined the rest of us in the family room. Parker tuned the TV to an '80s movie, *Beautiful Girls*, which held up surprisingly well. The kids laughed at some of the posturing and quirky phrases. Ethan loved the soundtrack, and Alice wrinkled her nose at the feigned crush between the teenage character played by Natalie Portman and the much-older next-door neighbor played by Timothy Hutton.

"It's not like they actually hooked up," Ethan chided her, but she wasn't having it.

"It's just gross," she said. "Too much of an age gap. Predatory."

I thought about what Boden had shown me, all the children James had fathered. While he'd been my partner, living with me, sharing my bed, he'd slept with some women who were decades younger than him. Hell, I was a decade his junior and his student, for goodness' sake. What would Alice and Ethan think if they knew about my past? I was ashamed and vowed not to let Parker's kids be tainted by my sordid past. It was bad enough that he knew the depths of my mistakes. And still he loved me—I didn't understand why, but I'd take it.

It was after eleven when Alice and Ethan ambled off to their rooms for the night. Parker clicked off the TV and latched the front door. Lights lowered, blankets folded over the back of the couch, he checked the kitchen door, peered outside at the quiet night. I came up behind him, laced my arms around his torso and leaned my head against his back. The house vibrated with silence.

He was warm through his sweater, and he relaxed back into me.

"Hmmm, you feel nice," he murmured.

I was stroking his chest through his sweater, swaying my body into his. Sparks were flying throughout my body, out to every nerve ending. The furnace hummed on in the basement. It was going to be a cold night, the first frost. I was glad I didn't have to drive home. Here, I could pretend everything was fine, that I was safe.

And maybe I would be.

Parker spun around and lifted me off the ground. My legs wrapped around him, and he settled me onto the kitchen counter. He nuzzled my neck, little butterfly kisses and tiny bites that both stung and excited me. He pressed closer to me, the fullness of his body hard into mine.

"Should we go upstairs?" I whispered, threading my fingers through his thick hair.

"Mmmm." He nodded but kept tasting me, sucking at my skin, making it harder to imagine hopping off the granite and focus on putting one foot in front of another to head upstairs. "We'll have to be super quiet," he whispered then sucked my tongue into his. He was salty and sweet and familiar, and I pressed closer, wanting to slip inside him, to become one tight, hot web of a person, blending two souls into one searing dream.

He pulled me off the countertop and grabbed my hand. I thought we were heading upstairs, but he led me instead to the back of the first floor, where there was a guest room that doubled as a den and his home office. It was spacious and clean, carpeted in a low plush beige, a full-size bed tucked into a nook with a low window, a couch and a desk and a wall of bookshelves.

"I didn't even know this was here," I said.

"Shhhh." He put a finger to his lips and closed the door.

"Do we have to be quiet down here?"

He nodded and began undressing me, slipping my shirt over my head, sliding my skirt into a pool on the carpet. I reached for him, and he stepped back, shaking his head.

"I want to look at you," he said.

I felt the flush creep up my torso, engulfing my neck and face and covering my arms. He stood several feet from me, watching, as I dropped my panties to the floor, unhooked my bra and dropped it, too. There was no light in the room other than the gleam from his computer, which shone a calming mountain landscape. No light from outside either, with the lack of a moon in the sky and only far-twinkling stars to give a hint of life.

"Like what you see?" I said in a low voice.

He nodded slowly. "So very much."

Then he closed the distance between us and laid me gently on the bed, covering my body with the length of his. His mouth was on mine, but I mumbled, "Don't you think it's unfair that I'm the only one without clothing?"

His hands were running down my thighs, and I sighed, waiting for him to discover how wet I was. Then he stopped, stood up and unbuckled his belt, dropped it to the floor and his pants after that, then his sweater, under-shirt... He even unlatched his watch and laid it on the desk before returning to me on the bed.

I loved the look of him. For a man on the verge of fifty, he was trim and fit and beautiful. The sinews of his shoulders rippled with muscles, his arms pulsing with strength. His legs, too, were finely sculpted and covered by a light fur of soft hair. He kneed my legs open and planted himself between them, diving in so fast that it took me by surprise and my breath hitched in my throat.

"I can't go so long without feeling you," he said, thrusting deeper into me. I grabbed a handful of his hair and arched my back to pull him deeper.

"You like that, Charlie?"

I nodded and bucked against him.

He was biting his lip, and I didn't know if it was to hold back the power-hungry words that would send me into a mute ball or because of the intensity of our connection, the chemistry between us that was a lifeline. He thrust deeper, harder, then faster, and I lost all sense of time and space, catapulting into a new dimension of being. When he gasped with final pleasure, I was so close to joining him, electric with wanting, a bundle of nerves on fire.

He withdrew and knelt at the edge of the bed, pulling me down low so he could cup my behind with his hands and bury his face in my wetness. It didn't take long for me to match his release, and I cried out then clamped a hand over my mouth to stifle the sound. Over and over and over the waves came, and he didn't stop, didn't slow, didn't cease licking at my most tender spot until I fell quiet, a silent tear of release rolling down my cheek.

He sat up and looked at me with a satisfied smile. "Good?"

I nodded, unable to form words.

Parker helped me up and handed me my clothes then pulled on his own. "We'll sleep down here," he said. "It's too soon for them to see you in their mother's bed."

Of course. I understood.

I reached for him. "You'll stay with me?"

He nodded. "There's no other place I'd rather be."

Chapter Thirty-One

I awoke to find myself alone in the bed, the sun dazzling in orange hues as it peeked above the horizon. Parker was in the kitchen, frying eggs and toasting bread.

He turned from the skillet and grinned.

"Good morning. Sleep well?"

I nodded. "Smells good."

"We'll eat before seeing them off and then go to the precinct," he said. He'd showered and dressed in dark jeans and a brown and orange flannel with a long-sleeved T-shirt underneath and dark-brown Chelsea boots. I wanted to slide my arms around him and inhale his scent, but I could hear Alice and Ethan moving around upstairs. He turned back to the stove.

"I need a shower and a change of clothes," I said.

"Can it wait until after?"

I nodded. I guess I could carry the scent of our lovemaking on my skin for a little while longer. I gathered my hair into a messy bun and smeared my lips with balm.

"At least let me borrow a toothbrush," I said.

He nodded and led me into the guest bathroom, where there was a stash of packaged toiletries beneath the sink. "Help yourself," he said then whisked back to the kitchen.

I closed the door and breathed in to calm myself. I splashed cool water on my face and brushed my teeth then returned to the kitchen.

"I poured you some coffee," Parker said, handing me a steaming mug.

I smiled thanks and his face pinked up.

Alice came thumping downstairs, dragging her roller bag over each step. Ethan wasn't far behind, an athletic weekender over his shoulder. Both were showered and clearly eager to hit the road.

While the three of them buzzed around the kitchen, I migrated to the living room, wishing I'd left before the kids came down. It felt awkward to be there in the morning since I had no idea what they were thinking. I flipped through magazines and coffee table books, listening for the thrum of conversation in the next room. They didn't talk much. Forks scraped against plates, water ran, dishes clinked into the sink or dishwasher, all in a flurry.

Finally, strident footsteps from kitchen to foyer. I peered into the front hall.

Alice was pulling on her coat. Ethan hoisted up his bag and thumped his father on the back in a half-hug. Parker didn't even notice me hovering in the doorway.

"How long is the drive back to New York?"

Parker whipped around, seeming surprised to see me there. Alice glanced between us. I wanted to shrink into the wallpaper.

Ethan looked up at the sound of my voice. "Six hours," he quipped, not quite making eye contact. "Shouldn't be any traffic until I hit the city."

I nodded, smiling in case he looked my way. "I'm so glad I got to meet you both."

Ethan smiled and nodded.

The hallway walls held a collage of framed photographs from decades of family life. The kids as babies, sudsed up in a bathtub, fisting mashed carrots in a highchair, on Parker's shoulders laughing. There were family portraits, where everyone wore denim and white, and formal portraits with more relatives from weddings and bar mitzvahs. I knew so little about Parker's family. Were his parents still alive? Was he close to them? Did he see them often? How close had he remained to Sylvie's family? Did he have siblings?

And how could I not know any of this?

Memories of James's black-hole background came barreling back. And while I knew deep-down there were no similarities between Parker and James, my breath hitched in my throat at all the evidence of him happily linked to another woman for so many years. I was only there because she wasn't.

In particular, I couldn't stop staring at the big, framed portrait of Parker and Sylvie on their wedding day in the center of all the beautiful photographs. She wore white satin with tiny rosettes cascading down lace sleeves and pearls shining on the bodice. Thick brown curls spilled down her shoulders and framed her face. Her blue eyes glowed. Parker was so handsome, so young. His brown hair moppy and thick under a white yarmulke and a white rose in the lapel of his tuxedo jacket. He wasn't looking at the camera, only at her, with longing in his eyes.

God, to have loved like that.

I wished someone would gaze so adoringly at me.

Could Parker ever see me the way he saw Sylvie? Was it even possible, when he'd already had one love that had lit up his life? And a whole family they'd created together?

The door slammed, and I startled. The kids had left, and I'd missed their goodbyes. Then Parker was standing beside me, lifting my hair and kissing my skin, his breath hot on my neck.

I turned to him, hoping he couldn't see the envy in my eyes.

"You have a beautiful family," I said, throwing my arms around his neck and burying my face in his soft shirt.

"Thank you," he said into my hair, rubbing circles on my back. "The kids liked you."

I pulled back to look at him. "Did they?"

He nodded vigorously. Then his face grew serious. "Are you ready?" He laced his hand into mine, holding tight.

I nodded and gulped.

"Do you think it'll do anything? I mean, we have nothing—just a hunch."

He shrugged. "It can't hurt, right?"

I hesitated. "I mean, we could just wait and see if anything comes that is alarming—phone calls, letters...or anyone..."

"Or a car coming at you head-on in a narrow road on an icy night?" He shook his head. "I don't want to chance it, Charlie."

I exhaled, feeling shaky.

"Okay. Let's go."

His face brightened, relief written across his eyes. If he was that concerned about me, this must be love.

The nearest police precinct was a small headquarters with a middle-aged sergeant (according to the name tag pinned to his uniform) monitoring the desk and fielding calls. Behind him were three desks and two other officers. My hopes sagged the minute we walked in—it was too small-town to do anything significant.

"Hey, Rabbi, happy new year!" the officer called out.

"Hi Bruce, thanks very much," Parker said, holding out a hand to shake. The policeman took it and pumped heartily.

"Everything okay over at the temple?"

"Just fine, thanks," Parker replied. "We really appreciate your support."

"What brings you in today?"

Parker turned to me and beamed. "This is Charlie Tanner," he said.

I smiled at the policeman and held out my hand.

"Nice to meet you, Ms. Tanner. What can I do for you?"

Parker waited for me to speak. I sucked on my bottom lip, trying to figure out how to word it. Finally, everything just spilled out.

"Wow. That's some story, ma'am," he said, taking off his cap and running a hand over his balding pate.

I nodded, waiting for him to say more. Parker had hung back, letting the two of us engage, and I desperately wanted him to get involved, to explain whatever I had failed to convey, make it sound more threatening than I apparently had. I felt the fear like a chunk of ice lodged in my chest—why couldn't I convey the gravity of the situation in words?

The policeman seemed to consider what I'd said, and when he responded, he was equal parts sympathetic and questioning. He jotted some notes; I saw Armand's name scribbled in all caps across his notepad.

"I see why you'd be afraid," he started. "Unfortunately, I don't know how we can help—at least, not now or not yet."

He glanced to Parker, raised his eyebrows, and then looked back at me.

"We can certainly patrol your area more, keeping an eye out for suspicious characters," he continued. "And if you come across anything more concrete, I'd like to hear about it."

It was the best he could offer, but I felt deflated. There was nothing left to say except thank you.

He nodded and offered a sympathetic smile then grabbed a business card and scribbled a phone number on the back.

"This here is all the precinct information, including the hotline for emergencies." He pointed to the printed information on the front. Then he turned it over. "And this is my cell phone," he said. "Call anytime."

Bruce's eyes gleamed with sincerity. At least I had a friend in him.

I thanked him again and slid the card into my purse then followed Parker outside after he'd said his goodbyes.

The autumn air held a chill. The trees were changing colors, and the maples and oaks near the police station were a riot of reds and yellows and browns. We didn't speak; the wind whispered around us in soothing tones.

In the car, Parker turned to me. "I'm sorry, honey," he said softly. "I wish there was more that could be done." His fingers trailed down the sides of my face. "I'm disappointed. I honestly thought they could do something."

I touched his shoulder and smiled. "You're lovely to try."

He drove us back to his house, and I got out of the car and stepped over to mine.

"I'd like to follow you home if you don't mind," Parker

said. "Just to be sure you're safe, and no one's lurking about." He looked so worried and sincere, so I couldn't say no. And, my stomach knotted at the idea of going back there and finding someone skulking about. I nodded, and he returned to his car while I got into my Volvo, fired it up, and headed off. It was a quick drive, and I was surprised to feel relief when I pulled up in front of my cottage.

Our car doors slammed in unison, and he was at my side as we approached the house.

"Everything looks in order," he said, hands in his pockets, eyes darting around the yard.

Indeed, it was locked, just as I'd left it, and nothing was out of place. Inside, Parker peered behind every door, checked every bolt and window latch, and when he was satisfied, he came to me in the living room.

"Is everything okay with us?" I asked.

He was just standing there, not going, not sitting, buzzing with nervous energy.

I was ready for the blow, for the "I've had a great time, but…" I was waiting for him to sputter and depart, to tell me it had just been a dalliance, but he'd changed his mind, that seeing me in proximity to his kids had sent his heart reeling back to his beloved wife and he couldn't possibly love another like he'd loved her.

"Charlie," he started.

I held my breath.

"I can't lose another love."

They weren't the words I'd heard in my head, the words I'd feared.

Quite the opposite.

"I'm so busy at this time of year, with all the Jewish holidays and my congregants, so many things to take care of, and it's just me and the one part-time office assistant"—Sheila, the chipper, ancient secretary who clearly had a crush on the handsome rabbi.

Here was the blow, the brush-off. I closed my eyes and waited for the words to hit me with the force of a truck.

"Look at me, Charlie," he said.

My eyes flew open to see his shining with unshed tears.

"I can't be with you all the time to make sure that you're safe," he said.

"I wouldn't want you to," I said. "I have to live my life, Parker. I can't cower in fear and wait for someone to come and ruin everything."

"But what will you do? How can you feel safe when all this is swirling around you? I'm not... I'm not ready for us to live together."

"And even if you were, that wouldn't protect me, Parker." I placed a hand on his shoulder and peered into his eyes. "I don't want a round-the-clock babysitter. And besides, do you think you're that much of a threat if Armand sends a few guys to get me?" I huffed, and he cracked a weak, worried smile.

"I'm going to have to face whatever this is head-on,"

I said, feeling stronger. "I can figure it out. It's not your problem."

I regretted the words as soon as I'd said them. I wanted to be his problem, and I wanted him to want that, too. I refused to pretend I didn't want to be all-in with this man.

"I want you to be my problem, Charlie Tanner," he said, gripping my shoulders and pulling me close.

"Okay, but let's approach this as a team?" I said, and he nodded.

"Just be extra cautious for me. Please," he said.

He kissed me then, and it was a sweet, slow kiss, the kind that promised more kisses to come as well as a deep understanding.

Chapter Thirty-Two

The weeks that followed were surprisingly calm and quiet, and I began to forget my fear. The air turned cool, brisk, and I tended to my plants as if they were babies in need of twenty-four-hour attention. I covered some with tarps and spent more time in the greenhouse, sweeping and clearing space for the long winter. Parker had been right about how busy he'd be. Yom Kippur followed on the heels of the Jewish new year, and I popped in and out of services, which were long and heavy with contemplation. The fasting was triggering for me, bringing back awful memories from Anam Cara, and I needed the freedom of fresh air and autumn sunshine to quiet my racing mind.

Perhaps it was the inward focus of the Hebrew text that started me down the path of wondering more deeply about how, exactly, I'd ended up in a life not of my choosing and stayed there for such a long time. Mom had asked again if I'd consider therapy, and I hadn't resisted quite as strongly as I had the first time she'd mentioned it.

"I'm not saying there's anything wrong with you," she

insisted. "Every person can benefit from an inward look now and then. And having the help of an unbiased outside person can open new doors of thinking. A therapist might pick up on patterns or insights that you may not see. That's all I'm saying."

"I get it, Mom," I said, not wanting to sound short. Our daily calls had become an anchor, and I loved the silk of her voice, but I did not like being badgered. I tried to overlook any small annoyances and focus on how grounding it was to have my parents' support and attention, finally.

"I'm considering it, really. It's just...I don't know if I want to relive those years. I don't know if I want to unearth it all. I'm probably not going to like what I find."

She was quiet for a bit before she said, "But how can you move forward in a healthy way if you don't understand why you went there and why you stayed?"

I'd lain awake nights wondering exactly that—what had drawn me to James in the first place, why I'd believed he was my one true love, when he only wanted control over me and my endless adoration. It was all so clear now—how had I been so oblivious?

And then, on a Tuesday in October, a letter arrived. It was from Armand, in his hurried scrawl, with words that were clearly meant to convey kindness, but with a subtext lurking beneath them.

Dearest Charlie,

We miss you desperately at Anam Cara. There is a void

where you and James once stood, a gaping hole through which a cold wind blows. You left in such a hurry that we were not able to say a proper goodbye.

You likely already know this, but not long after you departed our community, our dear brother Boden left as well. I've learned recently of his tragic death—too many losses of men in their prime, forces of the Spirit! I can only imagine how your soul has been torn apart by the passing of two men close to your heart. How cruel the world can be!

I write to invite you back to Anam Cara for a memorial honoring dear Boden. We miss you and hope for your eager and imminent return.

Your friend and spiritual father, Armand

Friend? Spiritual father? My heart flapped like eagle wings, heavy and mighty and fierce. And now I had confirmation that he knew where I was.

I sank onto the couch, holding the letter, my mind racing as I tried to read between the written lines.

He wanted me to know that he knew about Boden's death. He wanted me to return to the community—like that would ever happen! And he wanted to tether me once again to him and to Anam Cara.

He couldn't possibly believe a letter would lure me back?

I shuddered. I'd never return to Anam Cara. No, Armand didn't expect me to come running back; he just wanted me to know that he was watching me from afar.

That I could never truly escape his reach.

I stalked over to the iron stove, added a log, crumpled some newspaper, and lit a fire. It glowed orange as it caught on, the flames licking at the wood. When it was going strong, I opened the grate and tossed in the letter, mesmerized by the speed with which the flames ate at the words until they were nothing but ash.

I sat in front of the fire for a while until it burned low enough to extinguish. Then I went to the kitchen, opened the pantry, reached for the highest shelf and pulled down the urn.

I'd had enough of mourning, of looking back with regret or cowering in fear. I pulled on a fleece, stepped into my boots and hurried outside.

So often in the summer, I'd wander off the edge of my property into the woods and lose myself under the trees. I could walk a short while and be deep in the belly of the forest, and it would always calm me, ground me, show me sense. It happened almost immediately, as if the trees were washing me in serenity, their heavy oxygenated breaths blowing new life into me, lifting me up. The breath of the trees replaced my own, a calming force flushing through me and literally changing me inside of a minute.

I became a person who could think clearly once again. A person who understood the gift of time and space. A person who communed only with nature and not with invented ideas of grandiosity and power. A person who could forget everything that came before and anything that might hover on the horizon.

I needed to be that person more of the time.

I hugged the urn against my body and ran. I ran and ran until my heart was in my throat and I could no longer think. My feet crunched on fallen leaves. It was so quiet in the forest that I forgot what day it was, what time in the day, what to-dos sat on the list I'd made out at the kitchen table that morning over coffee.

At the edge of the forest, the trees opened up into a deep ravine that trailed down to a cold, swift river. I crept sideways down the slope toward the riverbank, and when I got there, I looked up into the gray sky and felt my chest open.

"It's time to let you go," I whispered then tossed the urn into the river. It landed in the water with a *plink* and bobbed on the surface as the current carried it down and away, off into a future I couldn't see.

CHAPTER THIRTY-THREE

A week later, I sat in the office of a man named Hanley Stacey, waiting to see what secrets he could unearth from my regret-filled past.

"He's a good guy, and not your typical head-shrinker," Mary had said.

We had been eating cheese-and-apple sandwiches on a rock ledge overlooking the valley, midway up the Stowe Pinnacle Trail. I was the kind of calm that comes from hefting up a leaf-lined path in silence with a companion I trust. Mary had walked ahead, taking the lead, since I'd never hiked this trail before. The store was closed for the day—*always good to take a break for fall color,* she'd said, scribbling those words on a sign on the door explaining the midweek closure—and we headed out early to make the most of the daylight.

I'd been turning over the therapy idea and asked her opinion. Most of the hike, she just listened, as the wind fluttered the leaves and we stared up at half-bare branches.

Finally, we took a break, and I poured steaming tea from

a thermos for both of us.

"I'm wary of other people telling me about myself," I said. "Reminds me too much of James. Old habits and all."

She shook her head. "This is different than a guy controlling you, though I can see why you'd be gun-shy after living in a cult for two decades."

"It wasn't a cult," I started to say, but she raised her hand.

"Call it what it was," she insisted. "Not a commune. A cult. Let's be honest, Charlie. Once and for all."

I swallowed hard. Was she right? Had I given my life over to a cult for the majority of my adult life? Was this how Parker saw me, too? My parents?

Did everyone pity me?

It wasn't the first time the cult-vs.-commune question had wormed its way into my subconscious. But all the times before when I'd dared question what Anam Cara really was, I'd chased the thoughts away faster than they could come. I didn't want to believe I was that gullible.

"My mother's been mentioning therapy to me since they visited in the summer," I said, sinking my teeth into the sandwich. I'd spread a thin layer of horseradish-mustard over thick, grainy bread that I'd baked earlier in the week, and the tang of the spread against the sweetness of the apple and the softness of the cheese was a mighty combination.

"Good sandwich," Mary agreed when I hummed with

pleasure. "And your mother's right. What are you waiting for?"

I liked my friend's frankness. She said things as she thought them, didn't hold back. She was utterly honest, and it was refreshing. I was sick of subtext and of people tiptoeing around me. I needed everything out in the open. I thought about Boden yelling at me in my cottage and how it was the wake-up call I'd needed then. God, I missed him.

When we got back to the trailhead and into the car, Mary opened the glove box and took out an expired registration. She dug in her bag for a pen, then scribbled a name and phone number across the back.

"He rides with a Harley gang I'm friends with," she said.

I'd met some of her biker friends and loved them all—big-hearted, strong-voiced people who'd stand in front of a truck for you.

And so I found myself a week after that hike on a gray scratchy couch in Hanley Stacey's waiting room, waiting to begin my first-ever therapy session.

He was smaller than I'd expected, with a soft voice and dark eyes. He opened the door, smiled and waved me into his office. I settled into a brown, leather chair and waited.

"Charlie Tanner," he said, extending a hand. "Nice to meet you. What brings you in?"

I took a deep breath and looked around. There were books on a shelf, degrees framed on the wall and a vase with pussy willows against the windowsill.

"I need to understand some of the decisions I've made."

He nodded, smiling, and waited for me to go on.

"I'm a little nervous."

"First time in therapy?"

Now it was my turn to nod.

"Brave," he said.

"Is it?"

His eyes widened, and he nodded again. "Everyone would benefit from a little inward focus, but few people ever do it."

"That's what my mother says."

He leaned forward. "Tell me about her."

That was easy, so I started and the words tumbled out. I told him about my parents, my family, how we'd had no contact for twenty years.

"That's a long time."

I nodded, and he waited for me to go on. I bit down on my lip and jumped in—my impulsive choices, James, Anam Cara, going mute after James died, leaving and finding my voice again once I crossed the border, starting over, meeting Parker.

"Have you ever thought about what your parents contributed to your choices?"

I cocked my head and looked at him. "It's not their fault I cut them off."

"Really?"

Even though I'd pondered what led me to follow James in the first place and certainly spent time reliving my childhood disappointments and loneliness, it didn't explain why I was so gullible, so lacking in confidence that I'd put up with a straying partner, his lack of commitment and the cultish commune he took me to. I bristled with defensiveness.

Although I'd hinted at it when my parents came to visit, we'd never discussed how alone I'd felt as a child, how ignored.

I took a deep breath to calm my racing heart and let it all pour out.

Yes, I was relieved to reconnect with them. Yes, I'd missed them all those years, even though I'd been the one to sever ties. And yes even though I'd apologized for cutting them out of my life, I wished they'd apologize to me. I wished they'd see that their distraction is what caused me to leave in the first place.

I didn't notice I was twisting my hands as I was talking. My breath hitched in my chest, and I realized how nervous I was to bring this topic to my parents. I was afraid they'd reject me if I told them they had to shoulder some of the blame for our twenty years of distance, and once again I'd be all alone.

Tears stung my eyes, and I blinked to hold them back.

Hanley leaned forward, elbows on knees, and peered at me. "Charlie," he said in a soft, slow voice. "You are lovable just as you are." He was quiet for a moment.

"You are enough."

I bit my lip to keep the tears from spilling down my face. "I know."

He shook his head. "I don't think you do." He sat up, looked at the clock, then back at me. "I'm afraid we have to stop there."

My stomach fell.

"You're joking, right?" I was trembling, and a little annoyed that after reaching this pinnacle of emotion, I'd have to wait to see what would come next.

"Can't I add on a second session so we can make some progress?"

He shook his head. "It doesn't really work like that. Not only do I have another patient already booked, but the sessions are short and spaced out for a reason. The mind needs time to process between appointments."

I chewed on a nail while he opened a date book and turned the pages until he found the next available appointment, two days later.

"You'll probably want to come less frequently in time, but I can see that you're eager to go deeper."

I took the appointment and counted out cash for the fee.

"I don't often get paid in cash," he chuckled.

I shrugged. "Old habits. Fodder for another session."

Hanley stood and led the way out. "Thank you for coming here, Charlie," he said. "I look forward to seeing you again soon."

As I walked to my car, emotions swirled. I felt cut off, halted in the middle of my flow. I wanted to keep going, impatient to get to understanding so I could close the door on the past and move forward. I didn't want to wait even two days to learn what he thought. Although I intended to drive home, I ended up in front of the gardening store. The bell dinged as I pushed through the door and found Mary at the counter, reading from a collection of poetry.

"How'd it go?" she asked, smacking her gum.

I shook my head, searching for words. When I found them, they came out in a torrent.

"What's the point of therapy? It's so damn slow. I want to figure it out fast and move on. He wouldn't let me tack on a second appointment so we could cruise through."

She put down the book. Her mouth was a straight line, her eyes pinpoints.

"What?"

She shook her head. "You're incredible. You don't want to confront any of your dark past, and then you decide to try and it can't happen fast enough. What's the deal?"

"Not you, too." I was annoyed to be judged by my friend. Anger and annoyance and unkempt fury roiled inside me, ready to explode.

"There it is." She pointed at me. "Whatever's happening with you right now, that's the core of all this."

I stopped cold. "What do you mean?"

The door swung open, and a man walked in, whistling.

"Good afternoon!" Mary called out in a singsong voice. "Let me know if I can help you!"

"Will do," he said, tipping his cap and ambling down an aisle of rakes and shovels.

"You are your own obstacle," she whispered, poking my shoulder. "Your emotions aren't even adult. You swing from denial to anger in a heartbeat. Chill out, Charlie. And be patient—you'll get there. Not overnight, though. Nothing good happens fast. You just might be the most impulsive person I know."

I sucked on my bottom lip as I thought about what she was saying.

I'd always been impatient. And impulsive. Ever since I was young. And then it hit me: I'd jumped in with James before I could think it through and done the same when he asked me to go to Anam Cara.

"Admit it, Charlie," she insisted.

I nodded slowly. "You're right," I said. "But so what? Plenty of people are impulsive. How does it explain why I stayed for so long and put up with the way James treated me? Not every impulsive woman runs off to a commune—"

"Cult."

I rolled my eyes. "Fine, *cult*, and stays in a controlling, demeaning relationship."

She shook her head. "I don't pretend to understand you or your decisions, girl." She hiccupped a laugh. "That's why you're going to Hanley. Give it time. The answers will come, but they won't come fast. Take a breath and let it happen the way it's supposed to."

I sighed and smiled. "You're a really good friend, you know that?"

She was nodding. "Yes, I am," she said, smiling a little too big as she said it.

Chapter Thirty-Four

When the final fall holiday—Sukkot, an eight-day harvest celebration— was over, I saw a lot more of Parker. I'd missed him. Even though I'd attended services and eaten in his sukkah, the little hut on the patio where he hosted meals, it was different being with him as part of a crowd. I'd never even heard of the holiday growing up, but I found it fun and whimsical. I slurped squash soup, huddled into my down coat and marveled at the smart conversation. Although he'd put a hand on my shoulder or shoot me a knowing smile across the table, I'd yearned to be alone with him. He was too distracted planning sermons and running study sessions to focus on us.

We were approaching November, and since nothing had happened to confirm my fears about retribution from Anam Cara, I relaxed. After the letter about Boden's memorial, I hadn't heard so much as a word from Armand or anyone else.

Those weeks were like a bubble where our love grew. We were together every night, and at least one day a week we took off for the hills, hiking in shared quiet and admiration for the constantly changing landscape around us. At home, we couldn't keep our hands off each other or clothing on our bodies. We laughed about reverting to our teenage horny selves. If you'd asked me at twenty whether I could see myself at forty, wildly humping a nearly fifty-year-old man, I'd have been horrified. But I was reborn in this nourishing relationship, and though I didn't believe I deserved him, Parker's attention never waned. He was as enamored of me as I was of him.

Hanley cautioned me not to dive in too deep, but I laughed when he got all serious about it.

"Until you fully understand yourself, nothing will work entirely," he warned. "You went from a toxic long-term relationship and jumped right into a new relationship. Even if it isn't toxic, it still doesn't mean it's the best idea. And you didn't choose to leave James; you left because he died. It wasn't an empowered choice. That matters."

I was relaxing into the process of therapy, getting comfortable with it, overtaken with curiosity about what I'd learn about myself. But I wasn't worried that I was repeating old patterns with Parker. James was a one-off, an anomaly, or so I wanted to believe. Maybe I didn't even have a pattern since I hadn't had a string of relationships. There was James and then Parker.

The days held less light and turned dark early. The minty air hinted at snow. One night, we made pizza and a simple salad and ate it in front of the TV, checking off another throwback movie on Parker's list, this time *The Breakfast Club*, which we agreed still resonated so many years later.

"I'm so glad those days are behind me though," I laughed, watching the awkwardness of high school students trying to find their way amidst cliques and cast-offs. "I bet every girl had a crush on you in high school."

He shook his head and downed a slug of Guinness. "I was a nerd," he said. "Full-on dork. Had no sense of style whatsoever."

I giggled and inched closer. "Tell me."

"Total Jew-fro, hair out to here." He held his hands a foot from his head. "I loved being Jewish, which, in a public school in New York City, doesn't win many friends. I begged my parents to send me to a private Jewish school, but they wouldn't hear of it. They were old hippies who believed in free education no matter what."

"Who was your first girlfriend?"

"Sylvie," he said simply, draining the glass.

"You're joking. You never dated anyone else?"

He shook his head slowly. "My parents sent me to this hippie Jewish camp in the Adirondacks, and I met her the summer I was fourteen. I had such a crush! But she wouldn't look at me until two summers later, and then I was hooked. We never looked back."

Suddenly, the fun I'd been having hearing about younger-Parker disappeared, and fear gripped my throat.

She'd been his one and only. They'd grown up together. And she died a tragic early death. I couldn't compete with a memory of the perfect woman.

"Charlie..." He stroked my face. "I'm not comparing you to Sylvie. I never would."

"How do you do that?" I breathed almost in a whisper. "How do you read my mind?"

"You have no poker face," he said. "It's like your emotions are written across your forehead."

He got up, went into the kitchen and came back with another can of Guinness, popping the tab and turning it upside down in the glass then pulling it out slowly as the dark liquid poured out.

"Want a sip?"

I shook my head. I'd never liked the thick, sweet beer. I sipped the last of my merlot, and he tipped the bottle to refill my glass.

"So, what was high-school Charlie like?" He peered at me with a half-smile.

"I was on the dance team," I started.

"No way!" He rubbed his hand over my thigh and squeezed. "No wonder you're so limber." He flashed those hazel eyes at me, and the light from the lamp glinted off them, highlighting little flecks of amber.

"That was a long time ago," I said, swatting at his hand. "I was moderately popular, but quiet," I continued. "Almost like an only child. My sister, Willow, is five years older, and she was already at college when I started high school."

I chewed on a nail as I tried to picture those years. "My parents were always busy. My mother taught kindergarten, and my father was a high school principal—at my high school, if you can imagine. It was so humiliating."

I closed my eyes to get a glimpse of that time. My parents had been busy, never home. I was lonely, alone in an echoing house, Willow whisking in and out of our lives on school breaks and summers when she didn't have an internship downstate. It seemed everyone had a purpose...except me.

My parents never even attended teacher conferences because they'd already heard a full report from every teacher who had me in their classroom. It's like they glimpsed my childhood out of the corners of their eyes, content that I was doing fine and they could focus fully on all the other kids under their charge. Every child mattered to them—except me. At least, that's how it felt to me.

I sighed. Parker was watching me with fire in his eyes. It was an intense gaze but one that made me feel safe and seen.

"Although I didn't have the words for it at the time, I left to find belonging, to find a place where I'd be noticed. No wonder I fell for James! I was starved for attention."

His controlling nature was the exact opposite of everything I'd had growing up, and I'd mistaken it for love.

Fuck.

"Hey, come back to me," Parker whispered, reaching out to pull me closer. I nestled against his chest, and his arm came around me.

Suddenly, I wanted him desperately, wanted to pour all the new awareness bursting like little sunbeams inside me into desire for him and gratitude for his unwavering love.

I kissed him hard on the mouth and climbed into his lap. His arms were around me, and our lips pressed hard, deep. His tongue found mine, my hands were in his hair and he was pulling my sweater over my head. The air was cool against my skin but blazing under his touch.

"I want you," I whispered, biting on the edge of his ear. "Now."

He scooped his hands underneath me and stood up, placing me gently on the ground. He grabbed my hand and pulled me through the house and up the stairs to his room, where the big king-sized bed was waiting with crisp sheets and a fluffy comforter. The curtains were open around the windows, and the night sky winked with stars.

I fell back on the bed, and he covered me with his body, grinding into me as we kissed hard, so caught up in each other we were a tangle of desire. Since our first time together, when I'd freaked out about his domineering words, Parker had hung back, waited for me to become comfortable with more forceful lovemaking. Now, I was ready. I wanted to fuck him hard, to banish all the bad memories, erase all the mistakes of my long and winding past. I wanted the pounding desire of today to eradicate the missteps of all the years that had come before.

"I'm ready," I whispered.

He pulled back to look at me. "For what?" He searched my face for clarity, and then he found it in my gaze and nodded. "You're sure?"

"I'm sure," I breathed, pulling his mouth down to mine and tasting him as I bit on his lip and sucked it inside to my tongue.

He pulled my jeans down and off, throwing them onto the floor, then stripped off his clothes to join me naked on the bed. His body was hard and warm, rippled and soft. I ran my hands along the ridges of his torso as he bore into me, hard and fast, the searing heat of his entry piercing into me.

I moaned as he filled me.

"You like that, baby?" he muttered in my ear, pulling back and teasing me before diving in deeper than before. I nodded, but it wasn't good enough, and he whispered hotter in my ear, "Let me hear you."

His insistence sent shudders through my body, and I rippled with anticipation. "Oh, Parker," I moaned, and he rammed into me again, cupping my bottom in his hands and licking my neck then nipping at my skin with his teeth. I saw nothing behind my closed eyes. My breathing came heavy, my body tingled with every touch, every plunge, every grip. I wanted him to take me past the edge of oblivion, to push me off into the abyss, to grab and hold and pound hard, then harder, until I was screaming in ecstasy.

"More," I muttered.

He egged me on, saying, "Louder. Tell me what you want, Charlie."

"More," I chanted. "Harder, Parker," and he obliged, until it was like fireworks on the Fourth of July, everything exploding around me and into me and inside me. He shuddered as his orgasm followed mine, and I lay there, limp, connected to this man I loved and in full ecstasy of the moments just past.

"That was amazing," I said as he lay beside me, our bodies slick with sweat.

He smiled and trailed his fingers in a straight line down between my breasts, along the softness of my belly, making me shiver.

"How're you doing?" He turned on his side to face me, studying my eyes.

"I'm okay," I said, realizing that for the first time in a long time, it was true.

CHAPTER THIRTY-FIVE

We were in a groove of discovery and contentment, and life chugged along nicely for a while. Mary hired me part-time at the store, so I finally had something to do beyond house and garden. I embraced the new responsibility with joy. Winter had arrived, and the snow fell hard and filled up the yard with soft white that sparkled in the sun.

And now that I was beginning to understand what had driven me to fall for James, to follow him, and to stay for so long at Anam Cara, I felt better, less broken, less fragile. It was no one's fault, just a circumstance of my past, and the combination of my personality and my family's choices made fertile ground for me to fall prey to strong and controlling men. I worried a little that I was doing it again with Parker, Hanley's voice echoing in my head, but Parker set clear and firm boundaries, and though he was wild and dominating in the bedroom, he was anything but outside of it. You never know what someone is like when the clothes come off until you see them stark naked before you and their secrets are unleashed. Did anyone in his congregation have an inkling of what Parker-the-lover was like? I laughed at the image of some of the adoring older women learning the truth. He was a tantalizing combination of forces.

One day, the autumn wind whistled low and long. The trees in my yard were bare of leaves, the grass a carpet of colors. I'd been spending a lot of time in the greenhouse, filling the shelves for the long, cold winter. Mary had stocked some new indoor growing lights, which I'd strung up over my shelves as a cozy incubator for early plants.

Just the day before, I'd swept the house, fluffed the pillows, given every room a good deep-clean, and it smelled lemony and fresh. The sheets on my bed had just come off the clothesline, carrying with them a scent of seasons changing.

I was baking ginger muffins when there was a knock at the door.

I should have been surprised to find Indira on my front step, but I wasn't. I'd never seen her look so ragged. Her black hair was wild, her blue eyes hollow, and beside her stood her daughter, Lacey, a tiny girl with big eyes and black curls. The girl clung to her mother's side.

"Charlie, I am so, so sorry." Indira lunged at me and engulfed me in a gripping hug. Lacey shuttled inside the cottage with her, keeping to her mother's shadow, the three of us in a little emotional bubble.

Something about Lacey looked strikingly familiar. I'd known her since she was born, but in this light, or in my new life, she looked different to me. In the days after her birth, I'd baked a pumpkin bread and brought it with some apples for Indira. The community had been great like that, nourishing members through the momentous occasions of life. But eventually, I'd kept my distance the more I saw her with James.

Now, the girl looked more than just someone I remembered from a life I used to live. She seemed as familiar as family.

I closed the door behind them and ushered them over to the couch. Indira wouldn't sit, just paced the width of the small room, while Lacey perched on the sofa and watched her mother with wide eyes.

"Indira, what is it? Why are you here? And what is upsetting you?"

She stopped pacing and looked at me. "I came for forgiveness," she said quietly. "And because if I hadn't left there, I would probably be dead."

I glanced at Lacey. The girl looked terrified, her little legs pressed tightly together and her eyes wide. I walked over and put a hand on her shoulder then rubbed circles on her small back. She relaxed under my touch, but her face remained as still and unreadable as stone.

"Indira, please, sit and tell me what this is about." I reached for her and clamped a hand on her forearm to calm her. It seemed to work, as her eyes softened and her gaze relented. "Think of Lacey," I whispered, tilting my head in the girl's direction.

"Oh, honey." Indira dropped to her knees and wrapped her arms around her daughter. "Mommy's sorry for scaring you."

Lacey breathed heavily but didn't utter a word as her mother held on to her.

"Please. Sit," I said. "I'll make some tea, and then we can talk."

The house was filling with the scent of the baking muffins, a tangy, spicy aroma that was simultaneously awakening and warming. In the kitchen, I put the kettle on and pulled mugs from the cupboard, scooping loose peppermint tea into a pot. I'd let it steep and then pour mugs for each of us.

When the muffins were just about done, I reached for a plate to arrange them on. I filled the table with all the accoutrements—cream and lemon and honey for the tea, napkins and butter for the muffins, and three small plates. When the muffins were out and the tea was ready, I poked my head into the other room and beckoned for them to join me.

By then, Indira had calmed considerably. I poured the tea then offered Lacey a spoon and the honey jar. She lit up and dipped the spoon into the raw honey, scooping out an overflowing glob and dumping it into her mug.

"Tell me what's going on," I said as we palmed our cups. I'd tuned my speaker to a calming meditative instrumental, a perfect lulling soundtrack.

Indira sipped tea then looked me straight in the eye. "I came to apologize," she said plainly.

"For what?"

She swallowed. "I didn't want to do it, but I had no choice."

I reached for her hand. "Indira, what did you do?"

Was she being purposely cryptic because of Lacey? Or was she too hysterical to speak clearly?

"James," she whispered. "He's gone because of me."

I shook my head and blinked. "What on earth are you talking about?"

She swallowed and looked me head-on. "Armand asked me to get close to James, to keep an eye on him. He was worried that he was plotting to take over. It was easy for me to get close to James...because...well, you know..." Her voice trailed off, and she avoided my eyes. My heartbeat intensified, and I watched her carefully. That's when it hit me. Lacey was so familiar because she resembled someone I'd known very, very well. Someone who'd been at the center of my life for twenty years.

Lacey was James's child.

Why had I never seen it? How had I not known? I mean, James died in Indira's bed, but Lacey was five at the time! They'd been fucking all those years?

I pursed my lips and tried to steady my breath. That blasted man. It all came crashing down on me—the humiliation, the indifference, the complete lack of regard for me and my feelings and the bond between us.

Had there even been a bond between us?

I was face-to-face with evidence that, while he had insisted he'd never wanted children with me, he'd sprinkled his seed around the community and produced more children than any one man deserved. And none of them were mine.

Poor, sweet Lacey.

"Go on," I urged Indira to keep talking.

"Armand was right, you know. James was determined to unseat him as head of the community. He was a bit too ambitious for his own good."

"What did you do, Indira?"

My phone buzzed. I grabbed it off the counter and glanced at it. Parker, sending a heart emoji and a *how's your day going*. I would so much rather be focused on this life than the one I desperately wanted to put behind me.

I slid the phone in my pocket and looked at Indira.

"Armand gave me a bottle of tonic and asked me to add a few drops to James's drink," she said, tears pooling in her eyes. "I didn't want to. I didn't ask what it was, but I had a feeling."

She swiped at her eyes then looked to her daughter. Tiny crumbs dotted her little lips. Indira wiped the girl's mouth with a napkin and said, "Honey, why don't you go in there and read?"

Lacey scuttled off, and when she was out of earshot, Indira leaned in closer.

"He threatened to kill her if I didn't do what he asked." She sniffed as new tears shone in her eyes. "Her and my parents. And they've been there since Anam Cara started! They were among the originators. Can you believe him?"

I sucked in a breath then let it out audibly, planting a hand over hers.

"Honey, you had no choice, I understand." I couldn't believe what I was saying. But I knew now how Armand worked, how menacing his presence could be.

"I loved him, too, Charlie," Indira pleaded. "Please forgive me for taking James away from you."

"By sleeping with him or murdering him?"

I couldn't help myself. She stared at me. I was just being honest. It was about damn time.

"Look, Indira, we both know what Anam Cara was like," I said. "But there are bounds to human behavior. There's still right and wrong, and I'll be honest, I never agreed with James's passion for free-love. I went along with it because I believed I had no choice. I was weak. And a fool. I wish I'd had the strength to leave him years ago."

A knot had formed in my throat, and I tried to swallow it down.

"I get that you felt you had no choice," I continued. "I more than most. For all those years, I thought I had no choice but to stay with him and to stay there. But I was wrong. I was manipulated, brainwashed. And maybe you were too."

I cleared away the plates, dumping the crumbs into the trash before depositing the dishes in the sink.

"It's not me you need forgiveness from," I said, my back to her. "It's the law. You killed a man."

I heard my voice as if it were coming from someone else. Cold. Indifferent. The truth spoken plainly, matter-of-fact. It's not that I didn't care. There were conflicting emotions swirling within me. We'd all been caught in a sticky web of group-think—Indira more than me, even, because I'd had the benefit of living in the normal world for two decades. She'd had no influence other than the kooks at Anam Cara.

We were all guilty, and none of us were. The emotions were so heavy, and just when I thought I'd shed them, broken free of their chains, another blow came barreling at me and I was leveled.

There was a knock at the door.

What now?

I strode across the cottage, past the quiet girl on the couch, and flung it open.

"I was driving by and wanted to see you!" Parker's smile was radiant, but it drained as soon as he saw the pained look on my face.

He stepped inside the house. I closed the door and

sighed.

"What is it?"

He glanced at Lacey, who looked up with wide eyes. Indira had come into the room and stood beside the couch. Parker looked from them to me with a question in his eyes.

"Parker, meet Indira and her daughter Lacey—James's daughter, apparently," I said dryly. Indira's eyes widened at my words.

He smiled and nodded, taking a few steps into the room and reaching a hand to Indira. "Nice to meet you."

She forced a smile and took his hand loosely.

"They've brought news," I said.

"When you didn't respond..." His voice trailed off.

"I'm sorry," I said, all the energy draining out of me. I needed to call the police station, report what Indira had told me. She needed to pay for her sins. For ruining my life.

Or maybe giving it back to me.

I started to reconsider my rage.

"Are they staying?" he whispered.

I shrugged. Where would they go? I was exhausted from the immensity of this never-ending saga. What would it take to shake free of Anam Cara, once and for all?

"Can we?" Indira's voice was a squeak.

I spun around, the rage replaced with compassion. "Listen, honey, I forgive you for the whole James thing. He pulled women into his orbit and kept them there." I glanced at Lacey. Had James known she was his? Had he known about all the children he'd fathered? He must have! Had he been happy about it? Or was he really that cruel?

I was angry all over again at being robbed of the chance to have a family of my own, finally angry at him and at myself for letting him dictate the terms of my life. So many years wasted on a man who cared only for himself.

I knelt down at Lacey's eye level and took her hands in mine. "Sweet girl," I said, smiling. She hesitantly smiled back. She was a beautiful child, quiet. There were flecks of gold in her eyes just like there had been in his, but her hair was all glossy-black like her mother's, not even a hint of the warm red of her father. I wished for her to have a better life, to have choices and freedom. I pulled her little body into a hug, her fast-beating heart thrumming against mine, the delicateness of her bird-like bones. She was so small, with so much ahead of her. Shivers of wanting coursed through me. I wanted to be a mother more than anything, to give all the love inside me to a small, helpless creature with so much ahead of her and the chance to be better than me. He'd robbed me of that chance.

I stood up, straightened my shirt and dabbed at the tears forming in my eyes. "Indira, you can't stay here," I said. Her eyes were wild. "I'm sorry. I need to close this chapter of my life."

"But where will we go..." She glanced at her daughter, and my heart broke for the girl. I couldn't report what she'd told me to the authorities—they'd arrest her, and where would that leave the little girl? An orphan, alone in the world. I knew too well what could happen to people who believed they were alone in the world.

I looked from Indira to Parker to Lacey. "I'm sorry," I said evenly. "I need to break free of the past. I need to start over, and I can't do that with you here. I'm truly sorry."

I wasn't trying to be harsh. I was trying to be fair to myself. Finally.

She nodded. "We'll go," she said, sniffling. She gathered her coat and held Lacey's for the girl to slip into. "At least I got the truth out in the open," she said. "At least I can leave you with that."

At the door, she turned once again to look at me. "I really am sorry, Charlie," she said. "I never wanted to hurt you. I've always liked you. Envied you, really."

"Envied me?" I shook my head, chills running up and down my arms. "Why?"

She pulled me into an embrace, and I smelled lavender in her hair as she hugged me tightly. "Because you always had his heart," she whispered.

I was shaking my head, not believing her, as she pulled away, her gaze penetrating into mine.

"You did," she said, nodding with confidence.

Forgiveness washed through me as I watched her go. "Be safe," I said as she walked out the door and out of my life.

Chapter Thirty-Six

"Well, that was intense," Parker said, settling onto the couch.

I sighed and plopped down next to him. "Uh-huh." I nodded, numb.

"We should tell the police," Parker said, stroking my hand then lifting it to his mouth and kissing it.

"Probably," I said, leaning onto his shoulder and closing my eyes.

But we didn't. After Indira left, the idea of bringing James's killer to justice faded away. It didn't feel like an urgent responsibility or like anyone would care. Indira's bombshell evaporated after the door closed behind her as if it were a door to the past slamming shut. The only remnant that lingered in my aching heart was a haunting image of the little girl's wide eyes glinting with the light of her father's penetrating gaze. I couldn't forgive James for impregnating so many women and leaving their helpless children in his wake—especially when he'd denied me the opportunity. That was all I'd wanted, for so many years—a family of my own, a baby to hold close, a next generation to love me unconditionally and carry my legacy forward. And I was furious at him for literally spreading his seed and not doing anything to care for all the children he'd fathered. It was cruel to create new lives and ignore them.

At least my parents had been present, if distracted. How ironic, of course, that the man I'd chosen as my escape from their distraction had ignored me even more than they had.

They were trying to make up for it now, but I'd been reading about how the first five years of a person's life determine the course of everything after, realizing how true that had been for me. I was beginning to wonder how it had been for James. After being with the man for two decades, I knew surprisingly little of his early life. Only the disdain he'd held for his family and the glimpse I'd gotten after he died. What could explain his devious desire to conquer and own and control? What was at the root of his arrogance and entitlement?

"I can't make sense of it all," I said.

"Maybe you don't have to," Parker said.

I turned to face him. "It's never going to leave me, is it?"

Where could I go, what could I do, to make them leave me alone?

He shrugged, and a chill rippled through me. Did I have to keep running? Leave Vermont and head home to Traverse City? Or go farther, to a more distant, anonymous place?

But they'd find me. I didn't know how, but they'd find me anywhere. Funny how, when I first left, I knew nothing, was no threat to anyone. But then Boden came and now Indira, and now I knew everything. I held a wealth of information that I'd never wanted and the money James had stolen, and they were going to make me pay for it.

My head was spinning.

"Stop beating yourself up," Parker insisted. "Remember, they also controlled you, not just James. You had no money, no bank account. How would you have left, huh?"

He tilted his head, and a question filled his eyes.

"Come to think of it, how did you manage to leave, with no access to money?"

I swallowed slowly.

"After James died, I found a box of money hidden in one of the walls of our home," I said carefully, rubbing my lips together as I watched his reaction.

"And you used it to get free."

I nodded.

"Why didn't you tell me?"

Parker hadn't moved away from me, but he felt distanced, cooler.

"I didn't want it to change how you thought about me."

"Why would it?" He raked his hand through his hair and sighed. "I don't like secrets, Charlie."

My heart was thumping madly. "There's a lot we don't

know about each other yet," I said, as if that fact made it any better.

He was nodding, but his gaze was elsewhere. He sighed again and slumped back on the couch. "I don't think it bothers me that you took it," he said. "And I guess it wouldn't matter anyway. It's done. I think I'm more bothered that you didn't feel you could tell me about it."

My stomach was fluttering with nerves. I didn't know what to say.

"Please don't let this change how you feel about me," I said, uneasy with the sound of pleading in my voice.

He reached for me, and I clasped his hand. I wished I could find the reassurance in his eyes that had been there just a few minutes earlier.

"And anyway, that's not the most important thing right now," I said, trying to smooth things over. "How do I get out of this now?"

"Live your life, Charlie," he said, his voice forceful, growing louder. "Live your life honestly and cleanly. If they come, you'll face them. And I'll be by your side." He squeezed my hand.

"And if they want to kill me?"

He gripped my hand harder and shrugged. "I don't know. But you can't live your life on the run."

I shook my head. "No. But I can't always be looking over my shoulder, either."

"I'm not sure you have any other choice."

Chapter Thirty-Seven

I kept waiting for Bruce to call, to say that Indira had turned herself in, that Lacey needed someone to care for her. It was a fantasy, of course. Indira had probably fled, run with the cold wind at her back, and I hoped the little girl would be okay, would have a better life than her mother, or her father.

The cold was settling into Vermont, winter's icy fingers clawing at the hard ground. The evergreens stood tall against a white sky. I'd pulled the last of the cabbages from the ground and turned over the soil for the long winter sleep. Layers of mulch and tarp covered the garden, and as the first snows fluttered down, I watched my world become a blanket of white. It was hard to distinguish sky from earth.

In the greenhouse, I tended kale, chard, spinach, herbs, peppers and enough tubers and root vegetables to keep me content during the long winter.

Huddled on the edge of Canada's eastern coast, I hadn't celebrated Thanksgiving in decades, and I was excited to return to my American roots. Mom was begging me to come home for the holiday, to meet Willow's children, to finally be a family. But I wanted to stay with Parker. Alice and Ethan were coming home, and Parker's parents were coming, along with Sylvie's. He said he wanted me there, that he couldn't wait for them to meet me, but I was nervous. What role did I have in their family? I knew Parker loved me, but my background was a mess of bad decisions, especially when compared with the perfect Sylvie. I couldn't compete with the ghost of true love—I could never measure up. And her parents would surely resent me. As the day grew closer, I tried to find a way to escape, but I couldn't come up with a reasonable explanation for jumping ship so suddenly. So I kept to the plan, and the closer we got, the more my stomach was tied in knots.

It was a good thing we hadn't moved in together yet. Parker had come around to the idea, but just as I was building awareness and confidence, I wasn't ready to give up my newfound independence. And, I didn't want to leave my greenhouse or my garden. Parker promised we'd build both on his property.

But I also didn't want to live in the house where Sylvie had been a mother, a lover, a wife, as if I could be a stand-in or take her place in any way. There, her memories would haunt us both. As Thanksgiving week approached, I was beyond glad that I had my own place to retreat to.

Alice arrived the Friday before the holiday. As she was

settling into her old bedroom, Parker and I were putting the finishing touches on Shabbat dinner. We would go to services and then return home to eat and hear all about his daughter's fall semester.

But she had other plans.

Alice came bounding down the steps with her coat on and her purse slung over her shoulder.

"Bye, Dad!" she called out.

"Hold on, babe," he called back, wiping his hands. "Where are you going?"

"Out. With friends."

"Really?" His voice held a hint of sadness.

She scoffed and sent a pitying look our way. "Everyone's home," she explained. "I want to see my high school friends, catch up on all the gossip."

Parker sighed, raking his fingers through his hair. "I thought we'd have Shabbat dinner and catch up," he said softly.

Alice put a hand on his arm. Parker was wearing a navy sweater over a button-down. "Sweet Dad," she said. "I'll be here for a week. We can catch up over breakfast tomorrow!"

"But it's Shabbat, honey."

She nodded. "I know. And it'll be Shabbat tomorrow. So I guess not breakfast"—she rolled her eyes—"because you'll be at the temple, but we can do lunch after? Or pizza tomorrow night?"

Parker sighed. I hung back, not wanting to insert myself where I didn't belong. Alice flashed me a quick smile. At least she didn't mind my presence in her family home. I smiled back, grateful for her kindness.

"Go, have fun," he said. "Don't be late."

She pecked his cheek and laughed as she skipped out the door.

Parker turned to me, looking wistful. "I can't say I'm not disappointed. Was I fooling myself to believe she'd want to have a family Shabbat dinner?"

I couldn't bear to answer him, because yes, he'd been fooling himself. She was still a kid, home on break. I understood her desire to go in search of friends. Perhaps she was wanting to break free in her own way.

I let him talk, nodding when his eyes searched mine for a response.

At times like this, I wondered if Parker and I could really be together, when I stood awkwardly in the front hall of his family home, clearly an outsider. I wanted to be a mother but had no experience to help him in parenting his grown children. And there was the difference in our perspectives on Jewish identity and observance still bobbing between us. I wanted to believe the chemistry between us was enough to carry us through, to keep all these differences at bay. But when real life came barreling into our relationship, I began to wonder.

"It's okay," I said, stroking his arm. "At least I'm here."

He flashed a weak smile.

We went to services, and I sat in the back row, watching the man I loved orchestrate meaning out of ancient text for a meager crowd. I waited in the wings while he glad-handed, smiling, shaking hands, listening intently, providing reassurance and kind words. We went home to a regal meal, more food than needed for just the two of us, and a melancholy settled over the table like a suffocating curtain. I tried to pull Parker out of his funk. He moved the food around his plate and smiled when I spoke, trying to look interested, but his mind was elsewhere.

We were washing dishes when Alice slammed into the house in a fury.

"Honey?" Parker called out, setting the dish towel on the counter and hurrying out of the kitchen.

I stayed, washing dishes quietly, trying to hear what they were saying but not making out most of the words.

When Parker returned, he looked weary. "An old friend is now dating her high school boyfriend." He shook his head. "Her heart is broken. She feels betrayed." He sighed. "Sylvie would've known what to say."

My heartbeat accelerated. I didn't speak, cemented to the kitchen floor.

He pulled a chair out from the table and sank into it. I sat beside him, waiting for his next words.

"You miss her," I said, covering his hand with mine.

He nodded. "I'm sorry," he said, wiping tears that had

leaked from his eyes.

"Don't be." I squeezed his hand. "She was the love of your life, the mother of your children. Of course you miss her."

I believed the words, even if I didn't like them. I'd always be second fiddle. I'd known that from the start. I just hadn't known how hollow it would make me feel.

"I should go," I said, about to stand, when Parker grabbed my arm, his eyes wild.

"Please don't," he said.

Warmth spread through me, like sunshine inside my chest. She was gone, but I was here now, and I wanted to be by his side. Maybe I could live with three of us in this relationship. Maybe I'd have to.

A little voice in the back of my mind whispered, *Are you settling again, like you did with James? You deserve to have everything you want.*

He smiled thinly, a grateful smile, not one full of passion or desire. I couldn't expect that when he was mired in family turmoil and memories. I pursed my lips, searching my brain for a clue about what to do next.

His phone buzzed. Parker hopped up and grabbed it off the counter, looked at the screen.

"My parents are arriving tomorrow," he said. "Mom confirming." He flashed the screen in my direction, but I couldn't see the words.

"I should go home," I said again, standing.

"Please, Charlie, stay with me," he said, almost pleading.

I didn't want to leave him, but his daughter was upstairs nursing a hurting heart, and his parents were on their way. We could have this one night before the house filled with people connected by blood and memory, or I could give them the space to be a family without the demand to fit a new person in their midst.

"I want to," I said, my body inches from his, the heat between us palpable. "I want to be with you, Parker." My voice was low and, I hoped, reassuring. The chemistry between us was alive, buzzing, and I wanted him more than I could say.

But I needed to be strong for both of us. To finally do the right thing.

"Maybe it's best if you have this time with your daughter." I cast my eyes toward the ceiling, motioning upstairs to the sad girl who needed a parent's love. "It's okay if we're apart this week."

"But I want you with me," he said, nuzzling behind my ear, his hot breath on my neck sending shivers along my spine. "I want you, Charlie," he said, his voice a grumble. "You know, it's a commandment for a husband to satisfy his wife on the Sabbath," he murmured.

I nosed into his face, craving his breath along my skin. But the words *wife* and *husband* lingered in the thick air, words not belonging to the two of us, but to him and someone no longer here.

Someone not me.

"I'm not your wife," I whispered as he continued to rain little kisses along my skin, pulling the collar of my sweater wide to reveal my shoulder.

"You could be," he murmured.

I stepped back and looked at him. "What did you say?"

He blushed, wouldn't meet my gaze. "I'm sorry." It was quick and forceful. He didn't insist that it was what he wanted, only apologized for uttering the words. "You're right," he said, making it even worse. A slip in the heat of passion, not the true desire of his heart.

My stomach was hollow. For a second, I'd hoped he'd meant it.

I stepped back from him, turned and walked quickly out of the kitchen. My purse was on the table by the front door, and I grabbed it with one hand as I pulled open the closet with my other, searching for my jacket. When I found it, an olive green puffy down coat that was as warm as a sleeping bag, I pulled it on, flung my purse over my shoulder and reached for the front door.

"Charlie, wait." Parker had caught up to me, put a hand out to keep me from opening the door.

"Parker, I need to leave," I said, insistent.

"Please, wait," he said. He stood with his back against the door, blocking my exit.

I stared at him and sighed impatiently, almost angrily.

There was nothing he could say to make this right.

"It was a slip, fine. I'm not mad," I said, reaching around him for the door handle. But he stopped me, caught my hand in his and pulled me to him.

"I love you, Charlie, please don't leave me," he said, tilting my face to his. It was warm in my coat. I desperately wanted to go, to be alone in the screaming night wind, to feel sorry for myself at my cozy cottage.

"I believe that you love me," I said evenly. "And I believe that it is hard to be with me and with the memory of Sylvie."

His eyes went wide. He looked stricken, as if I'd said something I couldn't come back from. But it needed to be said, needed to be out in the open between us. If we were to go any further in our relationship, we'd need to address the shadow in the room—in every room.

"I can't compete with a ghost," I said, stepping back.

He let me go, released his hand from the door.

"And I wouldn't want to."

His eyes were downcast. He looked so incredibly sad.

"Parker, I don't want to replace Sylvie," I said.

He looked up then, searching my eyes—for what, I didn't know.

"I never could. Maybe it's too soon for me to be part of all this," I said, sweeping a hand around the house. "Maybe it's too soon for your kids and your parents, her parents. I think I might've been crazy when I said I'd celebrate

Thanksgiving with all of you. Or maybe just hopeful."

He looked embarrassed, shrinking away from me. I wanted to hug him, to kiss him, to pull us back into that last moment when we couldn't pry our bodies apart, when he was so certain about having me in his life. But I could see from the pain on his face that the moment was gone.

I wanted to call Boden, to run into his arms. I wanted to hear James's footsteps at the door, his booming voice coming home to me in the cold night. My parents would gladly welcome me to the home in Traverse City where I'd spent all my growing-up years then fled without a glance back, but I didn't want to go there. I couldn't go back. I could only move forward.

Suddenly, I realized that I was, and would always be, alone in the world. Even if Parker and I could find a way to be together, I'd be alone even with him. It hit me with stark reality that a person can never be truly fused with another. We were, each and every one of us, alone, always and forever.

A deep and heavy calm washed over me. The thought wasn't as terrifying as I'd expected. I could do this. Be alone and find my own happiness. I'd spent all these years waiting for someone else to bring me joy, to define me, to give me direction, tell me I belonged. I was at once sad and angry that I'd been so lazy, so dependent.

Parker hugged his arms, hunched into his body. I hated to leave him.

But I needed to get clear on what I wanted and not let myself settle for less ever again. And, it wouldn't hurt him to miss me a little, to think about what he wanted. He couldn't do it with me there—certainly not with his kids and parents and former in-laws filling the house.

And I could never be the one to heal his heart.

I stepped closer to him and placed a slow, firm kiss on his lips. "I love you, Parker," I said, my voice husky with unshed tears. Then I inched around him, and he stepped out of the way, as I pulled the door open and ventured out into the cold and blazing night.

Chapter Thirty-Eight

It was ten by the time I got home. I rushed inside, stomping my boots dry on the mat. The heat was humming in the cottage. I left my boots by the door as I bolted it and then threw a log in the stove before going into the kitchen to pour a healthy serving of bourbon, downing it in one gulp. Fire seared my throat. I sank onto the couch and pulled out my phone.

Mary answered after three rings. There was laughter in the background and low music.

"Charlie!" Her voice sang out. She was drunk.

"Never mind," I mumbled and hung up, throwing the phone on the floor.

An hour later, my phone buzzed. I was flipping through the channels, looking for something to watch and finding nothing. I'd given up on an easy sleep; my mind was too revved up, wondering if I'd ever see Parker again.

"Hey girl," Mary slurred into the phone. "Why'd you hang up on me?"

"You're drunk," I said calmly.

"You betcha!"

"Mary, we'll talk tomorrow. Go sleep it off."

"No, no, no, no, no!" she sang out. I could picture her twirling. A gruff voice called her name, and she barked, "Back off, Ben," then giggled. "My girl needs me, and I'ma be here for you," she chirped.

"You're stone drunk, you're not making any sense, and you won't remember any of what I say tomorrow," I said. The embers of the fire were a low orange simmer. I stared at them, willing them to lull me to sleep.

"You can tell me anyway," Mary said, her voice closer to the phone. "The guys are leaving now. I'm here for ya, hon."

I couldn't help but smile. She was a cute drunk and a good friend. Who cared if she didn't remember what I said? Maybe she'd offer some pearls of wisdom in her loosened state.

So I dove in, told her about the conversation with Parker, about backing out of Thanksgiving, everything.

"Wait!" Her voice was a screech. "That means you're free for the holiday to be with *me*!"

I hated that I perked up at the thought of an invitation from a drunk friend. And that she would likely be spending it in a biker bar with friends she'd known longer.

"Seriously," she said, sloshing the word. "Marisol is coming, and we'll make turkey, cranberries, all the things! You'll come. We'll be three single women together, eating a big bad bird."

"But you're a vegetarian," I said, laughing.

"Well, I'm not going to eat it, but you and Marisol can! I'll eat the stuffing and the cranberries and a big bad beer." I pictured spit flying as she over-pronounced her words.

"It's gonna be fine, Charlie-poo," she cooed into the phone. "Rabbi Romance will come flying back. He'll miss you too much to stay away. And until then, you've got *me*!"

Mary yelled, "OW," into the phone, followed by a torrent of curse words, and then the call ended abruptly. I chuckled as I put down the phone. At least I felt better.

I got up, filled a ceramic pitcher with water, and doused the fire. After checking window latches and the back door, I trooped into my bedroom, peeled off my clothes, pulled on soft flannel pajama bottoms and a worn waffle-print shirt, and climbed into bed.

A few minutes before five, I awoke with a start. Out the window, it was inky black, with stars winking. A cold wind whistled through the trees. I'd heard a noise—I was sure of it. Had it been a dream?

I crept from the bed, pulling a sweatshirt over my head, and then crept out into the cottage. And then, I heard it again—a thump against the wall then silence.

I was caught between wanting to investigate and wanting to hide. I reached for the phone to call Parker but then thought better of it. *You can't go to him now. Give him space. You have to save yourself.*

I slipped the phone in the pocket of my pajama pants and crept closer to the front windows to peer out without being seen.

The moon was low in the sky and full, its white light washing over the tips of the trees. The road was covered in new snow; no cars had been by since I'd arrived home hours earlier, no fresh tracks through the perfect white. I breathed a sigh of relief. Then, I heard it again—thump, thump, thud.

My heart picked up its pace, and I peered out the front. Nothing. No animals, no human footsteps in the newly fallen snow.

I slid to the kitchen, where there were no curtains to hide the windows, to keep me protected from view. If anyone was out there, they'd surely see me. Maybe it was raccoons, rooting through the garbage. But I'd secured the lid on the can, something we all had to do in these parts, to keep away not only scrounging rodents but bears, too. I chewed on a fingernail and sidled up to the solid piece of wall between the back door and the pantry. From there, I could see an angle out into the yard, where my dormant garden lay blanketed for the winter. Nothing moved there, not even a sigh of errant wild grasses long against the snow.

Nothing. I'd been hearing things, branches banging against the house, critters scurrying up along manmade structures. I was hardier than this, stronger, and I had better start acting like it.

I went back to my bed, climbed beneath the blanket and pulled it up over my head. I had hours to go before the day needed me, and I fell into a deep and dreamless sleep.

Chapter Thirty-Nine

I was tired when morning hit, my limbs heavy. My mouth felt dry and sticky, my face clammy. *Shit*, I thought. *I'm sick.*

I padded to the bathroom, shivering, and stuck the thermometer in my ear—101.5. I gulped down three ibuprofens, filled a glass with water and ambled back to bed.

That day, I surged in and out of sleep, kicking off the covers then pulling them back around my shivering body. I wished for tea, for soup, for someone to nurse me back to health, but no one was coming. Back at Anam Cara, when anyone fell sick, pairs of patrons would arrive with fresh-brewed teas from wild herbs or medicinals grown in the greenhouse, followed by carafes of soup steeped with bone broth and hardy vegetables. We were experts at nursing our friends back to health. Some of the older women had magical concoctions that corrected any ailment, and miraculously, most of us rarely got sick anyway. Something about living with our hands in the soil, building immunity from the natural world. And for those who did get sick, an illness lasted only a short time, healed quickly and expertly by the soothing foods cooked and served with love.

In my fever dreams, I wept for Anam Cara. My long-time home, my old friends. It wasn't all bad, I reasoned. They weren't all evil. They didn't wish me harm! How could any of the stories be true? Murder and intrigue, competition and conquest—ludicrous! They were all wrong. My sweet James came to me in those fever dreams, his angelic red hair gleaming like gold against a fan of light, his fiery eyes alive with laughter and love. I reached for him and buried my weeping face in his beard, let his arms encircle me, rock me back to sleep. When I awoke next, James was gone, but Boden was at my side, his legs extended long on the bed, his head cocked, his face smiling down at me.

"You're here!" I exclaimed, and he pulled my head into his lap, stroked my hair. "Oh, I love you so much, Bo! I knew you couldn't be gone. it couldn't be true. You're here!"

But he didn't speak.

"Say something," I begged. "Speak to me. Let me hear your rumbly voice. Your beautiful, sweet Boden voice."

He shook his head, blinking slowly, looking at me almost with pity.

"What is it? Why won't you talk? I need to hear you, need to know you're alive, that you've come back to me! It's awful being alone. I can't do it any longer. I need you here, I need someone to love me!"

And then he faded from view, and I wept angry, hot tears, collapsing on my pillow with exhaustion.

The next time my eyes fluttered open, the daylight had disappeared and the black night was back. I heard someone clanging in my kitchen, and my heart leaped into my throat. But then Mary appeared in the doorway, carrying a tray with a steaming bowl and a plate of soft rolls.

"How did you get in?" I mumbled, aware of my musty breath and the state of my appearance. My hair was natty and knotted, my clothes drenched.

"Looks like the fever has broken," she said, sitting at the edge of the bed and balancing the tray over my legs. "Sit up, and I'll spoon you some soup."

I did as she said, pulling the blanket up to my waist. I slurped the spoonful that she offered me—sweet carrot in velvety chicken broth—then repeated my question.

"How did you get in?"

"You let me in, honey," Mary said, offering me another spoonful.

The soup went down easy, warming my throat and spreading that warmth through my body. I sucked down every spoonful she offered until the bowl was empty, and I wanted more.

"I let you in?" I had no memory of it. I blinked the sleep from my eyes, stretched my arms overhead. "I can't believe how fast this came on. Must be a twenty-four-hour thing."

She shook her head. "Honey, I've been here since Saturday."

"What day is it?"

I glanced out the window at the lavender morning. The cold hovered in the air, frost painting the tips of the wild grasses white.

"Tuesday."

She lifted the tray off my legs and left the room. I sank down onto the pillows, pulling the blanket tight around me. Mary appeared a few minutes later with a mug of steaming tea and placed it on the nightstand.

"You've been here for three days?"

"Mmmm-hmmm," she said, nodding.

"How did you know to come?"

Her face flushed a deep shade of pink. Her gray braids were looped together at the base of her neck in a loose knot. She'd tied my gingham apron over her long-sleeved T-shirt.

"I came to apologize for my ridiculous behavior on the phone Friday night," she said, chewing on her lip. "Ben was over, and we got wild on tequila. Couldn't help it." She shrugged her shoulders up to her ears and cocked a half-smile.

"You love Ben..." I smiled, sitting back up and cupping the mug between my hands. The warmth of it was reassuring.

"Parker came by," she said, waiting for my reaction.

I blew on the steam coming off the mug, watched it push

away. A hefty scent of lemon and ginger drifted off the hot liquid. I pursed my lips to take a sip, but the heat of the ceramic had me backing away.

"Put it down until it cools a bit," she said, taking the mug and setting it on the nightstand. "Don't rush it."

I offered a weak smile. "There were people at Anam Cara, old women with satiny hair, who believed that illness came from the soul. That if you got really sick, it was emotion brimming over and spilling out."

She shook her head. "That place," she said. "What happened between you and the rabbi?"

"How long did he stay?" I stretched my legs out, clenching and uncurling my toes, which elicited several loud cracks.

Mary snickered. "Came Saturday and sat by your bedside. Sunday, too. I told him to be with his family for now, and I'd keep him up to date on your condition."

"That was nice," I said, reaching for the mug.

She swatted my hand away. "Five more minutes," she said. "He was worried. Didn't look like he'd slept much. I think he's pretty broken up about the way you left things."

"Oh?"

She nodded. "Smart to give him space. He needs to figure out his shit. His family's in town, and hers. They're really nice people, but it takes a long time to heal sad hearts."

I was nodding while wondering what that meant for me.

For us. If there was even an *us* anymore.

"Don't be in such a rush to figure it out," Mary said as if she could read my mind. "Now you can have the tea." She cocked her head at the mug, and I lifted it and was surprised to find that she was absolutely right about how long it had needed to cool. The woman was a magician. The liquid went down warm and easy, coating my throat.

"Is there honey in this?"

She nodded and smiled. "Raw, from Layton's bees." She settled next to me on the bed and laid a hand on my shoulder. "I know you're hurting," she said. "This flu is evidence of that. The emotions come out in the body."

I cocked my head at her. She'd been so quick to poo-poo the idea when I'd attributed it to Anam Cara, and now she was echoing those crazy people she despised so much. I smirked and covered her hand with mine. Friendship was good medicine.

"Did you sleep here?"

She nodded. "Every night. Been here for four straight days."

"Did you hear the knocking?"

Now it was her turn to cock her gaze as if I was crazy. She shook her head, and an eyebrow rose in question.

"Never mind," I said, sure that it had been the illness making me imagine things. I was safe. I'd say that as a mantra until I believed it to be true.

"Marisol's been minding the store for me, and now

we're closing for the holiday weekend," she said. "We're doing Thanksgiving the three of us, remember?"

"I'm surprised you do," I laughed, glugging another mouthful of tea.

"I'm a fun drunk, not a stupid drunk, and I always remember," she said.

"Ben coming?"

"To Thanksgiving? Nah." She shook her head and patted my shoulder. "Let the gnarly men have their holiday, and we women can raise the roof."

I winced. "I'm not sure I'm up for that."

She laughed. "Neither am I, honey. You're a lot to handle."

"Oh really?"

The mug was empty, and my heart was calm.

"When you're up for it, might I suggest a shower?"

I scrunched my nose and smoothed back my hair. "That bad?"

She nodded. "That bad." She smirked, took the empty mug off the nightstand and left the room.

Chapter Forty

I wanted to call him, and I was glad that I didn't. Having Mary around helped. My parents kept calling, begging me to come home, but I no longer had the energy to make the drive, and it was too late—and too expensive—to book a flight. Besides, I wasn't quite ready.

Would I ever be?

I had discarded past versions of myself like a reptile shedding skins. The Traverse City me was so far in the past that I could barely remember her, and I was in the process of letting go of Anam Cara me. I was focused on building the best me yet.

Mary and Marisol made a feast fit for a dozen, leaving days of leftovers in my fridge. I was too weak to do much of anything, but they didn't mind, and we stayed up late talking, eating, laughing, until we all slumped into sleep on my bed together.

On Monday, Parker knocked at my door.

He was beautiful on my porch. Winter hat, heavy coat, thick gloves and his breath puffing in the white morning.

His eyes held a sadness that I'd never thought possible in the always-happy rabbi.

"I've missed you," he said, striding into my cottage.

I wanted him there, and I didn't. I'd played second fiddle to everyone in James's life; I didn't want to do it for a ghost. But oh, how I wanted to wrap myself around him and never let go.

"I was so distracted last week," he said. "The kids could tell something was off. My parents, too. I don't know if Sylvie's parents noticed, and I don't know what I would've said if they had."

He threaded his hands through his hair as he paced in my small living room. The fire crackled, orange and yellow flames licking at logs. A pot of turkey soup simmered on the stove, and a loaf of sourdough was rising on the counter.

I was watching him as if I were a spectator, studying his every move. His hands gestured dramatically when he spoke, his words full of emotion. His eyes were big and bright. He couldn't stop moving.

I knew Parker the charismatic rabbi. Steady, calming Parker. Parker at the helm of a community, the grounded leader. Parker on the periphery of boring. Parker anyone could rely on. I'd never seen anxious, out-of-control Parker.

I reached a hand to steady him. He stopped and faced me.

"Come back to me, Charlie," he breathed.

I'd wanted him to miss me, but this? He was wild with emotion, and it scared me.

I studied his lips as he spoke, his sweet, simple lips. I longed to taste them. But I didn't know how to be the strong one in a relationship. Not yet.

He was close now, his body vibrating. I could feel his heat. I didn't want to feel it. I wanted to watch, to study, to think.

Then he was in my face, and I could smell him. I closed my eyes and inhaled his scent, woodsy with a sweetness and the musk of sweat.

His lips were suddenly on my lips, and I closed my eyes and kissed him, long and winding.

"Charlie," he breathed my name like it was lifesaving.

I opened my eyes and went to the couch, sank into it, and he followed.

"Say something," he said, lifting my hand and kissing it, turning it over in his, stroking the skin of my fingers. "Talk to me."

Where were my words?

I didn't know what I should say or what I wanted to say. I searched for the right words, but none came. All thought flew out of my brain; my mind went blank. I stared at him as if I didn't know him. This man in front of me—I loved him. I wanted him. He'd taught me the Hebrew word *bashert*, one's intended, one's destiny. Were we that for each other?

I shook my head.

"What? What are you saying no to?" His hands were petting me, and I sat there, unable to speak, watching his wildness go untethered.

Maybe it was easier this way, to not speak, to watch everything, let it unfold. It was fascinating to be a spectator in my own life.

Parker pulled me to him, stroking my hair. "Charlie, I miss you," he whispered. "I want you in my life. I want you." His words were breaths, hot and salty.

Where was my feeling? Where was the impetus to move, to do, to jump in? Had illness drained me of emotion? Or was I just tired of feeling so much, exhausted from too many years of wanting and yearning and being relegated to the sidelines?

I pinched my eyes shut and willed the memories to flit away like little insects winging toward the sky. His arms were around me, rocking me, stroking me, and I let the motion lull me into sleep.

CHAPTER FORTY-ONE

When I next opened my eyes, I heard movement in the kitchen. I sprang up and went to see who it was, surprised to find Parker with my apron tied around his waist, kneading the sourdough. He'd shed his sweater, rolled the sleeves of his flannel up past his elbows. The long lines of his muscles rippled like ropes as he pulled and pushed and pounded the dough.

"It's you." My voice came back in whispers. "You're here."

He turned, wiped his hands on the apron, and strode over. Both hands gripping my shoulders, he studied me intensely. "I want you in my life," he said. "I need you, Charlie."

"Do you?"

I went over to the ball of dough and poked it. It was elastic and smooth and sprang back under my touch. With both hands, I shaped it then reached into the drawer for a razor to score it and make a design of tiny flowers on the top. When it was done, I dropped it into a linen-lined basket for its final rise and draped a thin kitchen towel over top.

Parker came up behind me, his body mirroring mine. I could feel his wanting, and I wanted to consume him, but I was unsteady on my feet, too cautious for my own comfort. I didn't want to give in to the urge, to the wanting. I wanted to keep watching my life, to stay outside of myself, to wait and see what would happen.

He lifted my hair and kissed my neck softly. I closed my eyes and leaned into him, the wanting spiraling through me in waves of heat.

No. I could resist. I needed to. It was clear he wanted me. The desire wouldn't disappear. What wasn't clear was my own desire to move forward in a life constructed entirely on my own.

I spun around to face him, put a hand on his chest and pushed him slightly back. "Parker."

"What?" His eyes were a question as he tried to read my face, but he'd find no answers there.

"I need time."

He raked a hand through his hair, his eyes wide.

"Why? What for? Don't you want me, too?"

My lips a straight line, I nodded. "I do," I said carefully. "But."

"But what?"

He untied the apron and dropped it on the counter then pulled me to him.

"Please, Charlie, come back to me. Nothing is the same without you in my life." He was kissing me, his hands running up and down my body, and I wanted to give in. I wanted to let him consume me, to ride the waves of pleasure with him like we did so well.

But I pushed him back again, my palm to his chest, a simple line set on my steady face.

"I need time," I said, this time more forcefully.

He stepped back, his eyes filling with sadness. "How much time?"

I shook my head. "I don't honestly know."

He sniffled, dragged a finger under his nose, his shoulders hunched. He nodded. "Okay," he said. "Whatever you need. But can you tell me why?"

I swallowed and carefully considered my words.

"Because I don't want to be second choice for anyone," I said calmly, clearly. "I need to set the boundaries of my life, not have them set for me. I need to become my best self before I can move forward with anyone." I swallowed. "Even you."

He was in his coat and boots before I could say anything else and then out the door, the cold gasp of air from full-on winter shuddering through my house. I put another log on the fire and fell onto the couch. I was exhausted from the scene, fatigue leftover from the illness, which I now saw had purged me of all my pent-up questions and desire and emotion of the last few months. I was starting fresh, an empty vessel, and it took so much damn effort.

CHAPTER FORTY-TWO

I awoke to the heavy footsteps of the mailman trudging onto the porch and slipping whatever was meant for me into the tin box, which echoed as it slammed shut. He trudged away, and the puttering motor of his mail truck became faint.

I got up, opened the door, lifted the lid and dug out the letters and leaflets. Sifting through them on the couch, I pulled out one with familiar scrawl and a Canadian postmark.

I tore the envelope open and pulled out a letter in Armand's slanted handwriting. It started off nice enough, if formal—*My Dear Charlie, Your presence is requested at Anam Cara with urgency*—but it quickly took a menacing turn:

We are investigating some missing funds and are concerned about your role in their disappearance. If you are not present at the community by the first Thursday of December, we will have no choice but to come looking for you.

It didn't stop there. The letter became more threatening

toward the end, demanding my imminent return, my full confession and a hint of what might happen if these demands were not met.

I dropped the letter, my hands shaking. I grabbed my phone and started to dial Parker but then clicked it off. I couldn't depend on him to save me. I had to save myself. And I didn't want to put him in the path of danger.

I bundled into boots and a coat and drove the letter to the police station. A dusting of new snow was imprinted with tire tracks in front of the precinct. I tromped through the door, the biting air whooshing inside with a wail of wind until the door shut firmly behind me.

"Charlie Tanner," Bruce said dryly. "Nice to see ya."

I nodded and thrust the letter at him. "They won't leave me alone." I wished I hadn't burned the first letter before I'd shown it to him. Impulsive, indeed! When would I learn?

With concern in his eyes, he scanned the letter, his lips twitching as he did. When he'd finished, Bruce looked up, and there was a softness in his gaze that hadn't been there before.

"Well, that's something concrete, isn't it?"

I nodded, licking my lips, and told him about the letter I'd burned.

"A shame you didn't keep it," he said, nodding. "I think it's time to file a PPO against this Armand guy," he said evenly.

"What's that?"

"Personal Protection Order." He pulled a sheet from a shelf and started filling it out. "So if he attempts to come near you, there is legal recourse. Basically, he can't come near you, or he'll be in violation of the order, and that is prosecutable by law."

He put the sheet in front of me and handed me a pen. I read the words, saw the definite language forbidding Armand from coming within close range of me. If he did, he could be arrested.

I didn't feel better, though. A guy like Armand wouldn't follow the instructions on a flimsy piece of paper, no matter who wrote it or what the consequences would be if he violated it.

Which is what I told Bruce as I put down the pen and handed the paper back to him.

He shrugged. "That may be, but it's all I got, Charlie. I can't really do anything more. The guy lives in Canada. He's not a local; he's just sending menacing letters. It's a crime as it crosses international borders, but I can't go to Canada to arrest him. I have no jurisdiction there. And he hasn't technically done anything—only threatened to."

"He's good for it," I said, my heartbeat escalating. "He's killed people, Bruce."

"So you say."

I nodded vigorously. "Believe me."

"Oh, I do, Charlie," he said. "You seem like a sensible

person, and if the rabbi trusts you, I do, too. But like I said—there's nothing I can do, other than this." He held the PPO in the air and shook it. "Unless...until..."

"Yes, let's hope it doesn't come to that." I sighed. "Well, this is something, I guess."

"That it is," he agreed. Then the precinct phone rang, and a woman called out to Bruce to take the call.

After I filled out the paper and gave it back to him for processing, I meant to drive home, but my car found its way to Parker's house. The driveway had been cleared of snow, the walkway salted to melt ice. It was picture-perfect, the home of a responsible family man and community leader.

I was about to throw the car into reverse to head home when Parker opened the door and waved. I parked and killed the engine.

He took my coat and hung it in the front hall closet. "Tea?"

I nodded.

I waited in the living room for him to bring a steaming mug. The fire was going, and classical music played from a speaker.

"I'm so glad you came over," he said. "I was wild the other day. I'm sorry about that. But Charlie—I'm going crazy without you."

I offered a soft smile as I blew on the tea to cool it. I know he wanted me to say that I missed him, too, that I wanted to be back in his life, but I was devoid of strong emotion and couldn't fake it. I couldn't stop thinking about Armand's letter. I was scared. I didn't want to be alone.

But I knew what I had to do.

"We can get to that," I said after sipping the tea, "but not now. I need to tell you what's going on. I need to feel safe."

It all came pouring out, and his eyes were back to wild. I'd never seen him unhinged until these last weeks, hadn't known it was even possible for the easy-going, strong rabbi to lose it. It made me like him more, to see that he was human, that he wasn't always calm and measured.

Had he been like this when Sylvie died? I'd assumed he'd been stoic, stunned, frozen, but now I could see him in reeling pain, with long wails of despair.

Which Parker did I like better?

"Geez," he said. "I don't know what to say." He exhaled slowly and long. Watching him, my heart beat a steady tap-tap-tap.

"Are you scared?" He laid a hand on my thigh, and I wished desire did not ripple through me at his touch.

"Maybe I shouldn't have come," I said quickly. What had I expected? I was shaking my head, striding to the door, but he jumped up and stopped me.

"Wait. Don't go."

I turned, stared into his eyes, and saw my fear mirrored back to me.

"I don't want to lose you," he said. "And these people." He was combing his hand through his hair again, his eyes wide. "They might kill you, Charlie."

I nodded. "I've been telling you this, Parker. We agreed I can't live my life on the run. But I don't know what I *can* do. I don't know how to outsmart Armand."

He was about to say something like *we'll do this together, we're in it together*, but I couldn't let him. Because if he stuck by me, he was in danger, too, and I couldn't do that to him. Or to Alice or Ethan. They'd already lost one parent; I wouldn't let them lose another.

Which made me realize that I did, in fact, love this man more than I'd ever loved anyone. So I needed to save him. I needed to be strong enough to do what he couldn't do. I didn't want any harm to come to him or his family. I needed to protect them all.

"Look. This has been fun," I started, swallowing my hesitation. I inhaled deeply to gather strength for what I needed to say. "But it has to end. I can't play second fiddle to a memory of the perfect woman. I came second, always, in James's life, and I can't do that again. I won't."

It was all I could do to not show my true feelings, to not crumble under the weight of his gaze.

"You're better off on your own," I said. "It's only been two years since Sylvie died. I want to be with someone who loves me not as a consolation prize but as the focus of his life, and you won't ever be able to do that."

His mouth hung open, his skin pale. "Is that how you really feel? How can you say that, Charlie?"

"You'll never be able to leave her behind," I said plainly, not making eye contact. I couldn't look at him. I hated being cruel.

He looked stung. "Why would you want me to? I can't pretend Sylvie wasn't in my life. She was my wife, Charlie, the mother of my children."

I went in for the cold, hard stab. "Right. And I'll never be. I can't compete with a ghost, Parker."

"I can't believe you'd even suggest that I could forget her, or that I should," he spat.

Finally. It was working.

"If she hadn't died, we wouldn't even be here," I said, going in for the kill.

His eyes blazed with anger and betrayal. "You're right," he said plainly, coldly. "And if James hadn't died, you'd still be a pawn in his game at Anam Cara. A sad, lonely follower gullible enough to believe all that cult-y bullshit."

His words stung, but I'd started this and I would finish it.

"How can you be so cruel?" I said softly. "You know how much I'm wrangling with this, trying to understand myself, to be better."

His eyes were fire. He shook his head. "You'll never be more than a follower, Charlie." He strode to the door as he uttered the words.

I winced, trying to hold back the tears. I'd known what I was doing, but he hadn't. I had been play-acting, trying to distance myself from him to protect him, but he'd meant every word he'd said, and it stung.

He handed me my coat and stood stiffly by the door. I didn't even say goodbye as I left. The door clicked shut the minute I walked through it, and I heard the bolt slide into place.

The winter wind howled, and I shrank into my coat. Hot tears leaked down my cheeks in silent streams, scalding the air-bitten skin of my face. I'd finish this somehow, come out of it with my soul and body intact, and I'd do it alone. At least now the man I loved would be safe. If only he could know how much I was sacrificing to keep him free from the madness.

Chapter Forty-Three

"I don't know that I ever planned to stay in Vermont permanently," I said.

Late-day light cascaded through an old paned window in Hanley's office. I'd called to see if he could fit me in after the blow-up with Parker. Luckily, he had a slot for the next day, and I took it.

And now, the session almost over, I was no closer to clarity than when I'd arrived. Less angry, perhaps, but still melancholy.

"So what was the long-term plan?"

I shook my head. "I don't know. I didn't have one. Only to leave Anam Cara."

He leaned his arms on his legs and looked straight at me. "Leaving one place is not a plan. It's an escape. Going to a new place is a plan."

I nodded. "Right."

Outside, a fat-breasted robin flitted on a tree branch.

"Does everyone reach a point where they don't know their purpose? Does every person even search for a purpose?"

It was his turn to shrug. "Does it matter?"

"I guess not."

I flexed my fingers until they cracked, and then I sighed.

"What are you going to do, Charlie?"

I didn't know. I couldn't keep running. I couldn't go back to Parker, not until I'd resolved the threat from Armand. And I didn't know at this point if Parker would even take me back. We'd said things we couldn't erase.

But my focus for now was figuring out how to stay alive in the glare of Armand's threats. I couldn't evade his pursuit. If he was coming for me, I'd meet him head-on, which Hanley thought was a terrible idea.

"You don't have to go looking for trouble," he'd said when I told him I'd stay put and wait for Armand to show his ugly face. "It's okay to protect yourself. Some might say you have a death wish to take this approach."

I wasn't sure what the laws were around a therapist knowing that his patient might be waiting for death to knock on her door. I wasn't suicidal, so he couldn't have me admitted to a secure facility, and besides, that would only buy time. I wanted to live, fully and heartily, out in the open, and I needed to find a way to make sure that I could. What could Hanley do, really, except listen to my musing, my circumstances, my circular logic?

"Where would you go if you left Vermont?" Hanley's voice brought me back to the moment.

"Home, maybe?"

"Is Traverse City really home for you?"

I shook my head.

"And on that, why would you choose to go there, to go back?"

"Because my family is there."

"And how do you feel about your family these days?"

We'd spent several sessions picking apart the relationships of my family of origin, until I slowly saw the fractures there, the myth of a cozy family. I had more to reckon with than I'd realized about how my parents had treated me and how that had contributed to my choices. While my mother urged me to seek out therapy in the first place, I don't think she imagined I'd dig up childhood dirt that would cast a negative light on her. She didn't want me to interrogate that past, only the years when we weren't in touch. It pained me to hear the ache in her voice, but it angered me, too. I needed to get to the root of why I'd made the choices I had, what had drawn me to let others control me. I didn't want to lose my parents now that I'd found my way to closeness with them, and they were eager to embrace me. I'd always wanted to be loved and accepted without question or demand, and I was finally there.

"Would you consider choosing a life path independent of people?" Hanley asked. "Guided by instinct, by what you want to do, who you want to be?"

I sighed. "That seems like a lot of effort," I squeaked out.

"And it sounds miserably lonely."

"I'm not saying isolate yourself from the world," Hanley said. "Just take some time to be alone. To get clear. You're sort of doing that already."

He looked at the clock, and I winced. "Time's up?"

He nodded.

"Figures." I shrugged, gathering my bag and stuffing my arms into my coat.

"I'm proud of you, Charlie," he said with a warm grin. "You can do anything you want. Believe it. I'll see you soon."

That night, I warmed a bowl of soup and toasted a hunk of sourdough in the oven, onto which I smeared salted butter and blackberry preserves from my farmer-friend. The food was warm and soothing and went down easy. The wind outside was brutal, a winter storm revving up to slam the mountain towns without restraint. I pulled a sweater over my pajamas and huddled in bed with a book, listening to the scream of the wind, feeling it batter the sides of my house.

I was snowed in for three days. Parker called—twice—but I sent his calls to voice mail. After listening to his caramel voice in the messages he left, apologizing for his harsh words, I ached for him, wanting nothing more than to throw my arms around him and bury my face in his chest. He hoped I was safe. He missed me. He begged me to consider meeting, to talk things through, after the plows came and cleared the streets. We'd discuss the argument, he said, work things out. He pleaded with me to not give up on us.

I deleted the messages but held the phone close to my heart, as if it were an acceptable surrogate.

The storm gave me time to think. I pulled out my photo albums from Anam Cara, from college, looking at my younger self, those eager eyes, that innocent grin. I could see my passion for the environment, my enthusiasm for learning sustainable practices. I remembered how I couldn't learn it all fast enough, how I drank it in like life-giving nectar.

Did that girl exist somewhere deep inside me? Or had I buried her on the road to Canada, left her bones by the roadside as James drove fast across the border?

I tuned the speaker to acoustic folk music and took out a notepad and a pen, listing all my practical skills, all the work experience I'd amassed over the years, even if I hadn't been paid for any of it or earned a degree. The list was long and impressive. I sat back and read it through once, twice, three times, my confidence building with each glance. There were things I could do—things I loved to do, things I was good at. Could I turn any of them into sustainable, fulfilling work? A purpose? Was anything on this page a calling?

I could return to school, finally get my degree—though I wasn't sure I needed it at this point. I might just be able to build a career on the skills I'd learned in the garden and the greenhouse. I started to feel hopeful for the first time in a long while.

On the third day of the snow-in, I called Willow. My mother had been begging me to make contact, and I'd been hesitant. What did we have in common? How could we forge a friendship after an entire life of no contact, of living separate lives in the same family?

But I was curious. Who was this mysterious older sister? Was she a pawn in the stage play of my childhood, an influential character or just an extra waiting in the wings? Did she ever think of me? And if so, was it with kindness or contempt?

Mom had saved her number in my phone when she'd visited. I'd never planned to call. And then I wanted to know more, to learn what secrets lurked in the corners of my childhood.

Her voice was a question when she answered. Smooth like satin, strong like an old tree, and strangely familiar.

"Willow," I said, my voice a mouse hiding in shadows.

"Yes?" She clearly didn't know my voice, and I strained to make it louder, to match her strength.

"It's Charlie."

Silence. I could hear her breathing, in then out then in, to the back of her throat, caught there, pinned against a wall of blood and bone.

"Oh."

That was all. Not *hello*, not *finally*, not *I've been hoping you'd call*. No warmth, and no invitation to continue talking.

When she didn't speak, I mustered the strength to fill in the silence.

"Mom has been pushing me to call you," I started.

A *harumph*.

"I wasn't sure if I would," I continued.

"Am I supposed to be glad you did?"

A faint tapping, like a pencil against a countertop or a shoe on the floor.

I sighed. This was harder than I'd expected. I hadn't thought this through. *Fucking impulse.*

"I don't know," I said, choosing blunt honesty as a hail Mary. "I've been hesitant because I didn't know whether you'd want to hear from me." I paused. "I didn't know if I wanted to call."

"That's more like it," she said. Her voice eased, the anger thick. "You're lucky I have time to answer right now," she said. "I have a very full life without you in it. And I'm not sure there's room for a long-lost sister."

"That's fair," I said. "Let's agree that neither of us knows what this is or whether we want it to be something." I could almost hear her nodding. "I think I want to know you a little. To know where our lives intersect. To know what I've missed."

She sighed. Her background was eerily quiet. Were her

kids at school? I knew nothing about my sister's life, my only sibling a complete stranger to me. I had a string of facts, like a child's handmade bracelet, but no real knowing or depth. If I tugged too hard, the beads would scatter across the floor.

Finally, she spoke.

"When you left, it was all Mom and Dad could talk about," Willow said. "For years. They were obsessed with your leaving. They never forgot you or let me forget you. It was like you had died. They mourned you every single goddamn day."

I chewed on my lip. You had to care to be this angry. And this was entirely new information. They'd lamented my leaving for years? Possibly the entire time I'd been gone. God, how she must resent me!

"I was never enough for them. Never," she spat. "Not when I got married, not when I had babies... Nothing I did was ever interesting or impressive or worth celebrating."

"Is that true?"

"Well, no, not entirely. I mean, they celebrated all those things for me, but there was a ghost in our midst. You. Some missing presence, some hole in the happiness, hovering there, always."

I whistled in air between my teeth.

"Did you ever think about what your leaving did to anyone else?"

"No. Because I didn't do it for any of you. I was living

my life. It's not my fault they couldn't see that."

She was like a bull ready to charge.

"Willow, it's not my job, and it's not yours, to make our parents happy," I said evenly. She was dead silent. Was it possible my brilliant, charismatic older sister was at a loss for words? Had never considered this possibility?

"I don't mean this to sound condescending," I said, "but when you go away, you see things differently. I know I didn't make the best choices"—she *humphed* at that—"but I made choices based on what I wanted at the time. I went. I did. And I had to deal with the ramifications, too. It hasn't been easy for me, you know."

"You left us all behind without a glance back." Her voice was quiet now. "My kids don't even know they have an aunt."

I don't know why those last words hurt, but they did. I hadn't expected her to light a candle for me—but to never tell them I existed?

"Do you think there's room for them to know now?"

She sighed. "Maybe. If you're here to stay. How do I explain it to them? This sister of mine that you've never heard of is now here?"

I shrugged as if she could see me. "Willow, I just called to extend an olive branch. To try. One conversation. I have no expectations."

She fell quiet. The house was growing colder. The fire was down to embers, and I teepeed two logs over the seething cinders and crumpled some newspaper to get it going. Then I went into the kitchen and pressed the lever to heat up the kettle.

"One step at a time."

She gasped. "I used to say that to you, when you were little," she whispered.

A chill ran through me, as if I could remember it, too. "You did?"

"When you were starting to walk. You were the cutest little thing. I was six, and I said, 'One step at a time, sissy.' That's what I called you then. I coached you into walking."

I was silent. The kettle screamed, and I shut it off, poured the hot water into a tall mug.

"And then I walked away," I said quietly.

As I sipped the tea and the fire danced to life, I listened to my older sister detail her life. The anger dissipated, and an enviable sunshine filled her voice. I could hear love there, and pride. Thirty minutes later, I was clinging to the phone, wanting to meet all these new characters in the film of my life.

"Will you come home? Meet them? Let me know you?"

"I'd love to," I said wistfully. "I'll plan a trip. Soon."

"Maybe for Christmas?"

"You don't go for the whole Jewish thing like Mom and Dad?"

She sucked in a breath and chortled. "Well, sort of. We do it all. Colton is Christian, and you know we were never so Jewish, until you left. I was furious at the way Mom and Dad held a candle to your memory, so when we got married, I just followed his lead. We light the Chanukah menorah with Mom and Dad, though, and sometimes we go over there for Shabbat dinner. I mean, who can turn down challah and matzoh ball soup?"

I laughed, relieved that everything I remembered wasn't a figment of my imagination. It felt good to share the imperfections of my family with someone who understood.

"I'll come soon, I promise," I said.

"Don't leave me a second time," she said, her voice hesitant but firm.

"I won't," I said.

Chapter Forty-Four

Although another storm wasn't forecast to blow through, that night howled like wolves set loose in the woods. The day had inched above freezing, thawing the tree limbs and the roads, but when night fell, everything froze over and a crackling storm rained down, coating my world in a thick sheet of ice. Nearing midnight, the power snapped off, bathing the house in darkness.

I layered a sweater over my pajamas and piled two more blankets on the bed, but I couldn't sleep. Outside, the ice was alive with sound. After two hours of shifting under the covers, I got up, wrapping a blanket around me. I lit a fire in the stove and filled a saucepan with water and set it on the burner, grateful for the gas stove so I could make tea.

I'd never really watched the changing hues of night into morning. The house was still, pulsing with silent energy. The sky was a blanket of black with pinpoints of light. Then it was charcoal gray with a cuff of orange on the horizon. Then hues of lavender, soft blue and pink lighting up the sky until morning hit and the yolky sun showed its face.

By then, the cottage reverberated with cold. My breath puffed in front of my mouth, and I zipped up my down coat over all the other layers. I'd been feeding the iron stove all night and was running low on logs, but the last thing I wanted was to go outside. And yet, I needed to move. I was antsy, agitated, sick of being cooped up inside. I even wondered if the outside air might feel warmer than the stale stillness of the cottage. The roads were likely iced over; it would be a death wish to try driving somewhere, and anyway, where would I go?

I changed into thick wool pants, a turtleneck under a heavy sweater, and thick socks, stuffed a beanie over my hair, slid back into my thick coat and laced up my boots.

Cut wood was stacked in a shed behind the house, between the garden and the open fields beyond my property. I trudged through foot-deep snow to get to it, dragging a sled from the porch to fill with logs that I could lug back to the house.

While it was biting cold out, it was also a beautiful morning. The tips of the long, wheat-colored grasses were crystallized in ice, the field a silent sea of frost. The evergreen trees in the forest beyond were a beautiful contrast to the whiteness of the world. I surveyed the landscape and sighed.

I'd felt this way in Cape Breton, too. Hell, I'd also loved Traverse City. Which meant I could find beauty wherever

I went, despite what was happening around me.

The sled filled, I spun around to drag it back to the house, and that's when I saw him.

Standing twenty feet away, between my cottage and me, stood Armand Villencourt.

I gulped but couldn't swallow, fear lodged in my throat.

"Been wondering when I'd come?"

I froze in place, unable to move, unsure where to go.

"You little vixen." His words were slow, and a crooked smile spread across his hard-set jaw. His dark eyes blazed. "Did you think I wouldn't figure it out? Did you think I'd just let you have all of it?"

We were winter-hardened people, but the longer we stayed out there, the sooner we'd freeze. I needed a plan, an escape route, and I had no idea how to appeal to this imposing man.

Armand was over six feet tall and bald, his shiny head covered with a brown wool hat. His down coat made him seem even more terrifying than he normally was, his hardened gaze perfect for breaking down prey. He'd grown up in a feared family in Chéticamp, an Acadian stronghold in the corner of Cape Breton where French was the preferred language and anger reigned over centuries of bad treatment and colonization. Legend had it that his family had deep roots in indigenous culture, ancestry that had been wronged on two fronts over the centuries. Generational trauma coursed through his blood. Armand's fierce anger, which never left him, emanated from a long family history of fighting for what was rightfully theirs, for all they'd been robbed of, generation upon generation.

I'd never wanted to cross him. And when I was living at Anam Cara, I rarely had to interact with the man, let alone face him head-on. I was a nobody who had escaped his interest.

Until now.

"Armand, why don't we go inside where we can talk," I said, hoping to buy time but terrified of being alone with him in an enclosed space.

The sun was rising in the morning sky, painting the fields in its orange glow. I hoped the ice would melt, make the roads passable, bring the power back. I hoped someone would just happen to stop by, to find me there, with him. I wished I hadn't ignored Parker's calls.

My mind whirred, trying to come up with a plan as I dragged the sled closer to the cottage, trying for a soft face, to hide the fear that choked me.

"Lead the way, little lady," he said, hovering so close I could smell the sweetness of his signature cigar-smoking. I kept my head high, even though I was shaking.

He lifted the sled onto the porch as if he were trying to be a gentleman, and I wanted to scoff at the absurdity of it. I lifted three logs to take inside, and he held the door open for me to walk through before he slammed and bolted it.

As if I had the courage to flee.

Just then, the power flickered on, and the furnace hummed into action. The stove was down to embers. Armand watched as I carried the logs over to the stove, set them down, and fed in two to reignite the flames.

He sat on the couch and watched me, his arms slung like wings wide over the back of the couch. He'd always been a big presence, taking up all the space, and in my little cottage, he seemed to reach every corner. Once I had the fire roaring, I stepped back and waited.

"Did you think I'd just let you have it all?"

I whipped around to face him. "What are you talking about?"

"Don't play dumb with me, Charlie. You're too smart for that."

I would feign ignorance, make him say it and, in the process, buy time. "Seriously, Armand, I don't know what you're talking about. I don't even know why you're here."

His eyes blazed with anger, and his arms dropped from the casual stance as he leaned forward to peer at me.

"I think you do."

I was glad he couldn't hear my heart racing. My throat was dry. I licked my lips, wishing for a glass of water, for anything to distract him or me. "Why don't I make us some tea?"

But he shook his head and inched closer on the couch.

"Cut it out, Charlie. I know you have the money."

I wasn't going to acknowledge it. He'd have to pull it out

of me.

"Just give me the money, and I'll leave," he said.

I wanted to believe him, but Boden's face flashed in my mind and then the fear blazing in Indira's eyes. Nothing would be that easy with Armand. He didn't let anything go. Or anyone. Vengeance flowed through his veins.

Footsteps thudded on the porch. Armand's eyes opened wide, and his head whipped toward the door. He held a finger to his lips and crept over to it. My heart hammered in my chest. *Parker, you fool. What are you doing here?* It could only be him.

Knocking. "Charlie! We need to talk. Let me in."

His voice was like maple syrup, sweet and slow, and relief flooded through me, but this was exactly what I had feared. The last thing Parker needed was a run-in with Armand. I needed to divert him, send him away.

"Armand," I hissed. "Let me get rid of him. Please."

His head slowly shook back and forth. No. A hard, cold no. A vindictive gleam in his eye. He was in charge, and he wouldn't let me believe otherwise.

The knocking intensified, echoing through the room. *Please, Parker, leave. Go away and don't come back.* It was the closest I'd ever come to praying.

But he was too good a guy to forget me, to leave me alone to my own musings. Our love was real, and when you get a second chance, you want to grab it, hold it close.

Armand wrested the door open. His commanding

stance claimed the entryway to my house. I tried to peer around him, to make eye contact with Parker, to send a silent message to run and never look back.

"Who are you?" Parker's voice was stronger than I'd ever heard it, almost imposing, too. But he didn't know what he was up against.

Armand stared him down, and Parker tried to wedge his way inside, past the hulking man who filled the doorframe, but Armand wouldn't budge.

"I need to see Charlie," he said.

"She's busy at the moment," Armand said, crossing his arms in front of his chest.

"I don't believe that," Parker said, edging forward.

Please don't be stupid, I screamed in silence.

"Charlie!" he called out. "Are you okay?"

I swallowed and willed myself to say words that would protect my love and send him away.

"Parker, go home," I called.

Armand whipped around and glared at me, giving Parker just the space he needed to dart inside. Gratitude washed through me at the sight of him, and I cursed him at the same time. His brown hair was covered by a green winter hat, but his eyes gleamed golden as he caught sight of me.

"Charlie!" He ran to me and pulled me to him. I'd never been happier to see a person…and never more upset, either.

With his arms around me, his heart beating against mine, the smell of him heady and reassuring, I burrowed my nose into his neck, pressed my lips to his skin. For a moment, I forgot the peril we were facing.

But Armand wouldn't let us forget. He slammed the door and, in two strides, stood beside us.

"Well, isn't this cozy," he said. "I warned you, man. She told you to leave." Then he turned to me with a sick grin. "Didn't take you long to move on, did it? Has James even been gone a year?"

I bit back the responses I wanted to spew in his direction, willed myself to keep silent. Parker laced his fingers through mine and gripped tight. "You should've left," I whispered.

He just shook his head and squeezed my hand.

Armand closed in on us, his huge frame bearing down. "Give me the money," he insisted. "You don't know what you're doing, Charlie."

"I told you, Armand, I don't know what you're talking about."

"You think I'm stupid?" He was in my face, the hot sour of his breath rank and open. "How could you afford any of this?" He waved his arms around and snorted. "You had nothing. You *were* nothing. The only way you got out was to be sneaky and conniving and take what isn't yours."

I was shaking. Parker stepped forward, trying to show Armand he wasn't afraid, but he had to be. The hulking presence of this monster would scare anyone. Parker's normally calm countenance seeped around the edges of his anger. It rarely came out, but when it did, it was vicious, protective and well-founded. And now was the perfect time for it, though I doubted it would help.

"I'd like you to leave Charlie alone," he said calmly.

Armand shook his head and snickered. "You must be dumber than you look," he said. Fury blazed in Armand's eyes. He wasn't used to defiance, to not getting what he wanted. I wished I'd told Parker more about him so he wouldn't tempt his rage. But even if I had, I'm not sure he would have believed me.

In a flash, Armand thrust his fist into Parker's stomach. He doubled over, gasping.

"Armand, stop," I urged, reaching for him to hold him back and divert his attention from Parker to me, but he waved his arm to push me back and clipped my face in the process. Stinging from the blow, I held my cheek and stepped back from the fray.

"I didn't expect this to be so hard," he said, chuckling. "You people actually think you have a chance." He revved up and leveled another blow at Parker, who was curled in a ball on the floor, holding his middle.

"Stop it," I called, inching toward the stove, where the fire was roaring and cracking.

Parker moaned on the floor. Armand bent over to peer at him and said, "Had enough, buddy? That'll teach you to mess with Armand Villencourt."

He didn't respond, but just when Armand turned his

back with a sick laugh, Parker reared up and jammed his foot into the back of Armand's knee and sent him flying.

I hadn't seen it coming, and apparently, neither had Armand. He skittered across the floor, bucking into the wood coffee table and collapsing across it. A hand flew to the back of his leg, and he rubbed it, clearly hurt but not out of the fray. He was fuming. I could see it before he turned, before he'd gathered the energy to fight back.

I jolted over to him, a hand out to stop him, actually thinking I could have some impact.

"Please, Armand, stop," I begged. "He hasn't done anything to you. Leave him be. Your beef is with me."

But he was wild and out of control, mouth set, almost foaming. His eyes were glossy with emotion. He wanted revenge—for the single, deft blow Parker had dealt him, but also for all the imagined wrongs he'd suffered throughout his life. Armand was a walking regret, a six-foot-two-inch vessel of ancestral agony on hyperdrive, on a mission. And now, Parker was the object of all that rage.

"Please, please, please." I was crying now.

"You thought it would be that easy?"

I thanked God, or whatever force was bigger than all of us, that I had learned finally to feign a poker face, because I didn't flinch or glance at Parker as he picked himself up and snuck to the woodstove. Armand was focused on me, giving Parker a chance to grab the last log by the stove. Armand's hands came down on my shoulders, and he shook me. He was in my face, his eyes bright, his mouth wide. "Where is it?"

I stuck to my denial, shutting my eyes and waiting for whatever blow he'd deliver. I would not give in, not admit to having the money, not play into his hand. I scrunched up into my shoulders, waiting, waiting...and then a thud.

My eyes flew open. Armand lay on the ground bent sideways, his eyes closed, blood trailing across his forehead. Parker stood over him with the log in his hands, frozen, his mouth open, his eyes stunned.

I went to him, took the log and placed it gently on the ground. He was shaking.

"Come on," I whispered. "We have to go. Before he comes to."

His teeth were chattering, and he was shaking his head. "Is he dead?"

"Who cares? Let's get out of here. We'll call Bruce."

Parker turned to me, gripping my shoulders, his teeth set. "Charlie, I will stand by what I've done. I can't leave the scene of a crime."

"Don't be a noble idiot," I seethed. "He was going to kill us. He already hurt you—it was self-defense! You were protecting me and yourself."

He kept shaking his head as he stumbled forward. Armand's head twitched, a single finger fluttered.

"Parker, he's not dead. Look." I directed him to the man

sprawled across my floor. "We have to leave. For our own safety."

He was in shock, that much was obvious, and I couldn't believe how together I felt. With each moment, I grew stronger, more confident. I could command control. I could lead us to safety.

I settled his coat over his shoulders. Mute, his face incredulous, he glanced from Armand to me and back. I slipped into my coat and shepherded him outside.

My car wouldn't start, having sat in the cold for days, so I fumbled in Parker's pocket for his keys, helped him into the passenger seat and winged out of there as fast as I could. The roads were starting to melt but were still slick, and I took it slowly, glancing in the rearview mirror every few minutes to make sure Armand wasn't on our tail.

By the time we reached the police station, Parker was more himself, though still jarred and shivering. Bruce brought us hot coffee and sat us in a quiet room to tell our story. He took ample notes, listening attentively, and by the time we'd finished, I could see that the fear in Parker's eyes had subsided, and he was accepting the necessity of what he'd done.

"I've sent two officers to your house, Charlie," Bruce assured us. "We'll apprehend him." He laid a hand on Parker's forearm. "You did the right thing, Rabbi."

Parker nodded blankly. "I'm not a violent man," he muttered.

"We know, Rabbi," Bruce said as I patted Parker's shoulder.

"Never had to be," he continued mumbling.

"And you're still not," I whispered as Bruce scraped his chair back, shot a sympathetic glance my way and left the room.

When he was gone, Parker buried his face in my hair and cried hot tears of relief. Mine seeped out slowly and quietly in answer to his. I'd known Armand would come; I just hadn't known how I'd survive him.

Relief coursed through my body, and I shuddered as all the pent-up tension sifted out.

"You should give back the money," Parker whispered.

I looked at him with questioning eyes.

"It's not yours, honey." He cupped my face with his palm. I was shaking my head, new tears forming, every vision of my freedom vanishing before my eyes. "And you don't need it. As long as you hold onto it, you can't put the past to rest."

I was about to speak, when he went on. "I'm not saying you should give it to Armand," he cautioned. "No way. He doesn't deserve it. But it belongs to someone."

"To me," I squeaked. "All those years...I worked hard. I deserve it."

Instantly, we had changed roles. Now I was the shuddering mess, and he was in complete control of thought and body.

"Deserve is a funny word," Parker said, stroking my hair.

I was sweating in the warm precinct, all memory of the quaking cold of the beautiful winter woods gone.

"It suggests reward or punishment, and I've never wanted to live that way," he went on. "Do you?"

My lip quivered as I tried to hold back a flood of tears. I shook my head. I'd spent twenty years punishing myself, maybe longer. And yes, I wanted the sweet justice of a reward, of my due, of the freedom to have and to keep and to wander.

But he was right. I had all that, and more, and I could expand the possibilities of my life with a little effort and skill. I'd made the list. I knew what I was capable of. I had a lot to offer the world.

"Okay," I said. "I've spent a good chunk of it, though, to get on my feet."

He nodded. "So you'll give the rest to someone who truly needs it?"

"I suppose," I said, thinking. Who needed it more? To whom did it really belong?

"Maybe I could give it to Lacey."

A smiled dawned on his face like a beautiful sunrise in a stark cold day. He nodded and pulled me to him, and then the tears started in earnest, raining down on both of us, washing us clean.

Chapter Forty-Five

I turned forty-one that winter, determined not to waste another minute of my life. By the next fall, I was round with new life and standing in a grove of red spruce and sugar maple, on a damp carpet of fallen leaves and pine needles baked orange by the sun.

A rabbi friend of Parker's had come down from the Maine college town where he lived to officiate at our wedding, and our family and friends formed a standing circle around us as we shared promises and pledged to love each other until the end of our lives. Ethan and Alice were content to have me join their family, knowing I'd never replace their mother but hoping I could add some joy where she had once stood. My parents, my sister and her brood fanned out under the trees, while Parker's parents and Sylvie's, too, completed our circle. There was also Mary and Marisol, my farmer-friend Layton Spelman, and even Bruce, out of his blues and into jeans and a flannel, along with a few congregants who loved Parker so much, they wanted to witness the closing of one chapter in his life and celebrate the opening of a new one.

I held a clump of wild grasses tied with a blue satin ribbon and wore a long, ivory sundress with little flowers decorating the full skirt. A pale-blue ribbon tied my hair low on my neck. Parker wore his signature pressed jeans and a flannel button-down and a yarmulke that matched my dress. We'd wanted to marry in a place that we loved, in the way that we felt most at home in the world. Angles of sun glistened through the treetops, cascading light down on all of us, as if from the heavens.

The ceremony was short, poetic and full of tears. After, we all went back to the house Parker and I had bought after he sold his and I ended my lease. We'd agreed on a fresh start in a place that held no memories for either of us, only new rooms we could move through freely, paint the walls any color that spoke to both of us and fill the space with items that would hold memories we had yet to make.

Mom, Willow and I had spent three days baking and cooking, and friends brought trays of pastries and good strong coffee.

In the back of the house, my one fervent request, lay an acre of untamed land, all ours, that I could do with whatever I wanted. I'd begun in the spring, just as we were beginning to build the dream of our future, moments before we created this new life twirling inside me, to clear-cut the long grasses and introduce order. I'd left the back third raw and wild, respecting its need to blow in the breeze, admiring the organic view. I needed to feel part of the landscape, to be free to wander whenever I needed it. I'd planted my summer crops along another third of the acreage.

And there was a corner of this vast space where I seeded wildflowers, to add a shock of color to my view, images of a little girl with wild curls and bright eyes in bare feet stomping through the seedlings and stopping to smell the pretty pinks and blues. I didn't know if this baby would be a daughter or if there'd be any others after her. I wasn't young, but I was just beginning, and I believed in the endless possibilities of time and space and land and love.

Which was what I was thinking about, my hair lifted by the breeze, when Parker came up behind me and encircled his arms around my body.

"Happy?" he hummed close to my ear.

I nodded. There was no need to say a word. He could read it on my face.

Behind us, the people we loved most swirled under fairy lights strung across the yard. Jazz bounced from the speakers, and the buzz of eager bees vibrated along the sweetness of all we'd made and all we had yet to create.

"I love you, Charlie Tanner," he whispered, kissing me lightly on the cheek.

I smiled and nodded. Finally, I loved her, too.

DISCUSSION GUIDE

Themes in *I Love You, Charlie Tanner*

- Strong, complex female protagonist

- Second-chance romance

- Small town living

- Healing family ties

- Gardening + love of nature

- Hot rabbi

- Escaping toxic relationships & cult-like community

***

Key Ideas from *I Love You, Charlie Tanner*

Identity Is Chosen, Not Given

- Investigating ancestry can be enlightening & inspiring. Have you wandered down your ancestral path? If so, have you found surprises or confirmed what you always knew?

- It's not fair to assume that ancient ways resonate for everyone. However, anyone can find access into long-held customs and rituals. What rituals have been soothing or grounding for you?

- Each individual must take an active role in constructing their own identity. When have you deliberately defined yourself? Was it difficult?

- Only upon reflection does Charlie see how she spent most of her life expecting other people to tell her who she was. Is this familiar to you? If so, did you like the guidance others offered to you?

Connecting with Nature & Cultivating the Earth is Empowering

- Charlie processes her grief in the garden, and also finds power there. When have you experienced nature as a healing force?

- One of the exceptional qualities of Anam Cara is its cultivation of difficult land. Despite the community's controlling, cult-like tenor, it gifts residents the skills of sustainability. When have you experienced this kind of duality in your life?

- Research shows the many positive effects of gardening, including that exposure to sunlight lowers blood pressure. What have been healing experiences for you in nature?

Community Is Important

- The support Charlie receives in the wake of James's death, and her friendship with Boden, are anchors in an often-rudderless life. Who has been an essential support for you throughout your life, or at difficult times?

- While it evolved into a cult-like entity, Anam Cara connected people in meditation and communal gatherings as well as back-to-the-earth values of cultivating the land. What positive experiences have you had, despite challenging circumstances?

- Charlie later finds comfort and stability in the kind welcome of the Jewish community, and in the soothing rituals of Jewish observance. What has been your most welcoming community?

- Charlie's parents are soothed after the loss of their daughter when she cuts ties by reconnecting with their Jewish community in northern Michigan, and their renewed identity strengthens their lives overall. Where have you found comfort during difficult times?

The Best Relationships Involve Two Whole Individuals

- Love must be mutual to be truly beneficial—James's wild and promiscuous behavior often left Charlie alone and lonely, but her love with Parker grows out of a deep place of knowing and choice. Why did she stay with James for so long? How did it make you feel to read about her continuing to field his unreliable and often cruel behavior? Were you relieved when she found a healthier relationship with Parker? Why or why not?

- We must come to terms with uncomfortable aspects of our past choices in order to be whole today. Have you had to make peace with choices you made when you were younger? If so, how did you manage to move on, or even learn from past mistakes?

***

ACKNOWLEDGEMENTS

It's becoming a bit of a habit to write books about the places I visit. As I approached my 50th birthday some years ago, I resolved to go somewhere new each year and be there not as a tourist or visitor, but as a temporary resident. Longer than a few days—long enough to embed myself in local life, to learn the roads, to know the grocery store aisles. In 2023, I spent a month in Nova Scotia. The first week, I experienced the gorgeous landscape and friendly people of Cape Breton. I spent the next three weeks at a beautiful hilltop house an hour south of Halifax. Ironically, it was there that I finished writing my second novel, *Cave of Secrets*, but this book was inspired some time later by the time I spent in Nova Scotia.

I hiked. I met lots of writers, largely directed by the Writers' Federation of Nova Scotia. There is a strong literary tradition and community in Canada and while I am an American, my Detroit-area home is mere minutes from the border with that nation to our north. It's close enough that we've crossed over for dinner. The idea for this book percolated in my mind for a year and a half before I started to put my ideas on paper. In fact, Anam Cara was inspired by an agricultural commune in the north of Scotland that I visited on my 2022 writing sabbatical. But I didn't want to pigeonhole myself as someone who only writes about Scotland. And, I wanted Charlie to make her way home to the United States easily, without having to cross an ocean. Where better to place her than in an isolated community in a northeastern corner of North America?

There is archeological research that suggests at one point in historical time, Scotland's mountains were connected to the Appalachian range and when the continents broke apart, these ranges drifted and became separate. But the landscape, and perhaps the culture, retain certain similarities.

During my time in Cape Breton, I met Maggie and Kit Davis, who live on a gorgeous isolated slice of land, not too far from Bras d'Or Lake. There, they raise farm animals and grow incredible crops and gather their community for fresh-made meals full of local produce. Thanks to Maggie and Kit for reading an early version of this manuscript and guiding my cultural references to Cape Breton to make sure they accurately represent the land and the people of their region.

Thanks also to Judy Front, a master gardener who has been a mentor to me as I enhance my own gardening skills. Judy read an early version of this story to make sure the gardening references are realistic and sound. Thanks to Bob Levine, a member of my synagogue, Congregation Beth Ahm, who first introduced me to "The Piper's Refrain" by Gordon Bok. After my Scottish novel *Cave of Secrets*, made its debut, Bob told me at a Friday night service about this song and it somehow found its way into this story.

A lot of the character names in this book were inspired by names I found in the cemeteries on Mackinac Island, where I host a writers retreat every September.

As always, a big dose of gratitude to Dan, the love of my life and my partner in everything, who has always seen me as a writer. He's also my first reader whenever I finish a manuscript and his honest feedback helps me make each book stronger. I am so grateful that he is interested in what I write and supportive of this writing journey, even when it costs more than it yields.

All my love to my four wonderful children—Asher, Eliana, Grace and Shaya. My mother, Sonny Cohn, is one of the best cheerleaders of my writing, along with my sister, Jody Charlip, my sister-in-law, Darcie Cohn, my aunt Suzanne Zwiren and my cousin Amanda.

Thank you to Jean Meltzer, Christopher Locke and Sarah Ansbacher for blurbing this book. Thank you to my Michigan writers workshop, women I love deeply who have become an important part of my life— Susan Chaplin, Karen Hildebrandt, Pam Houghton, Kim Kozlowski, Carrie Nantais, Anne Osmer, Lisa Peers. Many thanks to my Tuesday co-writing group—Janet Bailey, Elizabeth Gowing and Rachel Weikel—lovely friends and wonderful writers.

Thank you to Jenny Rarden, my steady editor, and to Susan Jones and Patrick McEntaggart, my talented cover designers. I am so glad to be part of the Women's Fiction Writers Association and Michigan Writers. It's hard to live this writing life without the support and encouragement of others who truly get it. And thanks to Barbara Jones, my mentor and friend for more than three decades, whose guiding insight is a beacon of light in an ever-changing publishing world.

About the Author

Lynne Golodner is the author of twelve books and thousands of articles as well as a marketing entrepreneur, writing coach and retreat leader. (Lynne's work has been published with three different surnames: Lynne Cohn, Lynne Schreiber and Lynne Golodner.) After working as a journalist in New York and Washington, D.C., Lynne returned to her native Detroit to pursue a freelance writing career and teach writing. In 2007, she created Your People LLC, a marketing and public relations company with a focus on storytelling that helps companies, organizations and entrepreneurs build their brands and market their work.

Lynne's writing has appeared in *Saveur*, the *Chicago Tribune*, *Better Homes and Gardens*, *Midwest Living*, the *Detroit Free Press*, *Porridge Magazine*, the *Jewish Literary Journal*, *The Good Life Review*, *Hadassah Magazine*, *The Forward*, *Valiant Scribe*, *Story Unlikely*, *The Dillydoun Review*, *QuibbleLit* and *YourTango*, among many more publications.

Among the awards she has won for her writing, Lynne's

first novel, WOMAN OF VALOR, won an honorable mention in the Spiritual Fiction category of the Eric Hoffer Awards, and one of her essays was a 2022 finalist in the Annie Dillard Award for Creative Nonfiction through *The Bellingham Review*. Lynne's second novel, CAVE OF SECRETS, earned the #1 spot on Amazon in Jewish fiction, Gay Fiction and British and Irish Literature and has been named a Finalist in the FOREWORD INDIES award for Romance and LGBTQ+ fiction, and in the Reader's Choice Awards.

Lynne teaches writing around the world. A former Fulbright Specialist, she is a graduate of the University of Michigan (BA, Communications/English) and Goddard College (MFA, Poetry). The mother of four young adults, Lynne lives in Huntington Woods, Michigan with her archivist husband Dan.

Learn more at https://lynnegolodner.com.